VIKING
75 years

Welcome to My Planet

Welcome to My Planet*

*Where English Is Sometimes Spoken

Shannon Olson

Viking

VIKING
Published by the Penguin Group
Penguin Putnam Inc., 375 Hudson Street
New York, New York 10014, U.S.A.
Penguin Books Ltd, 27 Wrights Lane,
London W8 5TZ, England
Penguin Books Australia Ltd, Ringwood,
Victoria, Australia
Penguin Books Canada Ltd, 10 Alcorn Avenue,
Toronto, Ontario, Canada M4V 3B2
Penguin Books (N.Z.) Ltd, 182–190 Wairau Road,
Auckland 10, New Zealand

Penguin Books Ltd, Registered Offices:
Harmondsworth, Middlesex, England

First published in 2000 by Viking Penguin,
a member of Penguin Putnam Inc.

1 2 3 4 5 6 7 8 9 10

PUBLISHER'S NOTE

This is a work of fiction. Names, characters, places, and incidents either are the product of the author's imagination or are used fictitiously, and any resemblance to actual persons, living or dead, business establishments, events, or locales is entirely coincidental.

Library of Congress Cataloging-in-Publication Data
Olson, Shannon.
Welcome to my planet : where English is sometimes spoken /
Shannon Olson.
p. cm.
ISBN 0-670-89208-4
I. Title.
PS3565.L838 W4 2000
813'.6—dc21 00-024549

This book is printed on acid-free paper. ♾

Printed in the United States of America
Set in Weiss
Designed by Jaye Zimet

To My Family,
My Favorite Earthlings

Contents

In scenery, I like flat country.
In life I don't like much to happen.

—William Stafford

It's time for the human race to enter
the solar system.

—Dan Quayle

Welcome to My Planet

Forward

You have such trouble living in the moment, says the counselor, sighing. I believe she's losing patience with me. I have been here for four, going on five years now, clutching the small throw pillows in her office against my stomach as if they were life preservers.

"Have you looked around at the moment?" I say. "I have huge credit card bills, I'm thirty and single."

It sounds like a wonderful place to begin, she says. *To be an adult. To earn your keep.*

"I never thought I'd be single at thirty," I continue. One of my problems is denial. Another is not listening, which is pretty much the same as denial. Another is not taking her advice. "Everyone on *Love Boat* found someone," I say. "I watched it every Saturday night—those were my impressionable years."

Well, all those people didn't start out together. They started out alone, otherwise there would have been no need for a cruise. She often does not bother to humor me, but today she does.

"That's true, but it took them no time at all, a single vacation."

It's television.

"Yeah, but I didn't know that then. I thought all the people on *Love Boat* were just a slightly different version of adult than my parents, like a California version, with more eye shadow and more hair products, people who owned polyester ball gowns and went dancing, which my parents didn't. They wore wool and listened to Thelonius Monk. My parents had already found each other. You know, they lived in California for a while, and then came back to the Midwest to have a family."

I don't think I'm following you anymore.

"I've never really lived anywhere else. What if I never find anyone? I may as well go out and adopt a bunch of cats and start wearing macramé ponchos."

You're getting ahead of yourself, says the counselor, *and we went over this last week. Loneliness is a really honest place to be; it's the one human emotion that we all share. We are, each of us, separate, alone. The fact that you are feeling your own loneliness so deeply right now is a wonderful thing. What an empowering moment!* she says. I love it when the counselor goes on like this. It feels like a story, with me as the main character. Now what will happen? What will I do next? I want her to tell me. *You are really with yourself,* she continues, *with your own fundamental condition.* She is prone to saying things like this. *You'll make better choices from that place, from here on out. It's a wonderful place,* she says, *to begin.*

Part One \ Backward

Phone Home

I call my mother almost every day from my position as a Communications and Account Services Representative at a software company that I have begun to refer to as "The Jerry Corporation" or "Jerry Corp," named so for its president, a man three years older and much shorter than I am. At twenty-eight, Jerry is the thumbnail-chewing, bird-boned leader of a handful of office workers, including me. It is difficult to respect him because he is often mean and wears light-green dress slacks. He attributes his fits of verbal cruelty to his superior intelligence and Irish ancestry, and I am the only one who challenges him on this because I am part Irish, and I don't have a family to support, or even a decent car, and I don't care if I get fired.

"You Minnesotans are so reticent, you take everything personally," Jerry said to me once.

"I don't think it's only a matter of geography," I said.

"Well then," he said, "If you think I'm being an asshole, Olson, why don't you go ahead and call me an asshole."

"You're being an asshole," I said.

"Okay," Jerry laughed nervously and put his hand on my back, patting me gently and leading me out of his office and back to my desk. "Okay," he said, "I think we have an understanding."

Because he is shorter than me and perhaps by some reflex, I patted him on the head. "Okay, Jerry," I said. "All right."

For many reasons, only one of them my insubordination, my continued employment surprises me. Though it shouldn't, since my father got me the job; his best friend is the CEO, and also Jerry's father-in-law, and even *he* thinks Jerry can be a jerk.

"Hi, Flo," I say, when my mother answers the phone.

"Well, what are you doing today?" she says.

"Not much," I say.

"They pay you for that?"

"Apparently they do."

"No, seriously," she says, "don't they have anything for you to do?"

"Not really," I say. "I'm supposed to be writing a brochure, but they haven't finished designing the product, and they don't know who they're going to sell it to when they do."

"Well, can you *find* something to do?" she says.

"I already went and got a Little Debbie snack cake. I've had three cups of coffee. Now I'm calling you," I say.

"Well, I can't think of anything for you to do," Flo says, laughing at her own joke. "Things have certainly changed," she says. "Your grandmother worked so hard. If there were no customers, she'd dust the shelves. She'd dust every bottle of lotion in that drugstore."

"Grandmother was obsessive compulsive," I say. "She wore her bra to bed."

"She was afraid her breasts would sag," my mother says. "Her sisters did the same thing."

"How would you know if your breasts were sagging if you never took your bra off?"

"Well, what can you do to keep yourself busy around there?" my mother asks. "Can you help someone else?"

"There's no new business."

"How does that company stay afloat, I wonder?" my mother says.

"There's stuff to do, it's just not in my area."

"Oh," says Flo. "Well, I better go. I've been tired all day."

"It's only ten thirty," I say.

"I have a lot to do before my city council meeting tonight. I'm going to want a nap." My mom is on the city council in the small Minnesota town where I grew up. It means that every Wednesday night she's on local cable, arguing with the mayor about how high the sign for the new Kentucky Fried Chicken should be, and badgering him about planting trees in the new pharmacy parking lot. It means she's learned a lot about solid waste management and landscaping around the Minnesota River to prevent flooding. And it means that everyone says hello to her in the grocery store.

I call Flo again before my lunch break. "Hey there, Flo," I say.

"What is it?" says my mother. "Did you look at the clock?"

I look at the clock. *The Bold and the Beautiful* is on.

"Sorry," I say.

"Uh huh," she says, and hangs up.

Because it is Wednesday, I go to the grocery store to assemble a lunch. It's sample day, and I compose a meal of: New, Thinnest Ever! Crust Pizza; a Tyson Chicken Patty balanced on a toothpick; pasta salad in a tiny plastic cup; kiwi and papaya slices rationed out by a smiling lady with orange hair and a white laboratory coat; and a miniature ice-cream cone. I pick up a twelve-pack of Diet-Rite raspberry soda to take home.

At the bank I deposit my check and sign up for the Treasure Days giveaway, an all-expenses-paid trip to Cancún. Second prize is a TV with a built-in VCR. I drink some complimentary apple cider and nibble on a cookie. With my deposit, I am given a key to the treasure chest in the middle of the lobby, which pops right open when I try it.

I win a set of salt and pepper shakers shaped like cows, with big sad eyes and holes in the tops of their heads for the black and white specks of flavor to come out.

My Boyfriend

I have been dating the same person for three years now. I call him almost every day from the Jerry Corporation, too. He is often unemployed, and so when he's not asleep he can take calls.

We met on a street corner right after I'd graduated from college. I had my first apartment in Minneapolis and was working in a used bookstore and coffee shop, shelving battered paperbacks and struggling with the milk steamer. Mostly I had no idea what I was doing—my espresso drinks were always too watery, the steamed milk lukewarm—but I was good at making small talk. I was so good at making small talk with the customers, with my coworkers, with the people who worked in nearby shops, that eventually I got fired. Also, the boss was creepy. He mumbled a lot and had trouble looking us in the eye. His sad shuffle, coupled with his chain-smoking habit, made us believe he had a tremendous amount of pent-up energy. His hands often shook and I think he secretly wanted to sleep with all the female help.

My boyfriend was working at the Rollerblade shop down the street. For a while, we just exchanged meaningful glances on the street. He was hard not to notice, with his sculpted cheekbones and linen shorts that nicely cupped his firm little butt. He was hard not to notice, and I was eager to get laid. At twenty-two, I had never had a boyfriend and hadn't ever slept with anyone. In college I'd had a few flings with guys I knew, but mostly we were too drunk to figure out where to put anything, and the next day, in class, we'd pretend nothing had happened.

My boyfriend (I had already started calling him this before I ever met him; when I saw him on the street I'd say to my coworker, *There goes my boyfriend*) finally approached me one day when I was waiting at a stoplight, on my way up the street to get a sandwich. He was on lunch break, too, and sidled up next to me on the corner, just behind my right shoulder, and said, "Havin' fun?"

I always give people credit for trying in those kind of situations. "Not really," I said, watching the traffic go by.

This initial interaction would pretty much sum up our relationship for the next few years.

We went to lunch that day, and he told me stories about his childhood in Amsterdam, growing up on a houseboat, sharing one small room with his mother and sister. His father had long since left, and his mother had followed her ex to New York and then to Amsterdam, even though he was with someone new. She finally gave up when they all landed in Mexico; when they were south of the equator and in a tiny town where she couldn't speak the language, she returned to Minneapolis with her two kids. This was a mystery: *Why would she follow someone who clearly didn't want to be with her?* And it should have been some kind of signal to me, a red alert, "Distressed childhood! Take cover! Abandon ship!" But I was fascinated. I had never met anyone who had moved so much, who had such an eclectic background. I had grown up and lived in the same house, my entire life, except during college, but even then I could return to my home, my parents' home, on the weekends, in the summer.

"So, you're a rich doctor's kid from the suburbs?" my boyfriend-to-be said at our first lunch.

"Not really," I said. I explained that it was a small town, outside of the suburbs. That I had grown up with cornfields behind our house, and cows from the neighboring farm grazing in nearby fields. That I had spent most of my childhood just watching cows. That my dad was a general practitioner, and that I believed he sometimes took pies as payment, quilts and cartons of fruit. That he still made house calls and had lots of elderly patients who liked him because he listened to their stories.

My boyfriend told me that he was taking night classes at the university so that he could work during the day to put himself through school. His seeming self-sufficiency attracted me; I had grown up near the end of a dead-end street.

When I call my boyfriend around two thirty in the afternoon, he's just woken up. "What are you doing?" I ask him.

"Playing video games with Doug," he says, referring to one of his roommates. I imagine their gnarled bed-hair, that they are both in their boxers, wearing dirty sweatshirts.

My boyfriend is three years younger than I am. Still, it is hard for me, sometimes, to believe that I am dating someone who plays video games.

"Oh," I say. "I'll let you go."

He starts telling me about *Foucault's Pendulum,* how it's really hard, how it's really dense, but still, I should read it, have I ever read Eco? This is punctuated by video game noises.

"No, I haven't," I say.

"It's taking me forever to get through it," he says.

"I thought you had class today," I say.

"Ummm, no," he says. "No, I don't. I mean, I don't think I need to go. I got the lecture notes from someone else."

Because sometimes my boyfriend's voice simply irritates

me, I get off the phone, preferring instead to stare at my cubicle walls.

When we first met, my boyfriend was working at a Rollerblade shop *and* at the Kinko's up the street. He was also taking classes, he told me, or was getting ready to take classes again—it was never quite clear. He had taken some time off and was dealing with the bureaucracy at the university, trying to get some financial aid. He was interested in political science and Spanish, and wanted someday to direct films.

"What do you guys talk about?" one of my friends asked me.

"Well," I said, since mostly we had sex, made dinner, watched movies and had sex, "collating. How paper jams. He seems to know a lot about copiers."

My boyfriend was still living with his mother at the time, his mother and his two younger brothers. I would meet them only once. He didn't seem to like being around them. His brothers, he said, were brats.

One of them, a senior in high school, got a sophomore pregnant and they were still deciding what to do. His younger brother, he said, had three rabbits, a guinea pig, four salamanders, and bad personal hygiene. And wasn't I allergic to most animals? His mother, he said, was usually too exhausted for company. She worked long shifts in the pay booth of a downtown Minneapolis parking ramp, a fact that would later seem odd, when we were both seeing my boyfriend, her son, off at the airport, because he was leaving for six months to go live with his father in Mexico. As we left the airport together, she couldn't remember where she'd left her car in the ramp. I would spend half an hour helping her find it.

My mother had always made a game out of remembering where we left the car. It was a game to see who could remember where we had parked, and it always ended in a tie. We all always remembered. My mom always made sure that before we went anywhere, we knew where we had been, and how to get back.

Evelynn

I grew up next to Evelynn, who got smashed regularly and then went out into her garage and smashed old jars meant for preserves. "Goddammit, Ray!" *Smash!* on the cement floor. *Smash! Smash!* "Goddammit!" Shards of glass underneath the lawn mower, the snow blower, the trash cans. Back then I couldn't understand why a woman would be so angry.

It was her signal to Ray, my mother says now, *that he should come home.*

Ray was her husband, and he spent his days with married women, fixing their faucets, says Flo, adhering carpeting that had let go of the floor. Ray had grown up on a farm and knew how to fix almost anything, *and he loved women,* Flo says. *Nothing ever happened, that I know of, but he loved to flirt.*

Ray was retired, but he liked to work with his hands, liked to be busy. "He bought Evelynn the best of everything," says Flo. "Their basement had a whole wall of cupboards and shelves, built by Ray, that were stacked with boxes of things that Evelynn had never used. Steak knives, silverware, dresses and fur-collared coats, but nothing ever made her happy."

I remember Evelynn's fuzzy auburn hair, always looking as if she'd just woken up. Her thick, horn-rimmed glasses. Her house dresses made of polyester. Her sharp, crowlike voice that cawed *Ray, Ray, Ray.* The way she flapped around in the garage like an injured bird, stumbling and crashing into things, drunk at all hours of the day.

She drove around town on surveillance missions, looking for Ray and crashing into the occasional lamppost, piloting their Chevrolet back to the end of the block, and sometimes parking on the lawn.

"Ray is the one who finished our basement and made those blocks for you kids," says Flo. And when I ask her which came first? Evelynn's drinking, or Ray's wandering eye? she says she doesn't know. Ray and Evelynn had both grown up in the same small town, had married, owned a liquor store and bar, had retired and moved here, the last house at the end of the street. *Sometimes people come together like a bad chemical combination; sometimes two people bring out the worst in each other.*

My Boyfriend

Eventually moved out of his mother's house and took an apartment a few blocks away from me, though we spent almost all our time at my place. I didn't have a roommate then, and his roommate, he said, was a little nuts and was always there with his girlfriend.

"I thought he was gay," I said.

"He's not gay," said my boyfriend. "Why would you think that?"

"I don't know," I said. "When I met him I just thought he was gay."

* * *

My boyfriend has never owned a lot of things, because, he says, they moved so much when he was growing up. He's just never really had a chance to establish himself. And now, he says, he doesn't need much.

When he was living just a few blocks away, things from his apartment, bit by bit, started appearing in mine. At first it was a CD player, and then some CDs. Then it was some pots and pans, which he said he didn't need, since his roommate had a lot of really nice kitchenware.

"Where does he get all his money?" I asked. "I thought he worked retail."

"He does," said my boyfriend. "I don't know. Sometimes he waits tables, too."

I would usually leave my boyfriend sleeping in the morning, and I would go off to work at the bookstore. When I suggested once that perhaps we should begin to see other people, that I'd met someone I might like to get to know, I came home that night to find that my hardwood floors had been washed, the rugs vacuumed. There were fresh flowers on the table and he had almost finished making dinner. Pots were boiling on the stove and he had already cleaned and ripped the lettuce.

"You know," he said. "You're never going to find someone who will take as good care of you as I will." He had bought my favorite chocolate for dessert. "You don't know how to cook," he said, putting an arm around me. "Who else would put up with you?"

Our Level

At some point in my adolescence my father said to my mother, "Flo, you mustn't encourage them. Don't stoop to their level."

"Them" was my sister and me, and perhaps our older brother. What defined our level is not exactly clear, but he said it so that we could hear him—as if some feature of our behavior, some strange climatic condition of our level, had rendered us deaf. There had been, perhaps, between my sister and me, too many jokes about poop. Too much pounding and stomping. Airborne curling irons during our morning hygiene wars. "Let me in the bathroom, you bitch! Take off my shirt, you bitch! You used all the hot water, bitch!"

My father began leaving for the hospital at 6:30 A.M. to make his rounds, but my mother had no such escape. Her work was our home. We were her work. So she stayed in bed until we left for school in the morning. She slept while we fought over clothes. She bought an extra curling iron so we wouldn't fight over the one we had. She had a second bathroom put in downstairs so my father and brother could shower in peace. The men's room.

Was she making concessions or just managing?

"Don't encourage them," my father said, when she couldn't help laughing at our dirty jokes.

But it was too late. It was the seventies. She had already admitted to us that she wasn't a perfect parent. "I make mistakes, too," she'd say. "Do you think this job is easy? I love you but I do not love your behavior right now."

* * *

Our father had drawn the lines of power and control more exactly. When, for instance, my brother, in the throes of a heated argument with my mother, called *her* a bitch, my father came storming out of the bathroom where he had been reading and smoking and whapped my brother over the head with a rolled up *Time* magazine, chasing him down the hallway as he attempted to retreat to the safety of his bedroom, his stereo, his piranha tank and science journals. "Do *not* talk to your mother that way!" *Whap, whap, whap.* My mother stood, stunned. My sister and I giggled: new territory had been forged, the envelope of disrespect pushed, and my father's belt had still been undone, twanging back and forth as he marched my brother down the hall, hitting him over the head with a weekly periodical. We giggled, but we also felt sorry for our brother, because in our own hormonal states we realized these things could happen: you were bound to say things you only meant for the briefest moment. And we believed our mother understood that.

The family joke years later would be that at least *Time* was good for something.

My Job

I have trouble getting up for my job at the Jerry Corporation, and am grateful for "flex time." This means that I can show up at 9:30, take a short lunch break and leave at 6 P.M. Or, take a long lunch break and leave at 6 P.M. When I leave for work around 8:30 A.M., my roommate, Karen, is often eating cereal and watching *Phil Donahue.* She's gone back to grad school and doesn't need to be anywhere in the mornings, and I deeply resent her for this.

I drive out to the suburbs from our city apartment, five days a week in my big, brown Delta '88, my grandmother's old car—huge and reliable—a car Jerry has taken to calling "the ghetto sled," because he lives in a barn-sized suburban house and not in the city like I do. The office is halfway between my apartment and my parents' house, and in some ways, they are similar. The carpeting is beige, the cube walls are beige, except Jerry has a thing for the opulence of Oriental decor, while my mother prefers the simplicity of Scandinavian design. There is a gong in the office, which will apparently be sounded when one of the men on the sales force has managed to get us a big contract.

Mostly, the office is quiet, with the clicking of keyboards as background noise, and Jerry's muffled profanities coming from behind the thick doors of his executive office.

Being a Communications and Account Services Representative means that I also test software, its limitations and capabilities. Last week, I tested cotton ball data and shampoo data. This week, I am testing our software on a fictional personal lubricants category, to make sure it retrieves the data that it should without exploding or shutting down the system.

I enter my request, wait for the software to retrieve the data, write down how long it took for the report to show up on the screen, and then enter another request. We need to make sure that everything works smoothly, that there are no bugs.

Friendly Neighbor personal lubricating jelly is selling extremely well in Rockport.

This took five minutes and twenty-eight seconds to come back to me.

The system, today, is slow.

* * *

I call my mom while reports are running.

"Hi, Flo," I say.

"What do you *do* around there?" she says.

"I'm running reports," I say. "They're running as we speak."

"What kind of reports?"

"It's just a test. I'm testing software."

"Oh," she says. "Is that part of your job?"

"No," I say, "You mean my job as CEO? No. But it's a little thing I like to do to help out."

"Say," says Flo, "when's your little friend leaving for Mexico?"

Flo and I don't talk about my boyfriend much. It's obvious that she doesn't like him, and since I'm not always sure that I do, I feel I have to protect us both from her middle-aged clairvoyance.

"I don't know when he's going. Soon, I think. He's trying to get his passport and he doesn't know if he needs a work visa. His dad already found him a job."

"He really needs to go live with his father," says Flo. "He needs a stable influence," she says, as if he were a horse. "He needs some direction," she says.

My boyfriend often says that I need to learn to form my own opinions about things. "Especially with your mom," he says. "You let her run your life. You go to her for *everything*. You totally listen to everything she says."

He also tells me that I should be taking vitamins. He's been reading about free radicals and other things that are supposed to be bad for our systems. "You should be writing, too," he says to me, "You'd be happier. You have a decent job," he says, "You don't have to take work home, and at night you could do freelance work."

"You should be taking vitamins," my mother says sometimes. "And calcium supplements. That's so important," she says. "Women need calcium." When she sees me she gives me handfuls of Tums samples from my dad's clinic, each tablet separately packaged. "These are good for your bones. All you have to do is chew on them."

"You know," she says, from time to time—and I always suppose she is thinking of my father when she says this, since when he *is* home, he's always dictating piles and piles of his patients' charts—"aren't you lucky? You don't have to take work home. It gives you room to have a life."

My Job

Jerry walks into my cubicle and puts his arm around me. "How's it going, sport?" he says, jiggling my shoulders a little. I believe this is some kind of apology. Earlier this morning he had asked me how the software testing was going, and when I told him that there was a bug in the trend reports, he barked at me, "That's the wrong answer." He has said this to everyone at one time or another and for a variety of reasons, a sort of occasionless greeting card, but I usually take it personally and desperately want to say to him, "Then tell me what the goddamn right answer is, and I'll repeat it, *word for word*."

I figure he must want *something* from me today, or soon, because he pats me on the shoulder and says, "Take care," as if I am going somewhere.

It is his habit to touch the female clients on the shoulder before making an important sales point, before indicating some deficiency in their current system, some void he can fill with his product. He doesn't do this to the men—he pats them on the back as they leave.

"Touch can be very effective," he once told one of my male coworkers, who had been surprised to see Jerry put his arm around a female client—the vice president of information systems for a multinational food corporation. "Never underestimate it as a sales weapon," Jerry had said.

I had been dating my boyfriend for about a year before he told me that he'd never graduated from high school.

When I stopped to think about it, it wasn't like he'd ever lied about it, he just never mentioned it. I figured that you had to have graduated from high school in America if you were over the age of eighteen, because there were barely any requirements besides showing up.

My boyfriend told me that he was deeply ashamed, that it was humiliating, and *could I ever understand?*

"Well," I said, "It's not like anyone really learns anything in high school, anyway." I figured that if he was taking classes through Continuing Education, perhaps he had been a restless genius in high school, bored in his classes.

"My high school was terrible," he said. "It was an awful place." He had gone to a city high school, which I had actually heard, even growing up in a small town, had a pretty rough reputation. Since he'd been kind of a skinny kid, he said, he got beat up sometimes.

I never got beat up in high school and figured this was enough to get anyone off track.

"It's okay," I told him. "I'm glad you told me. How are your classes at the university going? I never see you study."

"Oh," he said, "they're really easy."

Steve is a member of the sales force and walks quickly, even if he's just going to the kitchen for coffee. He is forty-five and recently divorced, and sings Def Leppard songs, "Love Bites," and "Bringin' on the Heartbreak," as he circles our island of cubicles on his way to meetings, to the bathroom, to the kitchen—sending his loneliness up like a flare. Steve drives a Jaguar convertible, and I am occasionally invited for a ride, though I always say no.

Today, I'm leaving my supervisor's office as Steve is coming down the hallway, careening toward me like an out-of-control plane trying to stop on the tarmac. "Hey, cool jacket," he says to me, from about twenty feet away—far enough away so that half the office can hear him. I change course and start heading for the kitchen. "Or would you call it a blazer? Are you blazing?" he says.

"Excuse me," I say, continuing to walk away from him. Someone chortles from behind a cubicle wall. Most people in the office find Steve to be an irritant, like a chemical sprayed into the atmosphere that makes your eyes itch and your nose run.

He follows me and catches up, turns and touches the lapel of my jacket, a few fingers brushing against my collarbone. He rubs the fabric between his thumb and forefinger. "Cool texture," he says. "Funky stuff. But I'd think it would start to itch." He winks at me. "Is it scratchy?"

"I don't think that's your concern," I say, continuing in the direction of coffee. Steve is always complaining that it's hard to meet women in Minneapolis, and I would feel sorry for him, but I can't. He whines about the fact that all of his friends are married and says things like, "We need to get out of here more often, the two of us, and do something besides work."

"None of your concern!" he says now. "God, you crack me up."

"If I have an itch, I'll attend to it myself," I say.

"'Attend to it myself'!" he says. "Oooh," he says, winking at me again and turning red.

And then, just to be cruel, as I'm walking away, I say, "It's a matter of finding the right person to scratch it."

Later, when I'm back in my cubicle, on the phone with my mother while Jerry and the sales force are guffawing and making a big graph to chart the Red Sox and the Cubs for the rest of the season, she says, "Think about it for a few moments and learn from it. And then don't dwell on it."

"I just wish I hadn't said it," I say.

"Well, try to pause for a few seconds before you speak next time," says my mother. "That is, if you think, more often than not, you're not saying what you mean to."

"But I was just walking down the hall," I say. "Why can't he bug someone else?"

It took me a while to notice that my boyfriend had been sleeping late in my apartment during the day, going off to work, coming over to my place late and staying there. He was always carrying around a kind of duffel bag that had extra clothes in it, and I finally realized that everything else he owned was already in my apartment.

"I want to be alone tonight," I said one night when he came

over. It was two o'clock in the morning and he'd just finished his shift at Kinko's, his new job. I was sitting up in bed in my pajamas and he was standing in the doorway of my bedroom.

"But I want to be here with you," he said.

"Just one night," I said, "I want to be alone."

"But I don't have anywhere to go," he said, and this is when I would find out that he and his roommate had been kicked out of their apartment for not paying rent. That his roommate had been arrested for shoplifting and was now out of jail, living with one of those electronic bracelets on his ankle.

"Get out of here," I said. "Now."

"But I don't have anywhere else to go," he said.

"Just get out," I said, "Go stay at your mom's."

"I don't want to go stay at my mom's," he said.

"GET OUT!" I screamed at him. "I don't care where you go," I said to him, "JUST GET OUT!"

We yelled at each other for about half an hour and it occurred to me then, in the middle of our argument, that my life had become like a bad television show, like a bad neighborhood where the police were frequently called in. I had never seen my parents fight; they had *discussions,* and neither of them really raised a voice, not like this. I was sure, now, that my boyfriend and I were waking my neighbors, and I had never imagined my life to be this way. In my wildest dreams, it could have been anything else.

He refused to leave and so I told him he could sleep in the living room, on the floor, since I had no couch.

"I don't want to sleep on the floor," he said, "God, you're *so* overreacting."

"I don't give a fuck," I seethed. "Shut my door and get out." He finally closed the door and I assumed he had resigned himself to sleeping on the living room floor. I lay in bed staring out the window. I had always expected my life to be so much more than this, but perhaps I had been wrong.

There were two beds in my room, shoved against adjoining walls and meeting in the corner to form a kind of V, the way my bed and my sister's had been when we were little.

In the morning I would wake to find him in the other one, his head near mine, his arm draped over my pillow.

Eventually, we would both find new apartments. I would move in with Karen, and he would move across the Mississippi River, closer to the university, where he was planning on signing up for more classes, as soon as the financial aid thing got straightened out.

The office gong finally goes off when Steve gets a big contract with the cotton ball people.

I happened to be standing near the epicenter when Gil, the executive officer in charge of the sales force, created the first vibration, connecting his baton with the gong's round middle. The gonging brought the tops of heads poking up from cubicle walls throughout the office, and in an increasing herd, they all marched toward Gil, their heads gently bobbing up and down along the walls of the cubicles, a gentle wave of obedience.

"They look like tiny worker ants," said Gil, not realizing I was standing nearby. "What a riot."

Gil congratulated our sales team on another super effort. "We got out there, we were aggressive, we grabbed the ball, we made the call. Nice win, guys," he said. "People are finding out about our product," he said. "This market is wide open for penetration."

For many reasons it is difficult to take Gil seriously, but on this occasion, mostly, it is because he is holding a baton with one swollen end, covered in lamb's wool, designed to create a softer and more lasting reverberation.

I notice, one evening, when no one else is around to know that I am inspecting, that there is a brand name on the back of the gong, a painted-on decal—and that the gong is suspiciously the same size and shape as a garbage can lid. I give it a little tap, a flick with the nail of my index finger, to determine its weight and density. It has suspiciously the same tonality as a garbage can lid—that thinly metallic and utilitarian clank. Spray paint can do many things.

I am sent to do training in Santa Fe for a group of forty pharmaceutical representatives, only four of whom are women. The client has put us up in one of the most expensive hotels in town, where it is rumored that Kevin Costner, shooting a film, is also staying. For the pharmaceutical representatives it is a kind of "working spring break"; they drink until four in the morning, and then try to figure out how to use their new computers. "How do I turn on the skiing program?" they ask me, green and hungover, looking for games.

They decide I remind them of Vanna White, and begin calling me by her name.

"Vanna, my ski guy hit a tree, and he's stuck."

"Vanna, my mouse isn't working."

"Vanna, I can't figure out how to get out of the mail program."

They are supposed to be learning *my* program, the one I've tested, the one I've been sent to show them.

When it is time to give away extra software, something their supervisor has decided would be a fun incentive to get them interested in their new laptops, I am elected to draw names from the box.

"Who's our next winner, Vanna?" they ask me.

When the training session is over, we all meet for cocktails. This is supposed to be a time when we relax and socialize with the clients, developing long-term customer trust.

As the night wears on, I watch this group of men begin to bend and weave. Each time the waitress comes by, they poke her in the stomach, trying to tickle her to see if she will drop her tray. When she bends to set down their drinks, they rest their index fingers on the top of her head, as if she is a doll who should begin to pirouette. She shoots a look at me, once.

The man who I've been talking with, who's been telling me about his wife and kids and their new van, leans into me, elbows resting on the table, head bobbing slightly. He lets out an airy beer burp. "Hey," he says, "you don't look like you're having so much fun anymore."

"I just kind of think they should give the waitress a break," I finally say.

"Oh," he says. "Hey, hey, hey. Now watch it. I see the whooole harassment thing coming up here and this is heeeeeavy. Here's my view on the whole things," he slurs. "If a woman has a problem with the way she's being treated, it's her job to say, *Hey, I don't like what you're doing*. Otherwise, like this, it's all just fun."

The waitress walks by again and the same group of men

poke her in the stomach. "Hey!" she finally says, "Knock it the fuck off!" pointing a finger in any random face, in the general direction of culpability. "I'm fucking sick of this." She gives them their drinks and walks away to catcalls.

The man I was talking to says, "Hey, smile. I saw you smile earlier today, Vanna. I wouldn't be standing here, wasting my time, if I didn't know there was more to you than being grumpy."

Another man, standing next to me, swaying back and forth like a metronome, looks at me and says, "Well that wasn't a very Christmas thing to do."

"You mean *Christian?*" I say.

"Yeah, Christian Christmas," he says. "She's no Christian Christmas bitch." He lets out a big wolfy yelp and weaves his way in the direction of the bathroom.

After the Sante Fe trip, my boyfriend is happy to see me. He comes over to my apartment, on the bottom floor of a duplex, late at night, and raps on my bedroom window so he won't wake Karen with the doorbell.

I had been lying in bed thinking about calling him, but I hadn't.

"Wrap your legs around me," he says as he pushes himself inside me. "Now do you know why I came over?" he says. "I love you," he says, pushing himself in deeper. "I love you," he whispers in my ear, which fills with steam and heat.

In all the time we've been dating, neither of us has ever said it, and I begin to sob, going off like a fountain, bursting open like an overripe piece of fruit, surprising even myself.

He gets off of me and I scramble for my robe. "What's wrong?" he says.

I tell him that I don't think I love him. That I'm not sure we should keep seeing each other, even though I can't say exactly why.

"You have an unrealistic idea of what relationships are supposed to be," he says. "You think someone's going to come along and save you."

It seems true, but I can't figure out how he knew it.

"You could fall in love with anyone," he continues, "as long as you could fill in the blanks, make him what you wish he could be. You think life is like movies and TV. That someday it will be perfect. It's unhealthy."

Since my boyfriend is always encouraging me to strengthen myself with supplements and holistic remedies, I say, "Is there a vitamin for that?"

"Fuck you," he says, going out into the living room to watch TV.

When my sister and I were younger, my mother read to us after dinner, a chapter a night. Some kids get *Alice in Wonderland* or *The Chronicles of Narnia*; but we, soon to be approaching puberty, got *Where Did I Come From?* and *What's Happening to Me?* My mother has always had faith in preparedness and self-help books, and she carefully went over each page, explaining all of the processes that bring life into being, patiently answering all of my questions while my sister, I think, just sat there, hoping it would all be over soon.

The books featured these sorts of sexless cartoon characters, who, even though they had sexual organs, didn't really look like they had *longings*. They were sort of potato-shaped, with big buggy cartoon eyes. When the potato people made love they had these huge grins on their faces and the drawings showed them under a quilt, with little action lines to indicate movement.

I was looking forward to all of these changes, to the ways, it appeared, my body would be pushing its limits, stretching itself beyond its current borders.

In high school I wandered around the house saying things like, "Boy, I really need to get laid," just to see what my parents would do. They were in their fifties then, and it had grown increasingly difficult to rile them. I would say it as I walked casually into the kitchen to get something out of the fridge, or to put something in the dishwasher. I had grown up listening to my mother say, "Children need limits," and mostly, I was trying to test my own, to shock them, and also I was avoiding my homework.

My father kept reading at the kitchen table and said, "You know, if I had known that the eighties were going to be like this, I would have liked to have been born earlier."

My mother said, "You know, sex isn't everything. Sex does not make a marriage, or a relationship."

"Sure it does," I would say, just to irritate her. "Of course it does. Flo, it's the *only* thing."

How would I know?

Later my mother would say to me, when we were alone, "You know, sex requires a lot of emotional maturity. I don't think you're ready for it yet. You really have to be ready to handle it."

"Don't worry," I would say, "I'm not having sex." But everyone else seemed to be, and this bothered me.

All through high school and college I would wonder if I was ready to "handle it." Eventually, something else took over, a kind of hormonal executive decision, a contract signed without consulting the shareholders.

My Job

I missed some work last week because I was sick. Jerry has welcomed me back to the office by saying, "Hey, champ, glad you're back. We've got a lot of software testing to do and we need your special touch for breaking things."

Sometimes while I'm testing software I envision a stapler leaving my hand, flying through the air in slow motion and beaning Jerry in the head. Staples fall out on the floor, sprinkling around like loose teeth. Jerry falls against the fax machine and knocks over a plant.

Today I am testing toothpaste data for one of our clients. Their new whitening formula is gaining brand loyalty on the East Coast. This took only two minutes and twenty-one seconds to come back to me.

The system seems to be running today as it should be.

When I was sick last week, my boyfriend brought me some sherbet and 7Up. I had a fever and spent most of the week trying to sleep the bugs out of my system, trying to sleep off the aches in my bones. "This is why you should be taking vitamins," he said.

I was lying in bed with my hair matted to the pillow from sweat and sleep, my pajama top stuck to my chest with Vicks.

My boyfriend rearranged the pillows behind my head, pulled my blankets back, and reached under my pajama top to rub my breasts.

"I've got Vicks on," I said. "Could you get me a cold cloth?"

"Yep," he said, as he began to pull my pajama bottoms down.

"Please," I said.

And he kept pulling them down, a little further.

"Don't," I said, "I really don't feel well."

"Come on," he said, "This will make you feel better," he said.

"I'm really not in the mood," I said, pulling them back up, "my whole body hurts."

"Come on," he said, moving his hands again over my breasts. "Just a little," he said. "Please."

My head was pounding and my nose was stuffed with snot. There were used Kleenex littered around the floor by my bed. I shifted my weight a little and looked out the window. It was sunny outside.

Soon he was on top of me, pumping inside of me, still wearing his clothes, and as I came all I could think was, "Why would he want to fuck me when I look like this? When I haven't showered in two days?" Some part of me figured that I must be lucky to have a boyfriend who doesn't care how I look, who finds me attractive even like this.

Another part of me was glad that he would be leaving for Mexico soon. That he finally had decided to go.

Labels

When we were small, Flo labeled everything with masking tape and a black permanent marker. She says this was so we would learn to read early. So we would know what things were, where they were supposed to go.

I ask her now, does anyone *really* know this? What to call things? Does everything really have a place?

The places on the wall of the garage where the gardening tools went were all marked: HOE, BROOM, RAKE, FAN RAKE, CLIPPERS, DIRT SHOVEL, SNOW SHOVEL. We knew exactly what was expected of us: "Go get me the dirt shovel, please," our mother would say. We knew which one this was. We knew where it would be.

The floor of the garage was divided up like a parking lot: RED BIKE, GREEN BIKE, WAGON, WHEEL BARROW, TRICYCLE. Our spots were up near the door, at the front of the garage.

I tell Flo now it was the only time in my life when I've had such a fabulous parking spot.

Flo says she did it so she wouldn't have to move our damn bikes every time she wanted to park her car. She didn't want to be the kind of mother who spent all her time nagging the children to pick up their things. And it worked. We felt important, pulling into our special parking spots, putting the kickstand down with authority.

I tell Flo now, that in some ways, I wish she hadn't done this.

I expected the world to be so much more organized. I expected to know what to call things. I expected there to be a place already marked for me.

An Evening of Theater

Flo and I walk on a frigid night in December from the Dudley Riggs comedy theater to my apartment a few blocks away. We walk slowly, her pace. She says she hasn't been feeling well lately, that she's been tired, that tonight she's dizzy for some reason. She walks with uncertainty, weaving a little. "My equilibrium is all off," she says. "I don't understand it. Yesterday Jane and I went to the Walker for our art group, and I got so dizzy," she says. "I had a muffin, you know, and I thought that would help, but who can make sense of art when it's spinning around? I was so wiped out when I got home. I slept for three hours. I didn't wake up until dinnertime."

I don't know what to say. She has always napped. Often when I call, if she doesn't answer, I assume she is napping. Then I leave prank calls on the answering machine, telling her that I am from NBC and would like her opinion on *The Bold and the Beautiful.* Or that I'm sorry she missed this opportunity to win a thousand dollars—all she would have had to do was to wave her bra out the front door. I leave fake names and numbers, and she gets back to me eventually. She seems to me to have been tired for years, still recuperating from having all of us at home. The napping is not new; only the dizziness is a new development. "So you're tired?" I say tonight, as we walk in the darkness.

"It's been like that lately," she says. "This week, especially."

"Have you ever thought of taking a painting class," I ask my mother, who has a natural artistic ability I envy, a sense of color, texture, design, placement that I do not possess. "You used to take painting classes when we were little."

"I don't have the energy," she says. "I barely have the energy to do my work for city council. I finally got them to plant trees in the grocery store parking lot."

"That's good," I say.

"We need green in our lives," she says.

Suddenly Flo loses her balance and crashes against the dumpster in the alley near my apartment. "Yikes!" she says, teetering, grabbing for my arm, regaining her composure, balancing herself by holding on to me.

I ask her if she is okay. I tell her that in a smaller town the cops might throw her in the drunk tank for a display like that; that she's lucky she's in the big city where she's the *least* of their worries.

"It's frustrating," she says. "I never feel like I'm on level ground."

We walk quietly for a while, her hand clutching the crook of my arm, her dependence making me uncomfortable.

"My golf game last summer was awful," she says. "When I'd swing I'd practically whirl around and fall on the grass."

"You had this problem last summer?" I ask.

"It's getting worse," my mother says quietly.

My Boyfriend

Has been in Mexico for almost six months. He sends postcards, telling me about his job as a bartender in a resort, telling me I should visit so we can go up and down the coast. While he is gone I test software, watch TV with Karen, and take an evening pottery class; I work hard to center small bowls. He is planning on coming back soon, and though we've both been dating other people, but not seriously, I decide to go and visit him. I had cried when he left, surprising myself. And also, Northwest Airlines is offering special discount fares. And also, for some reason, I have begun to miss his warm body, his smell of onions and souring milk.

On the plane ride down, I meet a radiologist as I'm standing in line for the bathroom. He is nice, young and good-looking, and traveling with two female friends from medical school. It seems like a good sign that women are willing to travel with him, and so we exchange phone numbers.

At the airport, when I land in Mexico City, I wait for my boyfriend for almost two hours. No one answers at his house, and he is nowhere to be seen.

I sit on my luggage—in the airport for a while—outside the airport for a while, back in the airport for a while, wondering if something has happened to him, then wondering if I should get a hotel, then wondering if he's just not ever going to show, and if I should just head up the coast by myself.

When he finally arrives, he shuffles in through the automatic doors, lit from behind by the bright sun outside. Hands in his pockets, jaws clenched, he says nothing, just picks up one of my bags and begins to walk away with it.

Therapy

Here is how I finally break up with my boyfriend: I go to a psychic, hoping she will tell me what to do, and she sends me to a counselor, who says that psychics and counselors are basically the same thing. "From the minute you came in the door," says the counselor, "I could tell you needed help. You don't need to be psychic to see that." I had grown smaller; my posture was bent. I had stopped wearing much makeup or jewelry.

It takes me about five minutes of sitting with the counselor before I feel comfortable enough to burst out crying. Her office is littered with pillows and pink macramé blankets. She has plenty of Kleenex and says she does not charge extra for them. "Tell me about this relationship," she says. "Do you want to stay in it?"

My Boyfriend

Says "Fuck you!" when I tell him that I don't want to see him anymore. He also says that we were meant to be together, and when I wake up, I'll realize that.

I had woken up several nights ago to find him trying to push himself inside of me from behind, while I was sleeping. I swatted him away with my arm, as if he were a gigantic fly, and told him to leave me alone.

We've both been back from Mexico for a couple of months. He moved back shortly after I left, saying it was time to get back to school, and we still see each other, even though our vacation together was a disaster. We had fought for almost three weeks straight, almost the entire time I was there.

Since we've been back he seems to keep making a point of forgetting to show up for our occasional dates, for movies, walks, dinner. He forgets to call, or calls only during my favorite television shows. I have begun to think that he is purposely testing me by calling during *Northern Exposure.* He attributes it all to absentmindedness, which makes me feel crazy and paranoid.

"I'm tired of you showing up late for things, or not showing up at all," I say. "I'm tired of us. This isn't working."

"You're full of shit," he says. "Whatever."

"It's happened several times," I say.

"Several! Oh, right, several!" he balks. "I hate it when you exaggerate like that. Do you realize how much you exaggerate everything? You make everything in life into this big *drama.* It's unhealthy."

"Why are you being so cruel?" I say.

"Because I hate it when you get on me like this. And I'm not being cruel. I'm not. You just piss me off."

"Well, it has happened a number of times," I say. "You keep forgetting our dates."

"In your imagination," he says. "Name the times."

"I can think of three examples off the top of my head."

"That's not several," he says.

"Excuse me?"

"Three is not *several.*"

"Well, it's what I think of as several."

"Well, it's not. And it's not how most people look at *several.* Most people, when speaking of *several,* mean five or six. Five or six at least."

"Well, I have always thought of it as three or four, and what's the point, for Christ's sake, of all this? A couple is two, *several* is three or four."

"It is not. It's five or six. Or more."

"Well, fine! Who gives a damn! The fact is," I say, "that you continually fail to call or show up when we've made plans. And we don't even see each other *that* often."

"Oh, *continually*, now? Not just *several*? You know, you twist everything around to meet your needs. We have language in order to communicate. We have words that mean something so that we're all describing the same experience, and when some people don't know the proper definition for something—for example, mixing up descriptions of *quantity*—when language is used inappropriately, or in the wrong *context*, it creates all sorts of problems and misunderstandings."

"You've turned into an asshole," I say.

"Go to hell," he says, hanging up.

I will find out later that shortly after he got back from Mexico he had begun seeing someone else, and didn't know how to tell me, so he'd sort of been seeing both of us, except she knew about me.

I find it out in the same way I've figured out most things in our relationship, months after the fact. How I figured out, finally, that the reason my credit card had been missing from my wallet for about a day before my boyfriend's roommate found it, was because my boyfriend's roommate had stolen it in the first place, though it was maxed-out and wouldn't get him anything.

I found out about my boyfriend's new girlfriend in the same way that I found out that his old roommate, Ben, the one who'd been arrested for shoplifting, had hanged himself. Still wearing his electronic ankle bracelet, he had hanged himself for reasons no one could understand.

I was told everything casually, and much, much later. In the same way that he could never tell me about school, or work, because I expected, he said, too much of him. "You always say we're not right for each other, anyway," he said. Which was true. I had.

My Lease

When it comes up, I tell Karen that I don't think I'd like to renew it, which is fine with her, since she's graduated from her M.B.A. program and is thinking of buying a house.

A Tumor

Is the reason for my mother's dizziness, the spinning she's been feeling for so long.

When I call her from work she tells me that surgery is scheduled in a month in Rochester. "It's what your father thought it was," she says. He is a good diagnostician. "My doctor says it's almost certain that it's not malignant," Flo says. "That's what your father thinks, too. But it's a necessary surgery. So it's good timing that you're moving home," she adds. "It will be nice to have you around the house to help. I'm not sure how I'll be feeling."

Moving Home

I don't tell my mom and dad much about why I'm coming back. I tell them I want to pay off my credit card bills, that I still have huge bills from Mexico (I had paid for all of our hotel bills, food, snorkeling and our dolphin rides), and that I'd like to finish paying for my new car (the Delta '88, my grandmother's old car, had died). I tell them that I just need to be at home for a while to get caught up, to get myself out of debt. I tell them I'm thinking about applying for graduate school and that I should start saving up for it. And I add, of course, that I'll be home for the surgery. I can help out afterward.

I don't tell them much, because it's not especially clear to me, either.

I just come home the way birds migrate back to the same place, without thinking, assuming the nest will still be there.

Part Two \ Our Optical Biosphere

The Local People

The first morning I am home, Flo comes knocking on the bathroom door. "Excuse me, I need my Wet Socks and my bathing suit for water aerobics. Well, *someone's* taking her time getting to work this morning. What time did you say you get there?"

I try to explain to her, again, the concept of flex time.

"Boy, you'll never find another job like this one."

"I hope not," I say.

"They let you come in this late? What do they think about that?"

"They think I like to sleep in the morning. I stay until six P.M. They don't care."

"Oh. Hmmm," she says. She advises me to eat a sensible breakfast and to pack a lunch to save money. "You are interested in saving money, aren't you?" she says. "There's some real nice bread in the fridge," she says. "I brought it back from Santa Fe." Flo has recently been to Santa Fe, too, to look at art with her friend Pauline. "It's homemade by the local people," Flo goes on about the bread. "It's real good."

Thank you, I say.

"Is that your breakfast?" she says, looking at the coffee cup on the bathroom counter. She kisses me on the cheek. "Bye, sweet pea. I'm going to class. Maybe that blouse would look nice tucked in."

On Wednesday morning, as I'm getting ready for work, she wants to know if I have a "five-year plan," and how long I think

I'll be staying. "No pressure," she says. "I'd just like to know what to tell people when they ask. I've been saying that you're saving for graduate school."

"That sounds good," I tell her.

Wednesday evening, perhaps, I could devote some energy to organizing my space?

Thursday evening, perhaps, I should get some sleep so I wouldn't have to go to work so late in the morning.

On Saturday, my shorts are too ripped and worn-looking. "Why don't you go put on one of your cute biking outfits? You never know who you're going to meet around the lakes," she says, "but I don't know what you'll pick up looking like that!"

I tell her all my cute outfits are still in boxes.

"I got you all those nice things," she sighs. "And people will think you're a bag lady."

On Sunday, she thinks I would like her dentist. He has dazzling brown eyes and a beautiful smile; he's *very* personable.

On Monday, when I get home from work, I find my brand-new linen shorts in a crumpled mess on the ironing board. Flo has washed my clothes, which is nice. But I was expecting, as has been policy ever since I left for college, to wash my own clothes. She had always told us then that she was happy to have us home but that she wasn't "our weekend slave." Now it looks like my shorts have been tumble dried into the toddler department.

"Goddamnit," I say, throwing them on top of a pile of towels.

"There's no need to swear," says Flo. "Just steam them a little and spray starch and iron them. They'll be fine. And you know, Lady Aster," she says, "now that you're trying to save money, you might think twice about buying expensive shorts."

Instructions for ironing things out at home:

1. Place mother in wash tub. Soak several hours. Agitate.
2. Spin like hell.
3. Hang out to dry. In the wind.
4. Spray with starch. Steam. Press until flat.
5. Hang in closet and close door.
6. Send out to be handled professionally if necessary.

The part that's most agitating is that she is right. Once I iron the shorts, they are fine.

Aspirations

When President Bush tells the American public that it makes his heart sick to see thousands of college graduates unable to find "meaningful work," and moving home, my parents cheer.

"Go, George. Amen!" says my father. He and my mother both sit on the couch clapping, even though only one of them will vote for him.

"I didn't know he had a heart," I say.

I've been back home for two weeks. My mother had told me I was welcome, of course, but still she can't resist following me around the house and saying things like, "The thing I don't quite understand is, when I was your age I couldn't wait to get out and *fly*. To prove to myself, and to the world, what I could do."

I tell her the runways are more crowded now.

"Well, I just don't see any feisty survival instinct, or drive in you," she says. "What are your aspirations?"

The word conjures up an image of me choking, clutching my throat.

The difference, I tell her, is that she was raised in an era when Jell-O was an exciting new member of the Fruit Group. When your bra made your breasts look like dangerous cones. When your sweater must absolutely match your lipstick. Pausing briefly, I notice that her lipstick matches her sweat suit, a raspberry color.

I remind her that when she lived in California as a young teacher, there was still plenty of room for everyone to live near the beach. Why is she badgering me? I point out that she was a young girl during World War II, when there was a real and singular presence of evil in the world to fear, instead of a generalized one, hovering over us now more thickly than our dwindling ozone layer.

"Hmmmm," she says. "I guess I'm an optimist."

Therapy

My boyfriend, now ex-boyfriend, calls me at my parents' house sometimes, usually during *Northern Exposure.* Often we start fighting and then hang up on each other, like cars that have run out of gas but keep sputtering for a while before they die.

Once, my father comes upstairs from his office when I'm on the phone with my boyfriend, now ex-boyfriend. While I'm on the phone, my dad reaches in the notepad drawer, takes some scissors out of the scissors cup, takes a pen out of the pen cup and goes to sit at the kitchen table.

While I am still on the phone my father places in front of me on the desk a little star he's cut out. It says, in the middle, "For endurance."

Though I hadn't told my parents much about my boyfriend, my father would tell me later that each time my boyfriend called, I'd sink, literally, in my chair.

The counselor asks me if I'd feel comfortable asking my parents to answer the phone, and to refuse to give me any messages should my boyfriend call.

I tell her that I think that would be all right.

I write a good-bye letter to my boyfriend and read it to the counselor. She mails it for me. She does not charge extra for this.

We talk about the ways that the body becomes used to things, how the body often responds, even when the mind has gone to a different place, floated off somewhere else entirely.

At home, in my parents' garage, I have a ceremonial destruction of everything he's ever given me—a jacket, a shirt, some wine glasses, some tapes—I cut them and rip them and smash them until they are nothing but shreds and shards. "This is hard," I tell Flo. "I'm used to keeping everything. I'm not used to throwing anything away, especially if it's still good."

"Oh, I totally understand," says Flo, who was born toward the end of the Depression, who was a small child during World War II. "But some things, you just have to get rid of, symbolically."

He had loaned me a few books, and those, I mail back to him. A week later the package is returned to me, unopened.

"Just throw it away," says the counselor.

"Really?" I say. "I mean, books, I could give those to the library or something."

"Just throw them away," she says. "For once."

And I do, thinking about how the words and ideas will be dumped on top of a heap of rotting junk, how they will be consumed, eventually, by the smelly juices of decomposition.

"Letting go is so hard for you," says the counselor.

"I hate not knowing," I tell her. "What's going to come next. Him, at least, I knew."

A Tumor

The night before my mother's surgery, the nurses have asked her to shower and scrub with antiseptic gel and now, at 5:30 on the morning of her surgery, her hair has dried in her sleep and is flaring out on her pillow. She looks like Albert Einstein.

My father asks her how she slept, what she had to eat the night before. Have they given her anything yet? Any medications?

"They kept me up half the night checking on things," she says.

"Now, which leg are they going to take off?" I ask her, fiddling with the chart at the bottom of her bed.

"That's not even funny," says Flo. "Those things happen, you know."

"I know," I say.

My mother's breasts have slipped down by her armpits and she wiggles in the bed a little to adjust them. "Maybe I could get the surgeon to perk these things up while he's at it," she says.

"Like he's going to do that when you're being so fussy about keeping your leg," I say.

She is Florence Irene Tillman Olson, age 56, patient number 325, room 506, scheduled for removal of an acoustic neuroma.

"That sounds like some kind of new age musical group," I say. "Acoustic Neuroma."

She has no allergies to medications. She is one of hundreds of the sick, wearing a blue Saint Mary's gown and a white plastic bracelet. A healthcare convict.

"You know," I say, pointing to her plastic hospital jewelry, "that's what all of the kids are wearing in New York."

"You're kidding," she says.

"It's true," I say, because it is not.

When my sister was a senior in high school, my parents took her to Madison, Wisconsin, to look at the university there. On their way, they stopped and picked me up at college, thinking I would like a weekend off campus, doing something different. In my sophomore year, I was still having trouble meeting people, and I was happy to spend the weekend in Wisconsin with my family. I was looking forward to free meals and cable access, and I sat on my suitcase in the lobby of my dorm, waiting, a pillow next to me for sleeping in the car.

When my family arrived, my sister came bounding into the lobby and shouted, "Sorry this school thing didn't work out, but Mom and Dad think you'll like the mental institution. They'll let you paint and draw there if you behave." Then she grabbed my suitcase and walked out, leaving me standing in the lobby on a Friday night, holding a pillow, smiling at a group of students I didn't know who were loitering by the front desk.

So now, at 6 A.M., after the nurses have given my mother a Valium and as they roll her down the cold hospital corridor like a cart full of groceries, I shout, "Good luck with your sex change!"

Flo waves a hand in the air vaguely, a sign that the Valium has already taken some action. "You sex change!" she says, arm flopping back down at her side. "That's my daughter," she says to the nurse.

She is Florence Irene Tillman Olson, age fifty-six, and she had asked her surgeon the night before if he had a good relationship with his wife.

I don't want him to take his issues out on me," she had said. "I want him to know who he's dealing with, you know, so I'm not just a chart."

A Flo Chart

Before the chart can even start, there are your parents, Helen and Bill. You are an only child—though, when you are forty-five, you'll learn you have a half-brother. It is rumored that Bill had an affair when he was engaged to Helen, but having lived through the Depression, and unable to throw anything away, Helen married Bill, anyway. And since your half-brother looks like both your father *and* Franklin Delano Roosevelt, it's impossible to confirm anything.

You are born Florence Irene Tillman in a small town in Minnesota and move around Minnesota, to a new town, about once a year. Helen sets up the apartment, takes down the apartment, sets up a new apartment, over and over and over. She tries to save money for a house and starches all the laundry. You make friends, new ones, over and over. You learn that life is dynamic, fluid. You are the Darwinian champion of western Minnesota. You learn to change your spots.

When you are six, and you are visiting your aunts, your mother's sisters, up north in Calloway, Minnesota, near the Indian reservation, you ask your elders for ice-cream money. Could you have five cents to go to town for an ice-cream cone? You walk, with your nickel, to the lodge that's on the reservation, and you put your money in the slot machine.

When your mother thinks you need a bath, she doesn't say, "It's time for a bath," she says, "Something sure does smell around here," and puts her nose in the air to sniff, wrinkles up her face. After a while, you figure out the code, the hidden message of sniffing, though sometimes it really is just the garbage, or the particularly smelly exhaust system of a car that's driven by, and so you are never quite sure. *Is it you? Or is it something else?*

Sometimes, when your mother is angry with you, she hits you on the back of the leg with a flyswatter. You learn to tell yourself that you have done something well.

In high school, you make all of your own clothes, you put together the yearbook, you smoke sometimes with your friends.

You have smooth, round cheekbones, white teeth and pin-curled hair. You dream about marrying Edward Olson, who runs track and plays football and basketball. Who is the class valedictorian and class president and says odd things sometimes that make no sense. Who writes, in your senior yearbook, "Florence. We've had a lot of good times. Maybe we should start a gum collection. A Gum Club. Everyone loves gum!"

When your father, Bill, is working late, as he often is, you and your mother eat together. Your favorite: fresh green beans in cream sauce. The two of you talking. When you are much older, your daughter will say to you, "I can't imagine hanging out and shooting the shit with Grandma." You can't imagine, at this time, that you will ever have a daughter who would say such things. But you, much older, will say to your daughter, "People are different in different times and places. People are different with different people."

Go back a little, which interrupts the Flo chart. Go back to when you are eight and you're at the ice-skating rink, in the warming house. There's an old man there, who's always there, who always says hello to you. Today it's just the two of you, late in the ice-skating season, and he wants you to sit in his lap. He pulls you close to him, grabbing you by the jacket, putting a hand on the back of your skinny leg, surrounding you with his mothball breath.

You run from the warming house through the snow and all the way home.

Years later, when you are a young mother, living in a small town where people leave their cars running outside the grocery store on cold winter days, where no one locks up their homes and kids bike around town and to the beach not really having to worry about traffic, you will come out of the Ben Franklin to find your daughter Greta sitting on the lap of a very fat man, a man who sits in the park each day, all day during the summer, whose jeans are brown with dirt and who smells like garbage rotting in the sun. Your daughter is on his lap and he is bouncing her on his knee. Her older sister is nearby, on the playground equipment. You scream, run across the street, snatch her from his filthy grip, grab your other child and never let them out of your sight again. From now on, they go in to Ben Franklin with you, where they will spend what seems like hours poring through the penny-candy bins. Tupperware containers filled with Tootsie Rolls and Bit-O-Honey and bubble gum. They can choose three pieces each because it's important for children to have limits and to learn to make choices.

Go back again, further. You have only been married a few months, living in Milwaukee. Your husband, Edward Olson, has just finished his service time, having returned from Korea. When you leave Milwaukee and return to Minnesota, you bring a gigantic army-issue desk, which you will keep in the basement for years, where your husband will pile his charts and medical journals and jazz records. He joins a private medical practice in a small town on the Minnesota River, Chaska, which means, in the language of the Dakota Indians, "Oldest Son."

Your Oldest Son, on his way out of the womb, bumps up against your pelvic bones so many times that he has to be pulled out with forceps. For weeks afterward he has two big bumps on his head and all the nuns at the hospital think he is retarded. He will become a National Merit Scholar and a professor of philosophy.

Your second child, a daughter, is so small that she's almost born in the toilet. The nuns at the hospital will tell you "void yourself" before you go into the labor room, and your daughter will almost come out with everything else. Which will turn out to be, unlike the birth of your son, strangely appropriate and symbolic. While your son proved all the nuns wrong by becoming a genius, your daughter will remain, mentally, intellectually, emotionally, in the toilet. Delighted by all things scatological, she will challenge your sense of propriety and often puzzle you for other reasons. She has asthma, gasps for breath in the middle of the night. For her, you buy special mattresses and pillowcases, a vaporizor, a family dog with no dander. When her chest seizes up, you wrap her in a wool blanket, call your husband, rock her back and forth until the doctor arrives. You learn the sounds of her breathing in the way a sailor knows the wind.

You have a third child, who is born while the river is flooded. You and your husband take the neighbor's duck boat to the hospital, a small motorboat that takes you to Saint Francis Catholic Hospital, where your husband will one day be chief of staff and where the nuns make Jell-O and where you've driven to deliver your other two children. You are in labor during a flood, riding in the moonlight in a motorboat. This third child will be the most independent. She will have a theatrical sense, a loud voice like Ethel Merman's, and a yearning to get out in the world. Together with her older sister (who is shy unless she is at home), they will challenge your patience. You will find yourself saying things like, "There's no call for language like that around here" and "Could you girls tone it down a little?" You will make appeals to their sense of dignity, which you will realize later is like asking a polka band to play Vivaldi.

You have had, in between each child, at least one miscarriage, so you decide to quit after three kids.

You get one of those new IUDs, something like a collection of fish hooks hanging in your uterus, doing the opposite of fishing, casting off life. You have quit smoking for the children's sake and taken up chewing gum, instead. This is how your young children will be able to find you in the grocery store.

They will hear you snap your gum, all the way from aisle six. They will know it as your noise.

Your mother dies of leukemia when you are in your forties, when your children are still young. At the end of her life, she believes the intravenous drip is an angel; there are angels everywhere in her hospital room. Years later you will tell your middle child that you believe household chemicals killed your mother. "She scrubbed the life out of that house," you will say, remembering the harsh chemicals she used to keep everything spotless. "She scrubbed the life out of life."

When you are still in your forties, the doctors will find a grapefruit-sized lump in your uterus, will pronounce it benign and will pull the whole business out. Your children won't know what to make of it, you being in the hospital, the person who's supposed to be in charge of them. Their father is there every day. It's a fine place to be. You will come home, too.

When you are almost sixty, you go to Rochester for surgery, with a tumor like a wad of gum, stuck in your inner ear. Where do these things come from? How do they produce themselves and decide where to lodge? It's the kind of thing your middle child would have done growing up, shoving a wad of gum in her ear just to know what it would feel like. It's the kind of thing she would do now.

A Tumor

My father buys a *Time* magazine and we wait in the neurosurgery lounge, which has a glass cabinet displaying various quilted scarves made by women in Rochester and apparently on sale in the gift shop. I wonder what Flo might like to wear on her head, since she'll be missing a big patch of hair. She had told me before surgery that, like her summers in Hawaii when she was a high school teacher, she might just like to wear a hibiscus behind her ear.

"That's right," I'd said, "didn't you say that one hibiscus behind the ear means you're single, and two just stands for bald? Or was it 'hairing-impaired'?"

"Oh, stop it," Flo had said, but she was laughing.

When I was small, Flo rigged up an elaborate system for combating my asthma. She got eyelet screws and plugged them into the ceiling, ran a cord through them and then hung bedsheets from the cording. What she created was something like a shower curtain around my bed, to keep vapor in. Whenever I returned from the hospital, I'd spend the days until I got better in my vaporizing tent, with Vicks plastered on my chest and neck, a wool sweater over my pajama top, and a wool sock pinned around my neck, which I made a fuss about, saying that the safety pin might come open and stab me in the neck.

Flo gave me books to read, blank paper, crayons and markers, and left me with the kitchen timer, which I could set to go off every twenty minutes. This way, Flo could get some work done around the house without me bugging her constantly. When the buzzer went off, Flo would show up, taking requests for root beer or banana Popsicles, chicken or tomato soup, did I want the bathroom radio for a while?

My mother made designs for me on blank paper, squiggles that I was to make something out of, a shape or a picture.

She would do ten or twenty of these and then leave me in the vaporizing tent with this sort of Gestalt kiddie project, making forms from implied shapes, trying to make something real from abstractions.

* * *

When I was a senior in college, my mother told me that if I wanted to have breast reduction surgery, since I was always complaining about my boobs being too big, that I should make up my mind. I needed to do it while I was still in college, she said, while I was still on my parents' insurance.

I was a lifeguard and taught swimming lessons every summer, and it was hard for me to find a swimsuit. I'd cry when we went shopping for swimsuits, sweaters, bras, and blouses, and my mother always looked exasperated.

"Don't cry," she would say. "It's your body. It's nature. Boys are built straight up and down. Women were given shape for a reason."

I was, on one side, a 36DD. On the other side, my breast was off the charts, like some kind of genius child, precocious and over-achieving. I refused to buy specially made bras, and crammed both boobs in a 36DD, the smaller size. I believed there was something wrong with me that made me fundamentally crooked, inside and out, and I wasn't willing to acknowledge it with specially made garments.

What had I done to deserve this?

"You're always complaining that you can't find clothes, that you have to wear two bras to aerobics," Flo said.

"Well, it's true," I said.

"Well then do something about it," she said.

I agreed to go to the doctor for a consultation. He lifted up my breasts and made marks on them with a ballpoint pen. He took Polaroid photos of me, like some topless convict. Side and front shots to send to the insurance company.

"I'd take you down to a C cup," said the doctor. "With your proportions, that would look best." I took this to mean that I had a big butt.

The insurance company agreed to pay for half the surgery; since one breast was so much bigger than the other, they thought the surgery to be in part practical, in part cosmetic.

"Your father and I will pay for the little one," Flo said, thinking she was being incredibly funny. "So, what do you want to do? If you're going to do it, you should have the surgery at Christmas, when you're home from school."

It was the end of summer and we were driving home from Southdale with new school clothes. I had started crying, as usual, in the fitting room, and Flo had reassured me that I looked fine and that there was nothing wrong with having a *figure.*

Now I watched myself in the passenger-side mirror. *What did it mean to change your body? To not keep what you were given?* Was there a reason that I'd been given incredibly large boobs? Or had there been hormones and funny chemicals in the casseroles my mother served? And then why did they affect only me? Growing up Catholic, I had learned that things happen for a reason, though we hardly ever knew what it was, and that you should suffer quietly. Maybe in the afterlife I would be rewarded with the same kind of perky breasts I'd had briefly in grade ten. *Why had my body gone haywire like this?* Why, suddenly in grade twelve, had everything moved like the tectonic plates, an underground shift creating mountains on the surface? Why this embarrassing abundance of womanhood?

"You could talk to Sue McDonald," Flo said. "Dr. Lundeen did her surgery, too, and she'd be happy to tell you about it. She's thrilled with her results."

I wasn't sure that I wanted to talk to Sue McDonald about my breasts.

"I really think you'll feel better," she said.

I watch reruns of *Hogan's Heroes* with an eight-year-old kid named Rudy, while my dad reads *JAMA* and goes through some of the patient charts he's brought along.

After four hours of waiting, I begin to look up when the nurse comes in the room, thinking she'll bring us news.

The night before my breast reduction surgery, my mother gave me a new pink robe. "This is to take to the hospital," she said. "And to the health club tonight." She had made an appointment for me to have an hour-long massage, because she'd read an article that said massage before surgery promotes faster healing.

I had forgotten that she'd done it until after I saw her being wheeled into surgery, down the long, cold corridor, and it occurred to me that I hadn't done anything for her.

In the second bed of a small, moist and dimly lit room, my mother lies on her side, her head wrapped in so much gauze it appears that she is wearing a white helmet, blood soaking through on one side. Her skin is gray. When she opens her eyes they have a thick, milky film. She looks at me, at first, as if she doesn't know me, and then furrows her brows.

My father knows exactly what to say. He asks if she is in much pain. "How do you feel, Flo?" he says.

"Like shit," she says. This seemed obvious to me, but there must be some relief in saying it. Then he tells her the time and where she is. How long she was in surgery, and how long in the recovery room. That everything went well.

"Hi, Mom," I say.

She looks up at me and acknowledges exactly what I was hoping I could mask. "Hi, Shanny," she says softly. "Is it hard to see me this way?"

This is the person who brought you Popsicles when you were sick, and cleaned up your vomit. This is the person who made you a paper doll of yourself to keep you busy, complete with your own paper wardrobe. This is the person who crushed bitter pills in Hershey's chocolate syrup, who gave you a bell to ring when you needed something. So you want to say, "Hell, you look great."

"Well, it's sort of hard," I squeak out. "You just look like you feel really sick."

"Yes, I threw up once already," she says weakly. "I'm so thirsty," she says, and licks her oxygen mask.

My dad puts his hand on my shoulder, "I think we better get you out of here before you fall over."

Before we go, my mother looks up at me again. "They took all my jewelry," she says. "I had so much jewelry—Oh, I'm sorry," she says. "I'm not very good company right now."

"Neither is Dad," I say. And then it occurs to me that people coming out of anesthesia don't want to hear dumb jokes.

A few days later Flo is sitting up in bed, still wearing her blue Saint Mary's gown. Part of the tumor had been sitting between two of her facial nerves, and in the process of removing it, the nerves have been bruised. The left side of her face, the neurologist tells us, will be temporarily paralyzed, and they will need to test her hearing to find out if she'll lose it on that side. She has a plastic bubble taped over her left eye. "It looks like the Hubert H. Humphrey Metrodome!" she laughs, the right side of her mouth turning up, the left unresponsive, as if it still hasn't awakened from surgery. I start calling her "Humphrey." She must wear the eye bubble to keep her left eye moist; because of the nerve damage, it cannot blink or produce tears.

I tell Flo that if she is embarrassed, we could give it a euphemism. I offer up: Optical Biosphere.

"I like that!" she says.

I take Flo on walks around the hospital. She does not want my arm, but instead grabs hold of the waist of my skirt, or a belt. She tugs a few times when she wants to turn or slow down. She directs me over to the Ear, Nose and Throat section of the hospital, where, before surgery, she had noticed the largest concentration of young, good-looking, available doctors.

"There's one for you," she whispers out of the side of her mouth that can move.

"I thought you were advising against marrying doctors," I say.

"That's true," she says.

We work on the jigsaw puzzles that have been left on the lounge tables and check them several times a day to see if other people have made any progress in completing them. Our favorite is a puzzle that is a picture of various cocktails. "Let's go visit the daiquiri puzzle," Flo tugs on my belt, interested in seeing which spaces have been filled.

I walk slowly with my mother, looking for cute doctors, noticing the humidity that builds up in her Optical Biosphere.

My mother has always had systems. Systems for keeping me alive and systems for maintaining her own sanity. So when her own system fails now, she comes up with a way to organize her experience.

"Sickness is a part of life," she said before going into surgery. "I look at this as an adventure, an opportunity to learn."

"I hate learning," I told her. "I wish we could all be dumb and happy." I couldn't stop thinking about the stories I'd heard about people who got cancer and then made radical changes in their lives, forgoing surgery, chemotherapy, any traditional medical treatments, doing something instead like selling everything they owned, quitting their jobs and traveling around the country by motorcycle. If you could heal by traveling around on a motorcycle, then there must have been something really wrong with the life you'd had before.

I had always wondered why I had asthma, why I couldn't breathe when other people could? And then, when I was dating the ex-boyfriend, I started to have problems, bladder infections that kept coming back. I believed it was my body's way of wanting to keep him away from me, though it didn't work.

And now I wondered why Flo's body had come up with this tumor, this little wad of gum jammed in her ear canal, cells gone wild and blocking the entrance of sound. It made me wonder what her body wanted, what it was missing, and whether it had had too much of something else. Maybe it was NutraSweet, all that raspberry soda. And maybe, I thought, it was something created by her body to get attention from my father, medical attention if nothing else.

Later the counselor will say, *You need to learn to mind your own business. You need to learn to live your own life instead of spending time coming up with theories. Your mother had a very difficult surgery.*

But shouldn't we wonder why it happened? I will say.

No, the counselor will say. *We shouldn't. This is your depression. Do you see that? This need of yours to create an explanation. It keeps you busy. It keeps you in your own head. You are in your own head the same way that tumor was in your mother's. Doing nothing but sitting there causing trouble.*

But there should be reasons for things, I will tell her. *Even for sitting. Why am I sitting here now? At this time? In this place? I could be training for the Olympics. I could have been someone entirely different. How did I get here? Life should make sense.*

Sense comes through movement, says the counselor. *Some day you'll see that. Answers come when you're out there living.*

Sometimes, I will tell her, *you sound exactly like my mother.*

And? the counselor will say.

And it drives me crazy.

It's hard to see a parent go through something like that, she says. *Suddenly they're vulnerable. We all want to run.*

The tumor, they found, was benign, as expected. But Flo has lost her hearing in her left ear. The color is returning to her face, and she seems more alert. The thick helmet of gauze has been removed, and she now wears a little cap, which looks more like a beige orthopedic stocking that's been cut and closed on top with a rubber band. I tell her she kind of looks like a gangster, with one side of her mouth turned up, the other benign, unresponsive. I tell her she'd look good with a cigar in her mouth. That she looks cynical.

"Oh, good," says Flo. "Now I finally fit in with the rest of the family!"

"I think cynics are realists," I say to her now, and she just looks at me, one side of her face showing concern, the other quiet.

Because only a bad daughter would be so insensitive, I go sit quietly by the daiquiri puzzle.

Finally we receive a call from my brother, who was biking in France and couldn't call sooner.

My sister also calls that day from Mexico. She's been bathing in the hot springs somewhere up the mountains and called to say that she was thinking about us.

My mother had told them not to worry, not to change their summer travel plans, that she had the best care. That she would be fine.

I go visit the daiquiri puzzle again, which is no nearer completion, wishing I could have been someplace else, too.

Priorities

We bring my mother home a week after surgery. Her hair's been washed, her stitches taken out. She puts on new "fun" pajamas.

I go shopping for her and buy a dozen or so headbands to try, in various colors and styles, choosing the ones I think are most likely to cover her new bald spot. I go grocery shopping and buy ice cream, sherbet, applesauce, two kinds of juice, and Diet Dr Pepper, her most frequent request in the hospital. I make 1-2-3 Jell-O, tuna casserole (soft and easy to eat), spicy chili ("It might wake up the left side of your face!"). I make her a sign that says: "WELCOME HOME, HUMPHREY! WE LOVE YOU."

On it I've drawn a picture of her, wearing a headband, with a hibiscus behind her ear, and her Optical Biosphere.

When I get home from work, my father, mother and I make dinner together. I do the laundry. I water the plants. Flo sleeps most of the day, waking up occasionally to sip ginger ale from a straw.

At the end of the week, I return from work in a funk. I tell Flo I've had a bad day. I am PMS-ridden and teary-eyed. Testing software sucks, I tell her. Jerry Corp sucks. The drive home sucked. I am having what my sister and I call, "One of those days when you cry just because you wear glasses," a category of experience developed after the morning my sister woke up, began putting in her contacts and burst out crying—so tired of dealing with bad vision, so tired of buying saline solutions. I tell Flo I can't stand my job anymore.

"Well, do you have any plans?" she says. "You know, I've been thinking. It might be a wise idea for you to give me your checkbook, and I'll give you an allowance. That way you'll be forced to spend no more than you can afford. I see you spending your money without thinking, making bad decisions. You don't limit yourself, or set budgets. You want to go visit your sister, but have you thought about how you'll eat, or whatever? When I was your age I borrowed three hundred fifty dollars to go to Florida, and we packed sandwiches and—"

"God, Mom! The only thing I've spent money on since I moved home is groceries, a million fucking headbands, a cookbook and a bra that I got on sale! Do you want my boobs to hang on the ground?"

"Well, cripes, I'll give you money for groceries and headbands," Flo says, looking down at the kitchen table. "But you know, people who don't have money don't spend money. They decide what's important to them and how they can afford it. They set priorities."

"Well, one of my priorities is not to have my boobs hanging on the ground!"

"Well, I don't know what I'm supposed to say about that." Flo looks back up at me.

I remind her that the trip would be to help my *sister* move after graduation and get settled in Texas. I tell her that since I've been home I've paid five hundred dollars off my Visa bill. That I've met my car payments and all my other loans. "I *am* earning money," I say. "I can't make the checks come any faster, Mom."

She says nothing.

"Forget it," I say, storming to the basement, as I haven't done since I was sixteen.

Sitting in the basement, in a pile of clean towels on the laundry room floor, I can't believe what a shitty daughter I am. I cry, I weep, I rub mascara on the clean towels. I think, God, I have to wash these again.

I think, I've been yelling at a woman who has a plastic bubble over her eye. A woman who can't move the left side of her face, and who's missing quite a bit of her hair. A woman who's been living on Jell-O and Tylenol with codeine. Who has a thick, ropelike scar running up her neck, behind her ear, halfway up to the top of her head. Who has convinced herself that being in the hospital is better than being home alone all day.

I've been yelling at a woman who has had a hole the size of a fifty cent piece cut into her skull, leaving a soft spot like an infant's, to be protected only by the eventual regrowth of muscle.

When I venture back upstairs my mother offers a truce: "Say, Shannon. You might be interested in this, although maybe you already have enough to read. Have you ever seen *The Hungry Mind Review*?"

"Yes."

"Well, here is some special offer for saving money on a subscription."

Here's what pops out of my mouth, something brilliant: "Well that'll be handy. Maybe I can rig it up as a bra."

She does not even look up at me, and I just leave the room.

I suppose it's a good sign, in a way, the fact that we're bugging the shit out of each other. It means she's feeling better, that she doesn't want to be taken care of and, instead, almost instinctually, returns to her role as professional worrier. It's, perhaps, a healing reflex, something to latch on to, in the way a physical therapy patient might grab a set of bars for balance.

Expectations

Months later, when Flo is feeling better, I place an English muffin on her head and crown her Queen of England. Queen Mum.

"Thank you," she accepts. "I think you got too much sleep last night."

I am in my pajamas at eleven o'clock in the morning on a

Wednesday. When the meteorologists predicted minus forty degrees Fahrenheit the night before, with no hope of warming up, the governor closed everything—businesses and schools—saying he didn't want anyone to be trapped outside if a car or bus broke down, didn't want schoolchildren waiting at the bus stop. On January days like this the sky is a deceptive Mediterranean blue and inside the house it's warm and bright; outside, car seats are frozen solid. Flo and I are drinking coffee and haven't even tried to start our cars. Of course, my father plugged the block heater into his car the night before and made it to the hospital this morning; and somehow the paper got delivered.

My mother takes the muffin off her head and resumes her daily front-to-back reading of the *Star Tribune*. "I should never start reading the paper," she says every day. "I can't stop," as if it is some erotic vice.

She tells me my horoscope, trying to find real-life applications for its predictions. "None of this will happen, you realize," she says, "if you stay in your pajamas all day."

"Where would I go?" I ask.

She asks me if I consider myself a "home person." Some article, no doubt, has spawned this interest.

"Well, here I am," I say. "I thought it was obvious."

"No, really," she says. "Is home important to you? Do you need a base?"

"Well, a sense of home," I say. "Does it have to be physical? Can it be a close relationship? An emotional tie?"

"No, I mean having a *space* where you're comfortable and in control. Where you can relax. A place you can sit and call home. A place you can return to, a place you need to *be* sometimes."

"Well, I think so," I say. "Here I am in my pajamas."

"I know your brother needs that," she says, licking her thumb, turning the page, noticing the dead leaf on the kitchen table plant. "You don't like it here, do you?" she says to the plant, picking off the crumpled gray leaf. "I'm going to move you."

"I think," she says, walking with the tiny plant to a less sunny corner, "you are an endomorph trapped in an ectomorph's body."

"Are you talking to me or to the plant?" I ask.

"You are someone with a need for comfort," she says. "In the wrong body."

"Do you want that muffin?" I ask her.

"It's been in my hair," she says, sitting down again.

Her next inquiry, after scanning the paper: "Name three things you expected to have in life, which you no longer are expecting."

"Three anythings?" I ask her. "Could it be experiences?"

"It could be anything," she says, looking at me across her bifocals, taking a sip of her coffee.

"I don't know if I ever expected anything," I say. "Then again, I expected everything." I stop and think for a second. "I expected to have everything, without having to do anything to get it."

"Did your father and I do this to you?" she asks. "Is it something we didn't do?"

"Women's magazines did this to me," I say. "Watching *Love Boat* did this. I did this to myself."

"It's true," she says. "You always wanted to be a princess. Maybe letting you live here just encourages that."

"I have a job," I say. "Just not a job I ever wanted. And I have a car," I say. "I just never pictured myself buying a car—but then, eventually you need wheels. See?" I say to her, "What good are expectations when life keeps throwing you new expenses? How can you plan?"

"I always expected," she says, "that when my children had grown, and had college degrees, that they would leave home!" She laughs at her own joke, closing the "Variety" section. "Goals are important," she adds. "You need to have things to reach for."

"Please pass the butter," I say, still holding the cold English muffin.

And she does.

The Grieving Conference

At this morning's grieving conference we are cheerful and eager to learn about our losses, our despair. We've been provided with miniature muffins and weak coffee in tiny disposable cups. With these we are fortified, stronger before the slide projector, the graphics of grief.

There are so many things to lose: clumps of hair, children, spouses, boyfriends, your appearance, your hearing. "Say that again?" the speaker jokes, cupping his hand to his ear. "No, seriously, the loss of your hearing is very difficult indeed."

"What did he say?" my mother asks.

"He says we should give floss and herring to those in need."

"He didn't, either," she says, nudging me, cocking her head to hear with her good ear, taking a bite of the miniature bagel she has stashed in her purse—a conference-sized bagel, a novelty breakfast.

We learn today that loss can be funny. But we also learn that if you do not cry at the appropriate stage of your grief, you will sweat three times more. You will urinate three times more frequently. "It's the body, emoting," says the speaker, Vietnam veteran, married twice. He knows about loss. He knows about letting loss out, not letting it well up.

I sip my coffee, which, not unlike grief, causes me to urinate more often. From my chair I look around for the bathroom. We have been told we can go to the bathroom if we promise to come back. We can sleep, too, because the speaker also does hypnosis and believes that in sleep we will still hear him.

My mom takes notes from the transparency that's humming at the front of the room and illuminating the stage: "The Onion of Grief, Peeling Away the Layers." The layers of the onion are marked by categories of loss, the things that make us weep: the dissolution of a marriage, for instance, comes with social adjustments, one layer, and financial loss, another. Sex, physical *contact,* is in the middle of this onion, but I think it could be the skin, the sprout, any of the rings that work their way toward the middle. The smelly onion of grief with sex at its center, sex smelling up the whole kitchen, sex ruining everything.

We learn today, too, that good things, marriage—childbirth, winning a million dollars—can bring you grief. They are, after all, changes. "Have you ever noticed," says the speaker, "the similarities between weddings and funerals? Cards, flowers, the receiving line. No one says, 'You have my deepest sympathies' at a wedding—but really, you have lost something very valuable: your freedom."

He pauses for dramatic effect. "What happens to the elderly when we put them in a home?" he asks.

"They get free cable," I whisper in Flo's good ear.

"They lose their freedom," says the speaker. "Independence."

"What did he say?" my mother asks. "You were talking in my good ear."

"He says he feels freedom in those pants."

"What does that have to do with anything?" she says.

"It's not clear," I say.

Flo punches me in the shoulder again.

The conference was her idea, since she's on the hospital mailing list, but I like it here, sitting in the dark with a group of people who aren't afraid to admit that they're missing something. That there is a void. Many of them are registered nurses getting seminar credits, but I think they feel empty, too. They nod and dab their eyes from time to time, like I do.

The speaker puts up more transparencies: a woman crying at her son's funeral. "This picture was splashed all over the national news," says the speaker, "and people said the press was being invasive, 'Let her grieve privately,' they said. But I tell you, that woman was so thankful that the world knew about her loss. She *didn't* feel alone then; she received hundreds of cards and flowers." I wonder how the speaker could possibly know that; the woman lived in Bosnia, or New York, or something.

Another image: a chart showing the clinical personality inventory of a schizophrenic, a series of peaks and valleys, a line that looks like an electrocardiogram. This image is followed by the clinical personality inventory of a woman who had just lost her husband, who was an abuser, an alcoholic. The peaks and valleys on the two charts are nearly the same. "She was depressed," says the speaker, "but she was also happy. He was a jerk and she was glad to see him gone, but you can see that she was also grieving. Grief can mirror craziness," he says. "The emotions of grief are pendulous, unpredictable."

He refers to the example of lottery winnings: "It's your dream," he says, "all your life, to win that Publishers Clearing House sweepstakes, right? Here comes Ed McMahon! So you win it, and then what happens? You quit your job. People start asking you for money. You have lost your old lifestyle. You have *lost* your old lifestyle," he repeats, wagging an index finger at us.

The audience nods. My mother nods. I think, *So what?,* still holding a disposable cup filled with bad coffee. If my life was so great, I wouldn't be *here.*

At the break my mother buys his book, *Grieving to a New You.* And I have to be honest, the picture of the mother in mourning made me cry. My mother noticed it, and as we stand in the bathroom line, she asks me why.

I tell her I don't know why. That anyone's loss makes me cry.

"You must still have a lot of undealt-with things," she says sympathetically, heading into a stall.

After the conference we go to Target. I get a bag of popcorn and my mother buys a big plant for eight dollars. "This should breathe some clean air into the house," she says, hoisting the plant into her shopping cart.

We run into a woman my mother hasn't seen in a while, and she asks how my mother's surgery went.

My mother explains that her face might still return "to normal," but that she lost her hearing in one ear.

The woman nods. I nod. My mother nods. For a moment we are all silent.

A Dream She Had

As I am getting ready for work I hear Flo tossing aside her sheets and covers. She comes ambling down the hall, scratching her leg through the fabric of her nightgown. Yawning, she wanders in through the open bathroom door, lifts her nightgown and sits down on the toilet.

"Good morning," she says, mouth wide open and twisted in a second yawn. Her hair is pressed flat against her head and fluffed up on top like Lyle Lovett's. Her face has bed marks on it, the impression of sheets or the pillowcase. "God," she says, "I had the weirdest dream last night."

She dreamed, she says, that an elderly couple, a prominent local businessman and his wife, were leaving town and asked her to take care of their dog. "They were strange, though," she says, "he kept the wife in a crib or something." Anyway, the couple left town and Flo was taking very good care of the dog; in fact, she and the dog became friends. Flo held it in the palm of her hands—it was small, a white poodle—and they had a conversation.

"Do you want to know what it said?"

"I'm not sure."

"It said, 'Cowboy wants to go to the toy store.'" Flo laughs, still sitting on the toilet. "What do you suppose it all means?"

I tell Flo there is a theory that you are everyone and every object in your dream. And since a little counseling can sometimes be a dangerous thing, I ask her what my counselor would ask me, "How did you feel as the pet dog in the dream?"

"Small and cute," she laughs. "Well loved, but tiny."

"How did you feel as the wife who was kept in the crib?" I ask.

"Oh," says Flo, pausing with surprise. "Now that's interesting."

As Well as You Should Be

It's all because of my junior high school guidance counselor, says Flo. I was in his office going over my grades, and I was getting C's and B's, which I considered to be average, really mediocre, and he said to me, "You're doing about as well as you should be."

I was indignant, says Flo. I was so angry when I left his office, because basically what he had said to me was, "You are supposed to be average." I vowed right then and there not to do things the way everyone else did. I was going to be better than that. I vowed never to be average, to do things differently.

So, anyway, when your father asked me when I thought we should get married, and he suggested maybe July, I said how about May? And he said, "Well, how about June?" And I said absolutely not. Everyone gets married in June. I refuse to be a June bride. I refuse to be a cliché. It's May or forget it.

And so we got married in May.

Piles

Flo makes this confession at lunch one Saturday: "The other day, I went to go look for something in your father's office downstairs, and there was so much crap in there, I could barely get in. So you know what I did? I took a few magazines from the middle of each of those big piles he's got stacked up, and I dumped them in the wastebasket, and then covered them up so he wouldn't know they were in there! And you know what?" she says, with a kind of gleam in her eye, "we must be connected telepathically, because he came home that night and started tossing magazines out left and right. He hauled boxes and boxes of those damn medical journals off to the trash." She rests, briefly victorious.

"You know," she adds, "I went to the clinic this morning to get my blood checked, and I couldn't believe the piles your father has there. Piles in his office, charts all over the examining room—do you know they've had to devote an entire examining room to your father's piles! And I thought: How overwhelming! To have all that looming over you every day. To wake up every morning having to tackle those same piles—to just shift them around and never see them, really, getting smaller. To wake up and have *that* to look forward to, every day."

Flo finally pauses. "Why are you smiling?" she says, her brows furrowing. "Tell me."

"Well," I say, "how are your piles?"

These are the piles she spends all day trying to diminish: the mail, the bills, the tax information, interesting clippings to send to friends and children, information for the city council meeting, investment information for her Retire Rich group, plans for the addition on the house (a place, probably, which will storehouse new piles).

"My piles?" says Flo. "Ah, well, the difference with *my* piles," she punctuates the air with her index finger, "is that they are hidden. I shove them all in the closet. No one else has to trip over them, or try to work around them."

I will learn later that *piles* is an old, folksy word for hemorrhoids.

"Oh, sure," Flo will say. "I forgot about that. Well, that's appropriate."

Wisdom

On my twenty-seventh birthday, when I am still living at home, I get a letter addressed to me in big, bubbly and unfamiliar handwriting, the writing of a young girl. It simply says, "Happy Birthday, Shannon!" and there is no return address on the envelope.

Inside there is a cheap silver ring hung on some leather cording. On the ring is engraved the word WISDOM.

My ex-boyfriend always told me, I say to the counselor now, that when I wised up, I'd realize that we were meant to be together.

"And so, you think this is from him?" she says, rubbing her chin.

"Who else could it be? He probably got some girl he's hanging out with to address the envelope. He thinks he's being tricky by not putting it in his own writing."

"Well, we'll never know," says the counselor.

"I don't know anyone else who would do something like this," I tell her. "He always believed that we were meant to be together. That it was fate and that someday I would see it. The funny thing," I tell her, "is that deep down, I always knew that wasn't true."

"Good for you," says the counselor as I am stomping the

ring out of shape and cutting the cording into tiny pieces. "You need to learn to listen to that voice."

A Good Coat

I wind up living at home for almost two years while I continue to pay off debts and work up the energy to go back out into the world. I stay with friends in the city on most weekends, and during the week I drive to the Jerry Corporation—it's the same distance as it was when I was living in the city, I'm just going in the opposite direction. In a fit of desperation and at the last minute I apply to the University of Minnesota's graduate program in English, because knowing English seems like the one thing I have always been able to do—though Jerry would often disagree, looking at my brochure copy and saying, "This is horrific." I am surprised when I get accepted and believe that I might be part of some kind of controlled experiment, an average mouse allowed into one of the advanced mazes: *Will she find the cheese?* And so, as a safety precaution, I keep living at home and working "reduced hours" at the Jerry Corporation. The CEO, my father's friend, arranges this, and Jerry has no choice but to go along with it.

For some of my coworkers who have gone to reduced hours—working mothers, usually—their time at work has an urgency, the concentrated impact of distilled liquor, of a sauce stirred down. But my time at work is the same gassy expanse that it's always been. The company has grown, our jobs have become more specific, more specialized, and yet, I am never sure what mine is. I am supposed to test software, sometimes. I am supposed to train clients, sometimes. I am supposed to help the woman who writes software documentation, but she tells me she doesn't want my help.

"Job security," she says. "They need to see me as overwhelmed."

"I think that's why they're asking me to help you," I say.

"There's not enough for two of us," she says.

I am supposed to help clients troubleshoot when they call with problems, but usually the problems are so complicated that I have to go get one of the programmers.

I walk around a lot with memos in one hand.

"Hey, champ," Jerry says whenever he sees me, "how's the student?" and then pats me on the back, a kind of gentle burping. I figure I'm working my way toward unemployment. I'm like some kind of dying patient—people patting me and recommending Tom Clancy and John Grisham novels. I am gradually leaving the world of the upwardly mobile, becoming an economic specter, one foot already in the afterlife of graduate school. "So, *why* are you doing this?" one of the salesmen keeps asking me. "Will it help you later?"

Often, especially when I am in class, I am not sure.

In my first fiction workshop, I turn in a story about a woman with an unfulfilling job and a boyfriend who follows her around like a parrot, verbally pecking at her. She ditches him and meets another man, who turns out to be a sociopath who sneaks things out of her apartment until one day she realizes that she has no silverware and that all of her travel-sized shampoos are missing.

"I just think she's like, really fucked up," one of the guys in my workshop says. We are seated around a white rectangular table and have just finished talking about his story, about a man who goes dogsledding in northern Minnesota. His character kills and skins things and also gets to make love to a beautiful woman on the rug in front of a fireplace. "It's like," he says, "I'm reading this and thinking, what's her problem?"

The woman sitting next to me, who spends all of class twirling her ballpoint pen, taking it apart, putting it back together, and twirling it some more, says quietly, "I like this story."

Our professor, a tall, thin man with a space between his two front teeth, is bent over the table like a wilted flower. "In the writing," he says, "I find it delicate but suffering from the literal. It fails to make imaginative leaps." He cranes his neck, looks at the ceiling, and the tip of his tongue appears at the open doorway of his teeth, like a tiny person greeting company. "For instance, what if they all went to Singapore, or Antarctica? Is there a reason why they *cannot* be dogsledding? Or could you incorporate Greek mythology? Some captivating element of fantasy?"

"Yeah," says the guy who wrote the hunting story. "I found that, too."

"Well I guess what I was trying to do," I say, "with the travel-sized shampoos—" but the instructor holds up a bony finger.

"What you were trying to do doesn't matter," he says. "Ms. Olson," he pauses, "we've heard enough from you."

In my playwriting class, we are mostly reading plays and are required to try and write one scene of our own. In mine, I send a fiction-writing teacher and a raft of his students to Singapore.

"What are the stakes here?" says the playwriting teacher. I like her. She offers us formulas for crafting drama *and* we get to say two things about our scene before the ravens are allowed to pick at the carcass.

"Well," I say. "Once they get to Singapore, they can't speak the language."

"In staged drama," she says, "everything must be a matter of life and death. And it needs to be obvious."

In revision, I incorporate dwarves, some of whom have magical powers and cellular phones. A tidal wave wipes out most of the class, including the fiction teacher, before it even gets to Singapore.

Do you want to talk about your anger? the counselor says to me later.

No, I say.

Having access to your anger can be a wonderful thing, says the counselor, *anger can be a very useful accessory.*

I was thinking of it more as a foundation garment, I say.

I often do my homework at the desk downstairs outside of my father's office. He has cleared all of his piles of charts, X-rays, and prescriptions off that desk and moved them to a different table, so that I have a place to work. My father mostly works quietly with his sliding office doors shut, a little Miles Davis or Thelonius Monk seeping out from the cracks along with his mumbled dictation, "Patient is fifty-five with no prior history of rectal bleeding, period. Recommended five hundred milligrams of blah, blah, blah, period." I try not to listen, since he's taken an oath, but I catch snatches of symptoms and body parts, and sometimes he lets me leave crank messages on the dictating machine for the secretaries, who seem to really enjoy it. I breathe heavily into the machine, "Josephine," I say, "Josephine, I'm watching you. You look hot today, Josephine," and my dad and I guffaw.

Flo comes downstairs for various reasons, and today it is with my father's old raincoat draped over her arm. She's been cleaning out closets; she seems always to be cleaning out closets. "Hello, you two, " she says to my father, working at his desk, and me, working at mine. "Ed," she says. "Would you like to say good-bye to your coat? Do you need any kind of special ceremony? Do you need to be alone with it for a while?"

"It was a good coat," he says, lifting his head from a chart, as if delivering a eulogy to an invisible audience.

"May I throw it away now?" Flo asks, forever tossing and replenishing.

Later that evening I am trying to finish my first graduate school paper, comparing structural techniques in *Glengarry Glen Ross* and *Waiting for Godot,* and my mother starts fiddling with the fuse box across the room.

"Oh, nuts," I hear from a dark corner in the basement as my computer goes dead.

I explain to Flo later how things that have not been saved can get lost.

"I'm sorry," she says, "I had no idea that would happen."

Therapy

The therapist and I are rehashing the trip to Mexico. I can never talk about a thing just once because new angles come up, things I had forgotten, glitches that seem to throw off my old theories entirely.

I tell her about how mad I was when my boyfriend, now ex-boyfriend, finally got to the airport. How he made excuses, said he couldn't get the car, that his stepmother had taken the car, not knowing that I was flying in that day, which was unbelievable to me because in my family, you know these things, you know when someone's boyfriend or girlfriend is flying in from another country, and you do *not* take the car. But his family was like that. They weren't planners. Or communicators. They often didn't have things planned for Thanksgiving or Christmas. And we always do, I tell the therapist. I mean, it's the same goddamn boring things over and over, and the same food and the same relatives drinking too much, but it always happens. It always gets planned. And we're together. Even if we don't know what to say to one another. Even if we just eat a lot and drink watery coffee, and burp and joke around about nothing.

Mhmm, says the counselor. *So he picks you up at the airport. Keep going.*

Then he drove me all over Mexico City and I swear we were lost, except he wouldn't admit it, and then finally we got to Cuernavaca, and we drove up a dirt road to the house where his father and stepmother lived, pulled in and parked the car on a patch of gravel above the garage. He showed me his room; they'd painted and put down nice rugs. It was private. He showed me his room and then he just sat in a chair in the corner and kind of looked off into the distance, except there was no distance, just a tiny window near the top of the room. We put in a tape and I asked him to come and sit on the bed. I was horny; it had been six months.

And do you have sex then? says the counselor, rubbing her chin. *I'm having trouble remembering.*

I think so. I can't remember, either. If we did, it wasn't good. He said he didn't want to, but in the end, I think we did. Yes, we did. And I was tired from the dry air of the plane and fell asleep for a few hours. And when I woke up, he was gone. He was in the house, playing video games. It was evening, and his stepmother was trying to make dinner for her four small children, who were worming around her legs and running around the living room throwing toys and crashing into things. I remember feeling ashamed for being there, like I didn't belong. I wasn't sure that I was welcome, or if they'd even known that I was coming.

My boyfriend had sent me postcards, I tell the therapist, begging me to write, asking me to come and visit, promising that we'd go up and down the coast together, that he'd developed an itinerary and that we'd go to all the places I'd seen on *Love Boat*—Mazatlán, Puerto Vallarta, Acapulco—but when I got there, he had no money and there was no itinerary and I wanted to kill him for lying, for showing up late, for sitting in that damn chair in his room and looking off at nothing. It was a thing he always did, and I assumed at those times that he was posing, trying to look like James Dean. I think I wanted to be on the beach more than I wanted to see him. I pressured him to call travel agents, to borrow money from his father, which I think he finally did. It never occurred to me at the time that not everyone can borrow money from their father, that sometimes having no money means *having no money,* but also, he was always telling me how successful his father was, and how he was going to be like him. Anyway, somehow we got up and down the coast together, and we fought a lot. We fought in hotels and in buses and on the beach.

On one of our last nights together, when we were on our way back to Cuernavaca, I wasn't feeling well. We had been on a bus for over twelve hours and were staying overnight in a little seaside town. There was a cool wind blowing and we were lying in sleeping bags on the beach. He zipped our bags together and said wouldn't it be romantic to make love on the beach? But it was the end of the trip and I was angry with him and I didn't want to make love. I was tired and the bus had been making me feel sick. I was hot and cold at the same time, like I was getting a fever, maybe from the water, maybe from something I ate, maybe from sleeping in the cold artificial air of so many tour buses, with my legs pulled up against my chest for warmth and my ass numb from sitting for so long, my legs cramped from being jammed up against the seat ahead of us. Anyway, I said no, that I wasn't in the mood, but soon he had pulled my shorts down and he was inside of me, scraping my insides raw. When he was done, I just lay there looking at the stars and listening to the crashing waves. He was my boyfriend. Wasn't I supposed to want to make love on the beach? I lay there burning on the inside and by the time we got back to Cuernavaca, I had a fever and a bladder infection and I was pissing blood and my eyes and throat were swollen and infected. His stepmother had a friend who was a doctor, and she came over and gave me some antibiotics. I missed my scheduled flight home and wound up leaving two days later. Everyone knew I was sick, too sick to travel, but I didn't tell anyone exactly why. I was tired, worn out, I told them, from sleeping on the bus, from too much sun, from the water. Shannon has asthma, my boyfriend told them. She gets sick very easily.

The counselor looks at me and nods, hands me a Kleenex.

My insides were raw, I tell the counselor. And I was so happy to be home. My mother picked me up from the airport, I tell the counselor, and she was on time.

Love Boat

All my life, for as long as I can remember, I've wanted to be married. I'm not sure why. I guess I just thought that that's when my life would *start*.

To counteract my romantic impulses, my mother gave me books about achieving my own potential, books like *Go for It!* and *Girls Are Equal Too*.

At the time, I couldn't understand why she gave me these things. As far as I was concerned, I *was* equal, just unhappy; and all I wanted was to find some dreamy *somebody*. I had always had lots of friends who were boys, and I knew I was as smart as any of them. Once I beat up a boy on the playground, I can't remember why, but we had a kicking fight and I won by kicking him in the crotch, which wasn't fair, but made me feel powerful.

I felt equal until I got to junior high school, and then everything changed, all the circuitry went haywire. The boys I had been friends with in elementary school were in different classes, and I had a hard time making friends because I was shy and considered to be "a brain." The new boys seemed randy and weird to me, goosing girls in the hallways and commenting on our nipple growth during study hall. When I tried to make friends with the girls in my classes, I chose the ones, inevitably, who weren't like me, who were popular and cool, and they, inevitably, wanted nothing to do with me. "Why don't you go sit with your friends?" they said when I tried to join them, "Or don't you have any?"

At that age, you're too mortified to tell your parents how miserable you are; instead, you project all your anger onto them, perhaps for having brought you into the world in the first place. It turns out, actually, that you can do this at most any age, because your parents have the unfortunate job of being the trampoline from which you spring, again and again, until you are comfortable being in the air.

In junior high I began spending a lot of time in my closet, sobbing; I thought it was a dramatic place to have a breakdown. I pictured myself in *Afterschool Specials*: I wanted to be Jennifer Jason Leigh, the anorexic girl who tries to commit suicide and garners all sorts of attention, finding out, in the end, that she is special. Or Helen Hunt, a drug addict who achieved similar results in after-school drama.

I devoted myself to talking on the phone and avoiding my homework, to watching *Popeye* reruns and eating cartons of ice cream after school and then going on bizarre diets of canned chicken and cottage cheese. I had always been thin, and remained thin despite all the ice cream (probably because of the sheer energy that went in to being so unhappy and so neurotic), but I kept trying these wacky diets, anyway, because it made me feel like a real teenager, a contender for high drama and hence, great rewards. I began to flunk my classes, and this is when my mother began buying me *Go for It!* and other similar publications, which I did not read.

At the time, I couldn't understand why I was being encouraged to be something else. What was I supposed to "go for"? What was wrong with who I was? Personally, I could find all sorts of things wrong with myself, but the fact that my mother saw places for growth and improvement disturbed me.

Instead of devoting myself to these volumes on self-actualization, I continued to try to make friends with kids who came to school drunk and who smoked in the building's corners—they were popular, although now I'm not sure why. They were, perhaps, the James Deans of Chaska Middle School; they seemed tough and alive, steeped in living. They wore dark eyeliner and lived in apartment buildings, had parents who were divorced, mothers who worked and older brothers who had been in trouble with the law. They seemed so alive that they were somewhere near death—chaotic and haggard.

I devoted myself to climbing inside their circle and to dreaming romantic dreams of the man in my future who would come along and save me. From what, I wasn't sure.

In my mind, he looked like Julio Iglesias—tan, with dark, wavy hair, chiseled features and a broad, white smile. He was always, for some reason, wearing a black tuxedo, just like Julio, and he was always, for some reason, in a wheelchair.

Later, when I tell the counselor this, she will say, *Why a wheelchair?*

I have no idea, I will say. But he was bright, creative, sensitive, loving and *at my mercy*. He couldn't wheel away fast enough. He depended on me to love and take care of him, to push him up ramps and about the apartment. *Why do you suppose that is?* I will say to her.

We could talk about control issues, she will say.

The point is, I had no other plans for myself. I flirted with becoming a psychiatrist, but I really had no idea what the practical steps were to achieving that as a career. Dear Abby and Ann Landers were my inspirations, and as far as I could tell, they had no qualifications. The career thing was more of a daydream. It was the man I really focused on, despite my mother's efforts to redirect me.

How would I meet that man? When would I meet him?

When would my real life start? This kept me up at night. It still does, even though *now* I know it shouldn't.

After all, my parents, as far as I was concerned, had no lives before they married. They were on earth as a couple to create me—miserable, overly dramatic me. This was their role. As I knew them, they existed only together.

Martino, Michael

I first see him in the cafeteria attached to the building that English shares with Mathematics and Engineering. The English Department is sandwiched into two hallways, surrounded by science and engineering students, recognizable by their calculators and sense of purpose. No one knows what to do with English anymore, where it fits, "a capacious field," the chair of our department calls it at our spring quarter assembly, then he makes a joke about Milton that everyone responds to with clench-jawed laughs. I look around for donuts, which are unlikely. The English Department, from what I can tell, is given all the bad office equipment and old furniture, while the business students, the medical students, the engineering students move one school of study at a time into new buildings with green-tinted glass. The students in our capacious field are recognizable for their grazing, their looks of ennui and hopelessness. If they are lucky, they will get jobs in other neglected English departments in Alaska, Tennessee or South Dakota. The writers will take jobs temping at American Express, waiting tables and teaching composition. We all know, going in, that our prospects are limited.

So when I first see Michael sitting in the cafeteria, with a group of women and men, some of whom I recognize to be graduate students in English, I have trouble placing him. He is wearing worn Levis and a white T-shirt with a black leather jacket; his long, wavy brown hair is tucked behind his ear, held back like curtains. Most of the people at the table are women, and they are all facing toward him. One of them looks up; I recognize her from my program, though I've met her only once. Her name is Jane and she has cropped red hair; she is tall and thin with no boobs and a long neck like Audrey Hepburn. She wears black combat boots, which is a thing I have always wanted to do but haven't felt I could pull off.

Jane gives me a light wave and I smile and sit at a table across the room from them. I pull out *Mrs. Dalloway,* which has been assigned for my British and American Women Writers course, and nibble at the soggy grilled cheese sandwich and chips that I've bought at the cafeteria. As usual, I've come straight from the Jerry Corporation and am still wearing my work clothes—plain black pumps and gold hoop earrings, wool slacks and a blouse that requires dry-cleaning. We'd had clients in that morning, and Jerry had instructed us to dress professionally, especially the computer programmers. "Pretend I'm taking you all out for a nice dinner," Jerry said, "and dress like you're going to eat steak."

Mrs. Dalloway is getting ready to go out for the day, and I am nibbling on carrot sticks when I look up to see Michael looking at me. He looks away quickly, the way a rabbit would dart under a bush. He has very good posture, I notice, and sits with his legs lightly crossed, fingers locked together around one knee. Every once in a while he runs his fingers through his hair and then rests a hand across his chest, on his collarbone.

He has a long nose and isn't handsome in a pretty way; he is handsome in the way you'd like your husband to be handsome. Someone you can look at for the rest of your life, who won't always be staring at himself. The ex-boyfriend was always checking out his profile in the mirror and asking me if I thought he could model. Michael doesn't look like someone who would want to stare into a camera.

When he gets up to leave, all the women at his table give him miniature beauty queen waves. He rolls up his napkin and empty plastic sandwich bag, jams them into a paper bag and tucks it into his backpack. On his way out, he looks over and catches me staring at him, and then looks away and disappears through the arched doorway of Nolte Cafeteria.

Still in my Jerry Corp clothes, I figure he probably thinks I work in the registrar's office, that I helped Jane get into a class that was already full.

The next time I see Jane she's in the graduate student lounge with a bunch of women in my writing program. They're talking about Edith Wharton and *Masterpiece Theatre.* One of the women says, "I *adore* Masterpiece Theatre. It's such a *guilty* pleasure."

Another says, "It's the only good reason to own a television."

"What about you, Shannon?" says Jane, with her head tilted back against the couch, stretched neck exposed. "What are your television vices?"

I have just walked in and am setting my backpack down on a table, digging around for the Aldous Huxley story I am supposed to have read for my Modern Narratives Workshop, which begins in an hour. Jerry had sent me to do training at a client site that morning, and the men there, in charge of marketing butter, milk, cheese and yogurt, had insisted on calling me "Dannon."

"*Roseanne* was really funny last night," I say, still digging around in my backpack, finally finding the folder with Huxley's story in it. Living at home, I have grown addicted to *Roseanne,* who is always locked in a power struggle with her daughters. "Did anyone see it?"

The woman who adores *Masterpiece Theatre* just purses her lips and gives me a heavy-lidded gaze. Another woman says, "*Roseanne.* Is that the show that stars that loud lady?" Jane says, "Oh, I don't watch much TV. I've never seen it."

"Well, it's good," I say. "The writing has really become sharp. They've really hit their comedic stride. Which means, I suppose, that they're about to go off the air."

The room is quiet until Jane starts telling people that she's teaching Elizabeth Bishop in her poetry class. The *Masterpiece Theatre* woman says, "I *adore* Elizabeth Bishop. Which poems are you teaching?" I was a French major and haven't read Elizabeth Bishop, and so I sink into an old, battered chair and focus on Aldous Huxley, a story about a family living a kind of well-intended but misguided isolation.

When I get up to leave for class, Jane says, "Shannon, I'm having some people over on Friday night for drinks. Why don't you come over? Bring something to read," she says. "We're going to share our work as a way of getting to know one another." She tells me where she lives and where to park, and that she'll provide everything. She will have it all.

I'll explain later how I wound up at a Lutheran college, and hated it, but stayed, anyway, for four years. The important thing to know now is that so far, I feel in graduate school the way I did as an undergraduate at Saint Olaf. The first-year students, like Jane, who have teaching fellowships, all seem to know one another and to have met the second- and third-year students, as well as the stragglers who have been around for no one knows how long. There is an established culture that is a mystery to me. At Saint Olaf, you were on the inside track if you were Lutheran and listened to Amy Grant and to inspirational classics like Aaron Copland's Amish barn–raising music. There was a wholesome air of achievement, of striving and Good Fellowship. Since I had never lived anywhere else but Chaska, I believed I had entered the *rest of the world* and all it represented. I believed I had better adapt. My older brother's campus was far more liberal, but he was a genius and I believed that *I* had entered the mainstream world that I'd live in for the rest of my life. So for my first few months at Saint Olaf, I tried to be more interested in God and to attend chapel at 10:05 every morning between classes. There was a peer pressure there about going to chapel equivalent to binge drinking at the larger state schools. My sister would later call it my God Phase.

It is with this same kind of desperate energy that I go to Jane's apartment on Friday. I'm not sure that I want to read my work as a way of getting to know anyone, but this kind of earnestness seems to be the programmatic culture, and I figure I had better get used to it, that I had better learn the customs or spend the rest of my life at the Jerry Corporation.

"So, Shannon," says Jane on Friday night. There are just four of us, drinking red wine and eating bread dipped in hummus. "You work off campus, is that right?"

"Yeah," I say. "I kind of applied at the last minute and I didn't apply for any of the teaching fellowships or anything like that."

"You should check the job board in Barrell Hall," says Jane. "Sometimes there are research assistantships listed, and if you get one it covers your tuition."

"Thanks," I say. "I didn't know about that. What do you do?" I ask the girl who watches *Masterpiece Theatre.* She has her dark, curly hair up in a bun and is wearing a velvet scarf, tossed around her neck as if she's going riding in a convertible.

"I write for the *Minnesota Review,*" she says. "I don't work on campus, either."

The other woman there is Jane's roommate, an architecture student with curly blond hair and short fingers. She downs a couple glasses of wine and fidgets with the bread while the rest of us each read a few pages of our work, at Jane's suggestion. The *Masterpiece Theatre* woman reads a short piece about travel in Italy, Jane reads some prose poems, and when I am done reading my story, something I'd written in college about a car ride with Flo, the *Masterpiece Theatre* woman just smiles at me and says, "It's nice. It's a shame I can't think of anyone who would publish it."

Jane puts on some bossa nova music and dances around the living room a little. I am never sure what to do at moments like this, moments of free-form antisocial activity. The *Masterpiece Theatre* woman says she should be getting back home to her husband, which surprises me. I can't imagine anyone wanting to live with her. Jane's roommate tells me to stay and goes into the kitchen to get another bottle of wine.

"So, do you have a boyfriend?" asks Jane.

I tell her that I don't, and ask if she does.

"I went on a date with a medical student this week," she says. "How about anyone that you're interested in?"

"Well," I say. "There was a guy at your lunch table last week. He has kind of long hair."

"Oh, Michael," she says. "You know, I could see you guys hitting it off. He's really nice. I'll introduce you. He's in the architecture school with my roommate." Jane stops and surveys me briefly. "You know, that just might work," she says. "In fact, why don't I call him right now and see if he wants to go out with us sometime?"

"Really?" I say.

Jane goes over to the phone and gets his number out of her organizer.

"Michael," she says, apparently into his answering machine, "I'm just here with some friends—this is Jane—and we were just calling to see if you might like to meet us for drinks. So, maybe some other time." When Jane hangs up she says to me, "I'll arrange something so that you two can meet."

I check the job board at Barrell Hall twice a week and finally, after a few weeks, there is an announcement for a research assistant position in the English Department. The professor wants someone who can translate computer disks and software programs, since she's putting together an anthology and the contributors are sending materials created in different software programs. She wants someone who can proofread and put the manuscript in the appropriate format, and when she interviews me I say, "Hell, I'll pick up your dry cleaning, I'll make us coffee."

"You won't need to do that," she says when she hires me. And then she says something that would make Jerry snort. "I'm so happy you have all this computer experience."

The job for now is ten hours a week, more if she can find

funding. "The essays should start coming in soon," she says, handing me the *Modern Language Association Handbook for Writers of Research Papers.* "But for now you should start reading this."

The next time I see Jane, she's in the Xerox room, making copies of Anne Sexton poems for her students.

"How's it going?" she shouts over the machine.

"Okay," I say. Jerry has let me cut back to twenty hours for the rest of the semester. Just software testing and customer assistance, though none of the customers ever call. "How's teaching?"

"Oh," she says, "my students are so good. I just love them. They're so *eager.*" Jane stretches her arms up to the ceiling and a row of bracelets falls down her forearm to her elbow, clanging like silverware. "One of them wrote me a poem, telling me how I've changed her life," she says, while the Xerox machine flashes behind her.

"Well, that's nice," I say. "So, have you seen Michael lately?"

"Hang on," she says, switching papers around, putting new sheets in the feeder. "He's been kind of busy this week. I haven't been able to pin him down. But I'll call you when I talk to him again. Here," she says, flipping over a student handout. "Write down your home number. You're out in Chaska, right? At your parents'?"

"Yes," I say, "but I can come in on the weekends and stay with friends. I mean, if you can arrange something with Michael. I saw him again, coming out of the architecture library. He seems really nice."

"Oh, he is really nice," says Jane.

At home that night I flip on the TV, turn the volume down to low and curl up on the couch with the MLA guide, reading carefully and trying to memorize the guidelines.

> 4.10.4 **A Performance**
> An entry for a performance (play, opera, ballet, concert) usually begins with the title, contains facts similar to those given for a film (*see* 4.10.3), and concludes with the site and the date of the performance.

Roseanne and her sister have opened up a sandwich shop, where they make some kind of "loose meat sandwiches" and are having difficulty with the health inspector.

> 4.10.1 **Citing a Television or Radio Program**
> The information in an entry for a television or radio program usually appears in the following order:

"Loose meat sandwiches." *Roseanne.* CBS. KBUN, Minneapolis. 7 March 1993.

I fall asleep while the health inspector is chasing Roseanne's sister around the counter.

As I'm walking to the student center one day, I run into Jane, waiting at an intersection.

"Guess what!" she says to me.

"What?" I say.

"Michael asked me out!" she grins.

"Huh?" I say. I have no idea what to say. What could she be thinking, when she'd been telling me for weeks that she was trying to get hold of him, that when she did she'd set us up?

"He asked me to dinner," she says, smiling like she just discovered fire. "Eeek!" she squeals.

"But I thought," I begin to say, and then the light changes and Jane crosses the street, waving until she gets about halfway across.

"See you later!" she says.

3.7. Tables and Illustrations
Example:
Fig. 1. Manticore, woodcut from Edward Topsell, *The History of Four-Footed Beasts and Serpents . . .* (London, 1658), 344; reprinted in Konrad Gesner, *Curious Woodcuts of Fanciful and Real Beasts* (New York: Dover, 1971)8.

When I see Professor Nelson in the student union, I duck behind a pillar. I had fallen asleep the night before reading about parenthetical documentation, and now I am afraid that when she sees me she'll ask me how to reference something from a weekly periodical that was originally quoted in a Liberian daily.

I wait a few minutes, reading the fliers that have been posted to the pillars, ads for student dances, bowling night and old cars for sale, and then I sneak around the corner to the coffee cart, thinking I will hide behind the awning as I develop an escape plan. Professor Nelson is standing there, holding a latté.

"Professor Nelson," I say.

"Hello," she says, "Well, how's the work going? Did you get the essays I put in your box?"

I don't know what to say, but I figure the worst she can do is fire me and I'll go crawling back to Jerry, offering to pick up his dry cleaning and spit-polish his shoes.

"Um," I say. I had hoped to at least get to the part about handling footnotes before seeing her again. "Um," I finally blurt out, "I am having trouble memorizing the MLA guide."

"*Memorize it? Oh my god,*" she says. "I just wanted you to become familiar with it, so if you have a specific question, you'll know where to look it up. *Oh, no,*" she says, "you should just start formatting the essays and look things up as you go."

"Oh," I say.

"So you haven't started formatting the essays?" she says.

"Um, no," I say.

"Well, you should do that," she says, and nodding at the cart says, "Are you getting coffee?"

I order a latté, too, and then we walk back to the English building, and Professor Nelson asks me about my classes and tells me stories about graduate school, when she was one of the only women at Yale. She tells me about the fierce competition between the men and women, and between the few women who were there. She tells me about how a guy that she went to graduate school with once took her paper out of the professor's mailbox after she'd turned it in. Someone had seen him digging around in there, and then several of the women's papers were missing, and then mysteriously reappeared, and even though they all went to the professor to talk to him, he gave them lower grades for turning their work in late.

I am relieved that she hasn't blown up at me. Instead, when we get back to the English Department, she gives me a key to her office and says, "If you'd like to work here when I'm not using it, you're welcome to do so. That would give you a nice, quiet place to be."

I run into Michael and Jane in a hallway, and even though she has declared his interest in her, and maybe because of that, I just march right up and introduce myself. I practically shove my hand into his chest, holding it out for him to shake in greeting.

And the next time he sees me, when Jane isn't around, he asks me out.

"I wasn't sure if you had a boyfriend," he says. "Jane had mentioned that she thought you did."

2.8.3. Italian
Personal Names
The names of many Italians who lived before or during the Renaissance are alphabetized by first name. But other names of the period follow the standard practice.
Boccaccio, Giovanni
Cellini, Benvenuto
Stampa, Gaspara

Martino, Michael

On our first date, we meet late, for beers. Michael is wearing a white T-shirt underneath a denim shirt, which is unbuttoned enough so that I can see the vague hint of chest muscles.

We talk about campus, what a difficult place it can be to negotiate, so much paperwork, so few places to park. He tells me about growing up in Italy, how he still remembers the smells and noises. He tells me about how they moved to New York when he was still young, how he misses the smells and noises of New York. His parents were Italian, but his father had died when Michael was in college. His mother has a summer house in Manzanita, Oregon, he tells me, where he loves to go. "It's the windiest place in the world," he says. "Someday," he says, "I'll take you there."

He asks me where I did my undergraduate work, and I tell him that I picked the wrong place, a conservative Lutheran school, where I was never happy. The wrong place for a Catholic girl to be, to say the least. There were no noises, I tell him, except the occasional choir member singing as he crossed campus. There were no smells, I tell him, except the Tater Tots Hot Dish served in the cafeteria.

"I know someone who worked there for a year," he says. "He's a transcendentalist."

I have no idea what that means, but I'm still thinking about how Michael had said he would take me to Manzanita some day. There is a way that I already feel like I know him, in a way that I can't explain. I don't have my usual urge to run, or yawn and call it a night. I love the idea of going on a trip with him.

"I don't even know your last name," I say.

"Martino," he says, which rattles me. When I was little, I had a handful of imaginary friends. One was named Steady Bee, another was Mrs. Nervous. Flo could never figure out where I came up with the names, but one of my favorites, the small, invisible pal I hung out with the most, was Martino.

Michael tells me about his father, how he believes that his father was never happy in his work. "That's why I picked architecture," he says. "My father made a lot of money, but I think his job killed him. He didn't love it." Michael keeps a firm grip on his beer mug. "I expect that I will provide for a family some day," he says, "but I also want to be involved as a parent. I want to get to know my kids. I want to spend time with my family."

I'm not sure I heard much beyond the word *provide.* I think I decided, right there, that Michael was the one for me. That there was nothing more I needed to know about him, that perhaps, in some odd way, I had known him all along.

The next time I see Jane, she just gives me a dirty look and takes the first staircase down the hall, slamming the door behind her.

And when I see one of Jane's friends, someone who is also in a class with me, she says, "You know, Shannon, you don't have anything to complain about. You can't criticize Jane for acting that way. The fact of the matter is, you got the guy."

Product

Michael and I are inseparable for the rest of the spring. He makes room in his closet for me and makes an extra desk out of file cabinets and an old door so I can work there. We go for walks, we drive to school together, he leaves little love notes around the apartment for me. We go grocery shopping and as he's wheeling down the isles he says things like, "I love grocery shopping with my sweetie!" Michael cooks for us most of the time, and because his kitchen is a tiny efficiency kitchen—a counter, really, on one wall of the bedroom/living room/ study—we most often find ourselves eating canned soup or spaghetti and frozen corn.

I study for my finals in his apartment, write my final papers, work on formatting the manuscript for Professor Nelson and querying the authors. When it's my turn to cook, we go around the corner to the hamburger place where we'd gone for beers on our first date. I usually treat on those nights, putting it on my credit card.

Michael has won a fellowship for the next year, based on his treatment of a public space, an indoor botanical garden. I had suggested putting a mini-donut cart near the rhododendrons, though he had rejected this. "I can't believe you won without following my good advice," I say to him. We dress up for his award ceremony, an annual black-tie gala sponsored by the College of Architecture and Landscape Architecture. As we walk into the building, a funny, sagging modernist experiment that will soon be remodeled, I hook my arm with his and Michael says, "Sweetie, not here. This is where I work. I need to look professional."

"Okay," I say. Except earlier in the week, he had asked me not to do that in the grocery store. He had said, "I love shopping with my sweetie!" and I had put my arms around him and kissed him on the neck. "Don't do that here," he had said. So now I say, "Do you have another job that you want to tell me about?"

"What?" Michael says, as we hang up our coats.

"Have you been secretly working at the grocery store?" I say.

"This isn't a time to be weird, Shanny," he says. "Now, about tonight, I just want you to know that some of my friends, or colleagues, might treat you funny, and if they do, don't take it personally."

"What do you mean, funny?" I say, walking next to him, keeping my hands to myself, acting professional.

"Well, they're kind of snobs," he says.

"I can be a snob," I say, *"Ma, we got volunteer rhubarb comin' up in the yard!"*

"They're kind of intellectual snobs," he says, "And they might judge you."

"Why?" I say. "Why would they do that?"

"Well, because you're blonde, and, well, you know," says Michael.

"No," I say. "I don't know. Are you embarrassed by me?" I say.

"God, no," says Michael. "You're my favorite person in the world. It's just that, these guys, well, they're really intense and they're just not always that nice."

Later, when I tell the counselor about Michael's award ceremony, she says, "You know that whole exchange about his friends was more about him than about you, don't you? About some inadequacy he feels? He feels uncomfortable."

"Well, why can't he just talk about himself, then?" I say, "Instead of making it about me?"

"It's a defense mechanism," says the counselor. "He doesn't realize he's doing it. My god," she says, "the whole world could be in therapy for that one."

"Well, it felt shitty," I say.

"*It* felt shitty?" says the counselor.

She is always trying to steer me away from unmodified pronouns.

"I felt shitty," I say.

Pick an emotion, she says. *There are really only five,* she says, and "shitty" is not one of them. Try *angry, sad, happy, guilty, lonely.*

"Pick a dwarf," I say, "Any dwarf."

The counselor readjusts her legs on the footstool, reaches for an Oreo cookie from the package we've been sharing during this session. "Come on," she says. "Let's go. Pick one."

"Sad," I say.

Try again, she says.

"Angry," I say. "Alex, I'll take Anger for 300."

There we go, she says. So, how were Michael's friends?

"They were nice," I say.

In the summer, I work on some research projects for Professor Nelson and I quit working at the Jerry Corporation. My hours there had become so few—I just hand a few files over, go out to lunch with the secretaries, and I'm done. When we come back from lunch, I say good-bye to everyone and Jerry happens to walk by. He pats me on the back and says, "Hey, champ, give me a call if you ever need anything." It makes me wonder, briefly, if I have misjudged him.

Michael spends the second half of the summer in Manzanita and flies me in for a week to meet his mother and his brother and sister-in-law. We go hiking and rent beach bikes. Michael's mother makes us big breakfasts. She is this tiny beaming Italian lady, who still has a thick accent. She gives me a huge hug when we meet, and then takes my hands in hers. "Every day I pray for each of my children and for the people who are special to them," she says. Michael rolls his eyes. "Every day I ask God to hold you and Michael in his hands."

Michael's mom asks me questions about my family, about Minnesota. "Michael says that your father looks so much like his, he almost fainted when he met him. Is that true?"

"I've only seen that one picture that Michael has," I tell her, "but from that, they look like brothers."

"Michael's father was reserved and gentle," she says. "Michael says that they move the same way, kind of talk the same," she says. She takes me around their beach house and shows me family pictures. "I like your new friend, Shannon," she turns and says to Michael, giving my hand a squeeze. Michael just smiles and goes back to reading the *New York Times*.

Manzanita *is* the windiest place in the world, and I keep finding sand in the pockets of my shorts, jeans and jacket. A fine dust of sand in my hair, on my teeth. I start having to take my asthma medication, and by the end of the week I've had to call my dad so that he can call in a prescription for prednisone to the Manzanita pharmacy. Michael and I had tried to go on a hike that day, but I was having too much trouble breathing and had to turn around. For the rest of the visit, I mostly stay inside. Michael and his brother windsurf, but since the prednisone I'm taking makes me feel uneven, fragile, I go to one of the coffee shops in town and read, or hang out with Michael's mom, except she, at sixty, is in training for a triathalon and spends every morning running on the beach. In the afternoons, she goes to the community pool.

Michael makes a reservation for us to stay in a little bed-and-breakfast up the coast, just for one night, just the two of us. It's less windy here, and we walk on the beach and spend hours looking in the tide pools at Haystack Rock. We order deep-fried scallops from a little shack and listen to the crashing waves.

"It's just kind of frustrating," I tell him, "not to have as much energy as your mom."

"It's okay, sweetie," Michael says. "The point was for you just to meet everyone. My family really likes you."

Even so, in a strange way I am relieved when I get back on the plane to Minneapolis, heading toward a place where I believe I will breathe more easily.

Though for the rest of the summer I find sand in my shoes, in the bags I took to Manzanita, in the pockets of my shorts, in every corner and crevice.

Before Michael had left for Manzanita, he said that he needed to find a new apartment. "It makes sense, Shanny, if you're going to be at my place all of the time, that we get a place together, don't you think?"

I loved the idea of spending all of my time with Michael, but the idea of actually signing a lease together terrified me.

"I don't know," I said.

"But we can't keep hanging out in my little apartment," he said. "In this little studio. It's too hard for both of us to be there all of the time."

"I just don't know," I said. For some reason, I didn't feel ready to do anything formal.

"Well then you need to get an apartment in the city, or you need to do something," he had said.

But I had lived at home now for two years, and I wasn't sure I would remember how to live alone, wasn't sure I wanted to.

"I'm not spending the extra money for a bigger apartment, just so we can hang out there together," Michael said. "When otherwise, if it was just me, this apartment would be fine."

Michael kept a careful budget and liked to plan ahead, so he started looking at apartments and finally he said, "I can't wait for you to make up your mind any longer. I have to do something before I go away for the summer."

Michael found an apartment and filled out an application. It was a nice place, and sunny, and the rent was pretty cheap because the landlord had this kind of Orwellian control over what went on there—he made it clear that his was a very careful screening process and that only the *right* kind of people would be allowed in the building. There were two women sharing an apartment across the hall from the one Michael took. There was a single guy upstairs who played acoustic guitar at odd hours of the day and night, and a single woman across the hall from him, a nurse who worked at the children's hospital in Saint Paul. Usually, when people in Minnesota say something about the *right* kind of people, they are my grandmother's age and they mean white people, and the landlord was my grandmother's age. But the nurse who lived upstairs was black, and one of the women across the hall was Japanese, so we weren't sure what the landlord meant by *right,* though he made it clear that it was a quiet building and that he expected people to take good care of *his* property. He told us about all of the good work he did through his Catholic church, and he told us about his standing in the community as a business leader. He was irritating, but the rent was too cheap to pass up. And there was no lease, which meant that you could get out of the apartment any time you needed to; it also meant that the landlord could kick anyone out at any moment, for no reason.

Michael agreed that I would pay the difference between his old place and the new one; it was still less than if I was paying half the rent. And I would keep paying for half the groceries. And I would pay for some of the utilities.

When we met the landlord at the building, so that Michael could hand over the security deposit, the landlord said, "Now, your friend here, what's her name, Maria?"

"Shannon," I said, "My name's Shannon."

"This apartment is just for you, right?" the landlord ignored me and kept talking to Michael.

"Yeah," said Michael. "Sure. I mean, she'll be spending time here, but it's my apartment."

"Because I only interviewed you," he said to Michael. He was a big old man with a barrel chest and a shiny head. Through his thin white work shirt I could see the outline of his pacemaker, the tube that ran over his undershirt and across his chest.

"Right," said Michael.

When Michael comes back at the end of the summer, we move all of his things out of the storage closet they've been in all summer and carry all of my clothes in covertly, in plastic bags, hanging them in the back of the closet. I bring a few books, and my computer, but that's about it. I leave most things at my parents'.

Since I'm not bringing much, my mother begins to offer advice and extra household goods. She likes Michael, thinks he is responsible and a vast improvement over "the other one," and seems to want to participate in my departure. "You know," she says one day when I'm home going through my things, "I just got in a big order of Amway detergent. So why don't you take that extra stuff downstairs—you know, that little box?"

Thanks, I say.

"It's not as good as Amway," she continues, "but you can have it. It gets real sudsy, and you know, with suds, you don't get the same cleaning action."

I wonder when my mother began believing in things like "cleaning action." My mother, who cringed as my sister and I sat down each summer day of our adolescence to watch *All My Children.* My mother, who now watches *The Bold and the Beautiful* each day with her lunch. "The Strange and the Dangerous," I call them. "How can you watch this?" I ask her.

"*Ssshh,*" she says, munching a baby carrot, sipping her Diet Dr Pepper. "Everyone thought she was dead," she says, pointing at the screen with a carrot. "Her husband loved her terribly."

"He needs acting lessons," I say.

"Quiet," Flo says, "you're ruining it."

The show seems to me to have been ruined in its conception, but I watch quietly. Flo eats her Diet Deluxe chili-macaroni lunch-in-a-cup. She's trying to lose weight, so she's bought all of the Diet Deluxe preprepared meals. I eat them, too, since they require no effort, even though the meat looks like dog food.

"This makes my lunch more exciting," she says, her eyes on the screen.

The point at which my mother began to believe in the promises of advertising—the hope held out by products, the half-hour daily serialization of glamour and intrigue—is unidentifiable. When we were small, she steered us away from it, refusing to buy things that were "overpackaged," saying that they were environmental disasters and overpriced, and that it was the same product inside, regardless.

When I brought home a twelve pack of Diet-Rite raspberry soda, for instance, my mother asked if she could try one. She approached me later, saying, "You know that Diet-Rite raspberry you brought home? I really like it! Thank you for introducing me to it."

Sometimes I catch her looking in the bathroom mirror, cocking her head, turning it from side to side, lifting one side of her mouth, then the other. Smiling a half-hearted, lopsided smile. When she sees I have noticed, she brushes real or imagined lint from her blouse, touches her hair, perhaps reapplies lipstick, hair spray, and goes into the kitchen, where she sits at the table and gazes at the mail.

I tell her, once, that I think she is brave.

And I take my mother's detergent to my new apartment, not expecting much from it, really.

Part Three \ The Depression

A Point

As a French major, I never encountered feminism. We read Flaubert, Baudelaire, Sartre and Camus, stories about dying women and loneliness, and I struggled to keep up. Like a beginning jogger who's trying to run a marathon, I panted up to the finish line of any book, still wondering who the main characters were, not knowing that some of them had died or fallen in love along the way, having confused things in the translation. Mostly I liked the cultural snobbery of the French, and their concern with alimentation.

Now, in my second year of graduate school, I take my first feminist literature course, in English, and promptly begin to grow out my leg and armpit hair. Though I spend all my time with Michael, I have begun to hate men as a general group and see my hygiene hiatus as an important retaliatory gesture; as a fallback I also think of it as a sort of international way of being, a European awareness.

Michael says he doesn't mind. And even though as my hair begins to accumulate into a kind of sorry, patchy crop, and I notice that my legs are beginning to look like those of a young Irishman, sort of knotty and sturdy, I keep growing it, anyway.

As Christmas approaches, Flo calls. "Say," she says, "I'm looking at your stocking-stuffer list here, and I'm noticing you've asked for razors. Is this is a mistake, or are you done rebelling?"

She won't actually use the words *hair* and *leg* in the same sentence, in the same way that people are uncomfortable saying *cancer* out loud. Instead she says, when I occasionally stick my leg up near her face to bug her, "I just think all those funny black lines are unattractive."

"You mean my leg hair?" I say. "And they're not black; they're brown," I tell her. "Light brown. Auburn." And what about those funny black lines people used to paint up the backs of their legs when panty hose were in short supply? I ask. And what about those funny brown lines people paint on as substitute eyebrows?

"Well, I've never understood the eyebrow thing, either," she says.

At least these lines are natural, I tell her. They are supposed to be there. Hair is there to keep us warm, to ward off the cold, I tell her indignantly.

"I'm sure you're warding off more than the cold," she says.

I tell her that I've decided leg hair is about control. When people are thrown in prison camps, what is the first thing done to them? Their hair is shaved off. It minimizes them, reduces their identity to one among many victims.

"Anyway," my mother says, "why are you asking for razors?"

"Well," I say. "I started shaving my armpits again, and my bikini line." The leg hair, I've become used to, I tell her, even though I really haven't and occasionally look down at my legs, pale and covered with curly auburn hair, and feel like Ron Howard, Richie Cunningham in his basketball shorts. But the armpit hair never quite grew on me, I tell her, I mean, not aesthetically. The bikini line, well, I swim a lot, I say, and that can get kind of gross.

"And who is dictating the aesthetic of your bikini line?" she asks me. "Who's controlling that?"

"Okay," I say. "Yeah, yeah."

"Ah ha!" she says. I can almost hear her lift a finger in victory, the way she does from time to time.

Michael and I have spent the last several months in the new apartment, which has only his name on the mailbox. We scrape frost off the car together in the morning and drive to school together; we go to the gym together; we grocery shop together. At home Michael drafts and reads books on modernist theories of space while I read or work on my computer.

On the mornings that Michael has to be at school early and I don't need to go in, I sleep until ten or eleven. And then, sometimes in the afternoons, I fall asleep again. More and more, my blood feels as though it's filled with cement.

Last spring, when I had been driving back and forth between Michael's place, my parents' place, Jerry Corp, and school, I didn't get much sleep. I had become thinner than I was in high school, my clothes were hanging off of me and the secretaries at Jerry Corp had started to call me Cracker Butt. "Your butt's disappearing," they said. "You look like all you eat is crackers." It's true that I was often too busy to sit down and eat, but it was also true that since I'd left the ex-boyfriend, I'd begun eating less, letting less into my body. I ate only enough to stop my immediate hunger, tiny portions. I wanted to winnow my body down to a manageable shape, something I could control. I didn't want to carry around anything extra.

One evening, an old man had followed me around the library while I was looking for books for Professor Nelson. He came up to me, licking his lips, and started asking me questions, *Was I a student? What was my name? What was I checking out? Where did I live?* He smelled of mustard and old socks, and my head began to spin. I had worked through lunch at the Jerry Corporation and eaten a bag of pretzels in between classes; I had been hungry while I browsed the electronic library holdings, hungry while I went through the stacks. I needed to get these books and then I had thought I would get something to eat. I backed away from him, turned and headed down the row of books. But the old man kept following me. *Did I recognize him?* he asked. *Had I seen him before? Did he recognize me from his biology class? Or was it Spanish? Had I taken World History?* I walked faster, carrying the armload of books I'd already collected, but I felt the stacks closing in on me, my peripheral vision going gray. He was still behind me, breathing his mustard breath on my neck. I was getting to the end of the stacks. *Which classes was I taking? Or did I have an office? In which building?* I felt his hand on my shoulder and I screamed, dropped all the books and ran to the information desk. When I turned back to point to him, there were just books on the floor, fallen in the shape of an odd star.

The librarian called security and they found the man hiding in the Quartos. He was homeless, a schizophrenic who had bothered other women. Mine was the last complaint they needed to be able to arrest him. *Would I agree to file a formal complaint?*

As the Minneapolis police dragged him away, the old man lunged at me, but was tugged back between two officers. *Ma'am!* He lurched and some spit flew into the middle of the room, disappeared in midair like a dying firework, *Ma'am! What did you tell them about me!*

Nothing that wasn't obvious, I thought.

I went back to Michael's that night; he had been worried about me, had been wondering why I was late, and he made me soup. "You've been working too hard," he said.

Now that we are sharing the apartment, Michael and I always pack lunches. And I figure that maybe my body, in needing more sleep, is getting caught up.

The week before Christmas, I am expecting a package. I've ordered some fleece slippers for my mother and am having them sent to the apartment I share with Michael, and I put my name on the mailbox, figuring it will only be up for a day or two, until the slippers are delivered.

It occurs to me now that maybe I should have had them sent in Michael's care instead, or sent to school, where the secretary would have put them in my mailbox, but part of me was in the mood, I suppose, to test the limits.

It took only one day before an envelope appeared under our door.

Mr. Martino, the letter inside read, *You are to vacate the premises by the end of the week.*

There was no explanation, so Michael called.

You know what you did! The landlord bellowed at him. *Maria's name is on the mailbox!*

"Shannon," Michael said.

That apartment was rented to you, not Maria. You have violated my terms, and you are to leave my property by the end of the week.

It was Christmas week and we felt like we were on some kind of bad network special. We called him a Grinch and secretly hoped that his pacemaker would seize up. We called the renter's association to see if he could actually *do* this, and they said that, unfortunately, he could. Around the apartment Michael, as we were packing boxes, would puff up his chest and then blow raspberries all over the room, marching around with his butt sticking out, bellowing, *"I am an old white man and this is my property!"*

I remembered what my mother used to say about how children needed to dramatize things in order to figure them out or work through them. My mother loved to tell people about how my sister and I, when we were small, would work through our issues at the dinner table by using green beans as little puppets. The green beans would fight until they had worked things out between them.

"It's always the green beans who have all the *issues,*" I'd said to Flo the first time she told the story.

It was important to Michael to do things well and right, and I figured this whole experience was hard on him, being expelled from a place, even if the landlord was kind of crazy. I felt bad that I had done this to both of us.

"I'm sorry," I said to Michael as we threw his kitchen things into a big cardboard box. "I should never have put my name up."

"It's probably better to get out now," said Michael, "than live waiting for the bomb to drop. He's a mean old man. With a sense of entitlement, a huge fucking Cadillac and those warped fucking Christian *values.* God, that shit drives me crazy. If he's so fucking Christian, why is he doing this now? It's fucking ten degrees below outside."

While we were packing, the women from across the hall came over to say good-bye. They told us it wasn't the first time the landlord had done something like this. "He doesn't like unmarried couples," one of them said. "Thank god he thinks we're like Laverne and Shirley."

"I wonder how often he came by during the day," I said. *"I wonder how much he was watching us?"*

We found a new apartment, available January first, that was

managed by a huge company with no interest in our personal lives, just our money. We put both of our names on the lease and moved everything into my parents' garage for the holidays.

I was nervous about how I would afford it, now that I had quit the Jerry Corporation, but Michael always seemed to manage. Michael and I were paid the same amount as graduate assistants, and he always had enough money.

At my parents' place, since Michael and I aren't married, I get the couch upstairs and Michael gets the couch downstairs. My brother and his girlfriend are home, and my brother has to share the foldout with Michael; they sleep together in front of the Christmas tree. My brother's girlfriend, who is thirty-four, gets the guest bed upstairs.

"Mom," I said, "this is ridiculous. We're all adults."

"Adults who aren't married," she said. "This is my house and these are my rules."

In his stocking, Michael gets some razors and chocolate and a calendar of the Minnesota seasons. My mother keeps hoping he will learn to love them as she does—he still can't stand the winters.

In my stocking I get shampoo and toothpaste, some stamps and stationary, a new toothbrush and an orange.

"I thought you were giving me razors," I say to Flo later.

"I thought you were still in your *feminist* period," she says.

I borrow one of the razors that Michael got in his stocking and I take a long, hot bath. Shaving every row carefully.

Boys

One day, my sister and I and the girl across the street decided to play topless basketball. We had no boobs yet, and besides, it was a dead-end street. Who would notice?

The next week, Mr. Henderson, who lived across the street and owned the shoe repair downtown, said to us, "Say, I thought I saw a bunch of boys playing basketball over at your place the other day."

No boys, we said. There were no boys.

I watched his hands adhere a new sole to a pair of old work boots.

I could have sworn they were boys, he said.

After that, we always wore shirts.

The Addition

In our new apartment, Michael and I put the futon in the main room, creating a kind of combination bedroom and social area, depending on whether or not the futon is folded up into a couch. We use the bedroom as a study, lining the walls with three old desks that Michael had salvaged from an old building on campus that was being torn down. Michael gets the desk by a window, so I get to spread my stuff out on most of the extra desk.

"My god, Shanny," Michael says, "Where do you get all of this stuff? Where does all this paperwork come from?" Michael keeps all of his designs rolled up in tubes, rolls them up every night when he's finished working.

Some of it is work for Professor Nelson, I explain, some of it is stuff I have to read for class. Some of it was crap I'd been carrying around for years and hadn't sorted through yet, but didn't want to leave at my parents'. Some of it is my thesis project, a collection of vignettes I was just starting to assemble about a girl who's having trouble figuring out what to do with her life, called "Plant Killer." I had been thinking of it as a kind of self-help guide, and had titled it "People Who Kill Plants and the People Who Love Them," but my adviser pointed out that you couldn't tell if some people killed plants and some people loved plants, or if some people loved people who killed plants.

"Am I in it?" Michael says.

"No," I say.

"But I water all the plants around here," he says.

"Sorry," I say.

"Is your therapist in it?"

"Sort of," I say.

"I want to be in it!" Michael whines and pitches a little pretend fit. "Can I read some of it?" says Michael. "You've never let me read any of it."

I give him a little section, a scene between the narrator and her mother where they are wandering around in a mall, and he goes to run some bathwater. Michael likes to read in the bathtub; it's where he reads most of his theory books, which is why almost all of his designs have pools and fountains.

"Sweetie?" Michael is digging around in the medicine cabinet, "where's the extra soap? My god," he says, still poking through the rows of asthma medication, birth control, the Prozac I've just started, the razors, lotions and nail polishes, "being you is complicated."

"I put it in the closet," I say.

Michael gets the soap and sinks into the tub with my pages

and after a while I say, "How's it going in there? You're awfully quiet."

"I think you need to vary your sentence structure," he says.

"You're awfully quiet and so I'm wondering how it's going in there," I say.

"In your writing," he says.

"Oh," I say. "That's all? That's all you're going to say?"

"I'm looking at this as an objective reader."

"But that's not why I'm showing it to you," I say.

He is quiet again, and I stare at my computer screen, where I've been trying to write a response paper on *Green Grass Running Water.* The professor has asked us to think about the author's use of experimental form and meta-narrative. The cursor is blinking.

"Thank you, sweetie," Michael says after a while. "You're my favorite writer."

A couple of weeks later, I drag Michael along to a reading put on by the graduate students. I don't have to read at this one, my number isn't up yet, but some of the people I've been in classes with will be reading. One girl gets up to the microphone and stands shyly with her hands in the back pockets of her Levis. She's wearing a torn T-shirt and an old cardigan; she has smallish boobs and her hair is clipped into a sloppy bun with the ends twanging out. Mine is always long and straight, hanging down below my shoulders, and I wonder if I could get my hair to do what hers does, or if mine would just droop toward the ground.

As she finishes a poem about Nicaragua, Michael exhales, "Wow," as if the wind had been knocked out of his chest. "She's amazing. She's an amazing poet."

"I thought I was your favorite writer," I say.

"You're my favorite writer because you're my favorite person," he says patting me on the hand. "I would love you if you were a check-out girl at Walmart," he says. "If you flipped burgers," he says. "As long as you were happy, I'd be happy for you."

I have trouble working in the study when Michael is in there, and so I go out to the combination bedroom/social area, where I socialize by myself while Michael works on his designs. I watch TV, or read, or call my mother. Or watch TV. Or call my mother.

Michael says that he thinks we will always be together, but when the subject of marriage comes up, Michael says he doesn't believe in marriage and says that he can't believe I do, since marriage is such an oppressive structure for women. He believes in *partnerships,* he says. He also wants to get rid of the TV because he says it's too tempting to have it around. "You know, Shanny, I don't think you realize that what I'm doing doesn't come easily to me; I really need to focus." *But,* I say, *if the TV weren't here, who would I hang out with?*

But, he says, *I can't focus when it's on in the next room. Why can't you think about the effect it's having on my work? About how hard it is to work when you're out there watching TV?*

And I say, *but I'm out here watching TV because it's hard to work when you're in the study.* And so on.

I need to work, he says.

Exactly, I say, and so I need to watch TV.

"Well, when you're out there," he says, "could you at least not leave toenail clippings all over the place?"

It's true that I have developed the bad habit of picking at my toenails. I pick at them through *Friends* and *Frasier,* through *The Simpsons* and *ER*. My fingernails, too.

Sometimes Michael takes a break from his work, walks into the kitchen and catches me sitting in the blue light of the television, furtively ripping off my toenails.

"Hey, little picker," he says.

Plant Killer

My grandma Tillman, my mother's mother, grew up above the grocery store that her parents owned, eating the rotten fruit and vegetables that weren't fit for customers. "Your grandmother," my mother likes to remind me, "grew up in the Depression, you know. People didn't take things for granted then."

My grandma and her four sisters lived up north in Callaway, near Detroit Lakes on the White Earth Indian Reservation. Her older sister, Alice, was kind of a thug, smoked cigars and lived to be ninety-five. Her youngest sister, Lavonne, was a model, and like Liberace, she was flamboyant, decorative, a lover. Another sister, Jenora, would marry the same man three times. The other, Celestie, never married, and lived at home all her life, working in the grocery store. "She was not a real healthy woman," says my mother. "She ended up dying of some kind of a—it's got a title—her fat cells or something weren't working right. I've got her coroner's report filed away around here somewhere—it was some kind of a 'malfunctioning of systems.' She was not a real sturdy person, health-wise. Except in size; in size Celestie was quite big."

My grandma Helen, born somewhere in the middle, was

small-boned but tough, and would grow up to marry and follow a man across the western Minnesota prairie, wherever his job on the highway construction crew took him.

My mom was born amid all that moving, and she got used to having very little, because they were always having to pack and unpack and repack; they were constantly re-creating a household.

I remember my grandma walking in quick, brisk and quiet steps, kind of like a fast-moving house cat. She wore cat-eye glasses, polyester pants and polyester blouses pulled tightly down around her narrow hips. She had her hair done once a week at the salon and often wore a rain bonnet to protect it, which I always felt negated having it done in the first place. She mowed the lawn with a toothpick in her mouth, twirling it around and around, rotating it wildly between her lips as she cut the grass in even rows.

My grandmother used to say of her husband that "Bill was nobody's fool," though it's not clear why. He was a big and gentle man, who loved women and chain-smoked, and died of emphysema when I was still in elementary school.

My grandmother was careful, deliberate, a planner. Her house was immaculately cleaned, spare and orderly, every countertop in the kitchen always wiped, the tobacco green carpeting always vacuumed, the decorative glass balls in their wicker basket never dusty. Everything had a place. The Pringle's were always in the same place in the cupboard every time we came to visit; the crème de menthe, which she would let us sample, was always in the same place high above the refrigerator.

My mother never wanted to be like her mother, whom she described as relentlessly dissatisfied, highly energetic and underemployed, a woman constrained by her generation, the great girdle of her cultural moment. "If she could have been a corporate executive," says my mother, "she would have been happy."

My mother never wanted to be like her mother, to speak so sharply, to follow a man around, to have to move so much. She wanted to put her roots down somewhere. So she and my father moved to Chaska, a tiny farm town, built a rambler, and have lived in it now for almost thirty years.

"I am so sick," Flo says now, "of bumping around in the same walls."

The Addition

My mother keeps trying to get an addition built, and the plans keep changing—they're unrealistic; then they're too expensive; then it's not what she asked for; then the contractor can no longer do the job, they have to find a new one; then the architect wasn't listening, the plan is still too extravagant. "Maybe Michael should look at the plans," Flo says.

"I don't want to have anything to do with it," Michael says to me, holding up a hand like a crossing guard.

Meanwhile, my dad is always working. They have been planning this addition for three years now and it's driving my mother crazy and she has given up, she says. "It's a conspiracy," she says on the phone one night. "Why? Why, when I just want this one thing? *Why can't it happen?* It's a sign," she says, "that I am doomed to just remain where I'm planted."

Why on earth can't you stop focusing on your mother so much? asks the counselor.

Because she seems depressed, I say. She's always napping, or picking at the little things, putzing around the house. I want her to want more for herself, I say.

Why? says the counselor. Maybe she doesn't want anything else. Maybe all she really wants is a little more room.

She doesn't realize it, I say. But she's capable of so much more.

We've had this conversation before, says the counselor. Why are you napping so much? What do you want for yourself?

I don't know.

You pick at your mother, says the counselor. You have to make her seem small and ridiculous in order to feel good about yourself. You make her seem like a child so that you can feel like an adult. How? asks the counselor, How do you think you could both be adults? How can you appreciate what both of you have?

But she has such a hold on me, I say.

How much of that is because you want her to? asks the counselor, directing me out into freeway traffic. I am naked and alone, standing on the Autobahn.

How much of that, she says, is because you still, fundamentally, want to be taken care of?

Is this The Depression? I ask. Since the counselor has diagnosed me with depression, and got me started on Prozac, I have begun to enjoy attributing things to my condition. To what the counselor calls, The Depression, her answer in the past few months for almost everything that's wrong with me: my sleeping, my avoidance behaviors, my chronic dissatisfaction.

"It could be," she says now, "if you want it to be. You could also try taking responsibility for it."

"I think it's The Depression," I say. A time of stark living. A time of few resources. "My grandparents lived through the Depression," I add.

"You will, too," says the counselor, rolling her eyes.

For Art's Sake

I often feel that I should spend time with my mother, though often I don't feel like spending time with her.

"That's because you aren't doing your own work," says the counselor. "You're either hanging out with Michael or watching TV or calling your mother or calling anyone else so you don't have to do your schoolwork. You can't enjoy your time with other people because you haven't been working on your thesis project. You said so yourself," says the counselor.

It makes sense, and I go anyway to the Saint Catherine's Art Fair with my mother on a rainy Sunday in May, though I have other work to do, and am having trouble being "engaged in the moment," which the counselor keeps telling me I would be able to do if I would just do my work, which I don't feel like doing.

"'Plant Killer' is not going so well," I tell the counselor. "All the plants have died and I don't know what to do next."

"Buy new plants," says the counselor, shrugging. "Things aren't as hard as you make them."

"Maybe we should just go sit and have coffee," I say to my mother, "until it stops raining."

"Where's your sense of adventure?" replies my mother, who is wearing a raincoat with a hood. "Where's your artistic spirit?" she says, handing me a Hefty bag. "Here, put this on. It will keep you dry."

Throughout the day, as we travel from booth to booth, my mother tells each artist who comments on the garbage bag I'm wearing that it is my artistic contribution to the show. She points out places where the bag has ripples or has torn a little and comments on their visual interest. The artists seem delighted by this, if for no other reason than humoring a potential customer, and I am crabby but acquiescent as my mother displays me.

The art fair is juried, which appeals to my mother because, in being selective, one avoids crap. Still, there is some crap, and Flo points out the pieces that lack a relationship between texture and composition.

She buys a jacket made of raw silk, and she buys me a big floppy hat, hoping that I will wear it, since I used to enjoy wearing hats as a toddler.

"I also wore diapers then," I tell my mother.

"But this looks adorable on you," she says. "It's perfect."

After browsing and shopping for several hours we sit down under a tree in the rain and drink the lattés we have ordered from a booth nearby. I drink mine straight, while my mother has decorated hers with everything she can find—cinnamon and sugar and mocha, having been unable to decide which additions would be best.

My mother asks me questions about my summer job at the university and about summer school. I tell her that I certainly won't be specializing in poetry, that I am having trouble with rhythm and method, and we giggle and make Catholic sex jokes. We talk about which exhibits we have liked best and agree that the fabric sculptures of women with their insides pouring out were the most disturbing—so much hair and yarn and wire protruding, wild and directionless.

"Did you notice that one artist has the same thing wrong with her face as I do?" my mother asks.

"It's not wrong, Mother, it's a feature," I say, sounding more and more like her every day, the way she used to tell me that my new adolescent curves weren't "gross," but aesthetically more interesting than my straight, prepubescent lines, and that I should learn to appreciate them.

"Well," she says, "the same thing happened to her face as to mine. Although she had a stroke. I asked her."

"What else did she say?"

"She wasn't very friendly," says my mother, hunched over her coffee and stirring it.

"That's too bad," I say. "It would be nice to talk to someone who has had a similar experience."

"Well, that's what I thought," says my mother. "But, obviously, she is doing quite well for herself. She doesn't seem shy at all about being out and greeting the public."

"Well, she's probably confident about her work," I say. "She probably doesn't think about it. Didn't you used to tell me that if I thought I was pretty the world would think I was pretty?"

"I can't believe you were listening," says my mother. "I knew all that mothering would come back to haunt me." She laughs and readjusts herself a little on the grass, pulling the hood of her raincoat up over the puff of her blond perm.

"Mom, can I ask you something?" And I go ahead before she even has a chance to answer. "It's just you've seemed so sad lately, and you've seemed tired, and I was wondering if you ever think that maybe you'd like to go talk to somebody about your surgery, or anything else that you might be concerned about." I step lightly, throwing euphemisms around like free product samples.

A tear forms in my mother's eye and she, always prepared, grabs her purse and begins foraging for Kleenex. "Well, thank you, sweetheart," she says, dabbing and sniffling. "It's so nice that you care about me."

"Well, it just seems that now that we're all gone from the house, you have more time on your hands, and that happens to lots of women your age. You know, because of June Cleaver."

"I have city council," says Flo. "That keeps me fairly busy."

"That's true," I say. "It just seemed like you were really interested in seeing the guy at the grieving conference until you found out he's not taking new patients. My counselor's partner specializes in women your age."

"Well," she says, blowing her nose, "I have thought about seeing somebody. I mean, sometimes I get really down in the dumps." She is dabbing her eyes with her Kleenex. "But then, on a day like today, when we're out and about, doing something fun," she says, blowing her nose into the Kleenex with a great honk, "I feel fine."

Up North

It would appear that Flo looks at our summer vacation as a way to get rid of leftovers.

She calls me the week before vacation with queries about my dietary restrictions. Since I moved in with Michael, I've had a series of bladder and yeast and bacterial infections. Like summer reruns, they are irritating and familiar. My gynecologist puts me on a diet of no caffeine, no alcohol, no spicy foods and no tomato products, nothing to upset my system's balance. "What reasons are there left to live?" I asked the doctor. "Those were all the vices I had left."

"There are worse things," she said. "Believe me."

"I'm going to make Mexican Casserole to bring up north," my mother says when she calls me. "Do you think you could eat that?"

"Does it have tomatoes?" I asked. "Is it spicy?"

"It's both," said my mother, "but I'll try not to make it too much of either."

It seemed to me that my mother was calling for some kind of a gastrointestinal hall pass, for permission to bring something that she already knew I could not tolerate. It was more of a warning than anything else, and at that point, at least, I thought she was following a recipe.

It's only halfway through our first dinner at the cabin we've rented that my sister—who's moved back from Texas and who now teaches at the same junior high we went to—recognizes some of the casserole's contents as reincarnations of previous dishes. This is the beauty of casserole, its indistinguishable ingredients, strange soupy mixtures of vegetable, bean and meat, suffocating in tomato sauce.

"Oh my god," says my sister, almost taking a bite and then pulling the fork away. "Mom, isn't this the—"

"Greta! Quiet," says my mother, shooting her a sharp and

silencing look. My sister often stops at my parents' house after work, and it is as if my mother has been waiting during the entire dinner to be discovered, her reaction time is so quick.

"But isn't this the—" says my sister again, who is quieted a second time.

"What?" I kick my sister under the table.

"What?" Michael says to me.

"What?" my sister's boyfriend, Cliff, says to her.

"What are you all talking about?" says my father.

"Nothing," says my mother.

"I'll tell you later," my sister whispers out of the corner of her mouth.

My mother is quiet for most of the rest of the meal, humming softly as she chews, looking alternately at us and at the large bronze butterflies decorating the cabin's walls. "Isn't it nice that we're all together?" she says, just as we're finishing up.

My sister reveals to me later that Mexican casserole was a reincarnation of a dish my mother had made weeks ago called Third World Hot Dish, from a recipe a friend had given her. Third World Hot Dish was a spicy combination of tomato products, beans, rice and corn. Though the ingredients are the staples of many world diets, its meatlessness in Minnesota called for special recognition.

"My god, you're right," I said to my sister, as if we were private detectives who had just solved a murder mystery. I remembered Third World Hot Dish because when I had stopped by one day, my mother had said, "Try this Third World Hot Dish," inserting a spoonful of it in my mouth. "It represents a complete protein."

Flo believes in protein, and asks me regularly if I am getting enough of it. Needless to say, when Third World Hot Dish became Mexican Casserole, hamburger was added, along with sour cream, some ancient guacamole from the back of the fridge, green peppers, salsa and tortilla chips sprinkled on top.

I couldn't tell if my mother was ashamed of being discovered or if I was just ashamed for her, for her use of old ingredients.

"It was the rice," said my sister later. "I remembered the rice."

"Thank you, Flo. That was delicious," says my father after dinner, who always says "Thank you, Flo. That was delicious" after any meal. I don't know if my father is lying to be kind or if after years of eating the nuns' food at the hospital cafeteria he truly believes it. "Coffee anyone?" he asks. "What do we have for dessert?"

"Bring over the mints," says Flo. "Eat these mints, kids."

"Didn't we get these for Christmas?" I ask.

"They've been in the refrigerator," says Flo.

"Eat them or you'll see them again," says my father.

"What did you say?" says my mother, spinning around in her chair to hear him better.

"Nothing," he says, popping a chocolate in his mouth and going into the kitchen to make coffee.

"Casserole con Chocolate," says my sister, who knows Spanish.

"What are you kids talking about?" my mother says, looking annoyed but trying to smile, since she has always believed in self-expression, creativity with food being one of those forms.

I know we are being mean, but for some reason I can't seem to help myself.

My mother has planned this vacation, rented the cabin for the six of us, looked forward to it, but now that we are here, she sits quietly and alone most of the time. She has been this way ever since her surgery.

In addition to Mexican Casserole, she has brought an assortment of half-rotted fruit, which I throw away, bit by bit, when she isn't looking. She has packed some kind of processed cheese puffs, which were intended as ingredients in some kind of caramel concoction that the League of Women Voters makes every year. "I just never got around to making them," says my mother. "I was too tired," she says, and she hands us the bag of unrealized ingredients.

She brings along some cookies she had made at Christmastime, which have been in the freezer since then in a large Tupperware container—largely because she made enough to feed an entire elementary school. She believes in economizing. She believes in large batches. She believes that doing it all at once, and then keeping it, saves something. She seems to believe that the ingredients will remain fresh, that everything can be recycled or rehydrated to good effect.

We eat the cookies, despite the slight flavor of freezer burn.

"Do you think we're just encouraging her?" I ask my sister.

Though my mother has assembled us as a group, she stays away from us.

When we are at the beach, she takes a nap at the cabin.

When we are in the cabin, she goes to read her magazine on the beach. When we are sitting on the dock sunning ourselves, she sits on a lawn chair, in the shade of a tree, licking her thumb and flipping through *Better Homes and Gardens,* getting ideas for the addition she and my father are planning on the back of the house.

"Come down to the dock," I shout up at her. "Are you embarrassed to be seen with us?" This is not unreasonable, given our behavior, and the load of sand my sister has just dumped down my suit.

"I thought it was the other way around," says my mother, who is given to saying things like this since her surgery.

When my mother takes a family picture after dinner one night, my father says, "Here, Flo, now you get in and let me take a picture."

"No," she replies. "I'm too ugly."

And I think she believes it.

"I need a new face," she says.

And we begin, I think, to believe it, too. At least I do.

And she becomes even more distant.

"It's so nice to have adult children," says my mother one night after dinner, sitting and smiling as my sister and her boyfriend and Michael and I clean the kitchen. "Responsible adults who can look after themselves," she adds. "This was a lovely dinner. You're becoming quite a cook," she says to me, squeezing my arm.

"It was mostly Michael," I say. My mother adores him, except she wishes he'd relax a little; he's brought his work along with him on vacation. He reminds her, she says, of my father, a little.

Later, she sits on the couch with the newspaper while the rest of us get drunk and play Yahtzee at the dinner table.

My father laughs at our dirty jokes and doesn't mind when we say "fuck" on a bad roll. He makes us gin and tonics and throws pretzels at us when we win. He tells us stories from his youth, like the time he and his brother put leaves in the daily paper, *The Willmar Daily Reminder,* and rolled it up and tried to smoke it.

"You kids like spending time with your father, don't you?" my mother says when later I go to sit by her.

"Sure," I say.

"He likes you, too," she says, smiling in a way that is both contented and disturbed, caressing my hand gently, carefully, the way you'd touch an old person, and with the familiarity of a lover.

I realize, for the first time, that I've never seen her touch my father this way. She would say, I know, that he is never sitting still that long.

Therapy

Even though I can get health care at the university, I go to my father for drugs. Since he is a physician, and since much of my childhood was spent trying to keep my lungs inflated, the nature of our relationship depends on this supply and demand. For years, most of our interaction revolved around my complaints of illness and his responding with a handful of antibiotic samples.

Now, though he rarely has free time, we drink beer together, we exchange books, we go golfing. The nature of our vices and interests has changed. *"Don't stoop to their level,"* he used to tell my mother when she got embroiled in disputes with my sister, brother and me, but now it is Flo who seems more distant, and my father who laughs at my dirty jokes while Flo thumbs through the newspaper and says things like, "There's no call for language like that around here."

For years, Flo was the one I told all my problems to, confided in, went shopping with, bought clothes only with her aesthetic guidance. I didn't know how to approach my father, and my mother was, well, so accessible—at our level.

But lately I tend to go to my father when I need advice, who doesn't direct me in simple tasks the way Flo does.

"Say," she said the other day when I was home visiting, "before you put this plate away, you might want to put that extra fruit in the bowl and place it on the table for people to nibble on."

"But we're the only people here," I said.

Or she might say, "Say, I've noticed that you used an unusually creative method in opening the prunes. If you're interested in *fresh* prunes, you might want to *cut* the bag open instead of tearing it, and seal it with a clothespin so they don't get dried out. That's only if you're interested in freshness."

So, anyway, for months, I tell the therapist, I have worried over my mother's interest in the mundane, in simple maintenance.

"Maintenance is the stuff of life," says the counselor. "I keep telling you that."

"But she's also isolated, disconnected, disinterested in life," I say. "My dad gets up every morning for work and deals with people all day. But she just keeps sleeping. And then, when she's awake, there's 'fruit to nibble on,' which she will continue to transfer to smaller and smaller bowls until it's all gone."

"It sounds like she keeps track of things," says the counselor.

Anyway, I say, this morning on the radio, I hear that laziness is our genetic and evolutionary condition. That our bodies gravitate toward this, *though social conditioning makes us feel that we need to be accomplished,* to constantly be accomplishing. I hear that many animals, if you watch them long enough, spend their days wandering around in circles, digesting their food, and sitting still. That ants and bees are like batteries: they are born with a certain amount of energy and if they use it all up early, they die. That many animals, for this reason, rest in order to survive, to ensure longevity.

I have long thought, I tell the counselor, that if I stood still long enough, I would continue to survive. Not only would I be safe in my own home, I would be conserving my resources. I would be stopping time, slowing down its process, removing my association with it, putting things on hold until I'm ready to deal with them.

"Meanwhile, life happens," says the counselor.

"Not to me," I say.

"Well then you're making a choice," she says.

Anyway, I say, I've always assumed this of my mother as well. I see her moving in circles, moving the fruit from bowl to bowl, shuffling the same piles of paper around, napping each day to restore energy, for what? To move more piles?

I heard on another radio show, I tell the counselor, that this is the nature of depression: that unfocused wandering, that need to sleep, that disinterest in life's business, a feeling of being overwhelmed by life's maintenance, subsumed by sloth.

So now I wonder if depression is not *actually the absolutely correct biological response to living in America.* If, in our society, the best answer is to nap, to move in circles around one's territory and digest slowly. I mean, there's just so much coming in, so much noise, so much junk mail, I tell the counselor. I mean, look at Flo, wandering around the house sipping Diet-Rite raspberry soda ever since I introduced her to it, and me, padding around the apartment, while Michael works, feeling dismay at the piles of paperwork on my desk, feeling a strong urge to climb up on my desk and lie down in those piles and nap.

I mean, why are so many people taking Prozac, me and Flo included, if not to counteract some instinctive drive, a drive that is not moving us toward death and inactivity, but, in fact, is moving us toward *life—a life of inactivity.* Maybe Prozac is a bad idea, I say, maybe it will just wear out my batteries. I think, perhaps, I tell the counselor, that by napping, my mother is *preserving* herself, trying to stay alive until the storm passes. I always thought that depression meant giving up, surrendering, but maybe it's a kind of vigil, a keeping of the faith.

"But see, that's the kind of circular thinking that is a symptom of depression," says the counselor.

"Well, it makes sense to me," I say.

"It's a way to work around the shame you feel at your own inactivity. To give it credence, when really, what you need to do is just get up each morning and begin to move with the world."

I explain to her that the radio show talked about this, too. That the world moves at a pace that has been established by a few—and that those people are feeling *particularly guilty* about something or they wouldn't be moving so fast. That if you are playing music in a room, and you ask someone to cross that room, she will do so at the pace that has been established by the music. That we move in rhythm with our surroundings. Society moves at the established pace and then tailors all its expectations to it. Perhaps my mother, I suggest, is a renegade in her napping; she's composing a symphony of slumber.

I go on to explain the other things I've learned from the radio show: that many of society's dysfunctions come from our *busyness, our frenetic movement.* That we need to operate in the moment, to wash the dishes when we are washing the dishes. To be with the dishes. "My mother is like that," I tell the counselor. "She has always been with the dishes."

"Of course she's always been with the dishes," says the counselor. "Only men who've quit high-paying jobs find dishwashing to be interesting."

"It's true," I say. "These Zen-dishwashing people are always men."

"Sure," says the counselor. "They have the economic power to make it a lifestyle instead of a chore. How many milligrams do we have you on now?"

"Thirty," I say.

"Hmmm," she says. "And you're worried about your mother, why?"

"Because she's always sleeping, and if she's not sleeping, she's worried about the prunes being closed tightly enough."

"So your mother's worried about the prunes, and you're worried about your mother," says the counselor.

"It seems like she's shriveling up, too," I say.

"For someone who's shriveling," says the counselor, "she certainly has an enormous influence on you."

"Is it possible your mom is still really worn out from her surgery?" says the counselor. "It can take some people years to get back on their feet after an experience like that. It's very traumatic."

"I suppose," I say. "I mean, that's what she says it is sometimes. But then other times she acts like it didn't matter, like the surgery was no big deal."

"Are you still napping a lot?" asks the counselor.

"Not as much as before the Prozac," I say. "But I still get tired. I get really, really tired."

"That might be the Prozac," says the counselor. "It makes some people tired at first. Are you getting up in the morning?"

"Sometimes," I say. "I mean, I'm trying."

"Seven o'clock," says the counselor. "Every morning."

"But not on Saturdays, right?"

"On Saturdays," she says.

"But not on Sundays," I say.

"Every day," she says. "You get up, you put on your robe, you go outside and touch the ground."

"But what if I wake Michael up?"

"Then he can get up, too."

"He usually sleeps until eight thirty."

"Well, you don't," says the counselor. "You're out the door at 7:05 to touch the ground and be a part of the world." The counselor has a theory that once I've been outside for a breath of fresh air, I'll be awake and ready to begin working.

"Can I have my coffee first?" I say.

"Only if it gets you out the door faster. Maybe it will take you around the block for a quick walk, too," she says.

"Oh, it will," I say. "I'm sure it will."

Later, when things are more clear, I will understand that being depressed is a little like being an alcoholic: you're always displacing and misplacing things, like a character in a bad made-for-television movie, shouting "I can quit anytime I want!" or "That's not mine!" when an empty vodka bottle is held up—you're always forgetting your own promises to yourself or stepping around them like sleeping giants—tiptoeing around life's great, rumbling energy, wishing it would just stay still.

On most weekends I visit my parents, and I go without Michael because he is always either playing soccer or working. Today I stop by my father's clinic to pick up some Prozac samples so that I won't have to pay for the stuff—the nurses are always loading me up with samples because sometimes I bring them donuts—and I wait around until my dad's done seeing a patient.

"Well, hello, Twinkle Toes," he says, coming out of an exam room and giving me a kiss on the forehead. "Let's have a quick cup of coffee."

We sit in the lunchroom of the clinic, picking at some left-over pizza and donuts and sipping coffee that has been idling on the burner for hours and tastes like motor oil.

We talk about Jon Hassler, new movies that have come out, and finally I say, "Dad, I'm kind of worried about Mom."

"Really," he says, brushing some crumbs from his fingers, lifting his coffee cup to his chest and then resting it in his lap. "Why do you say that?"

"Well, she just seems sad," I say. "She's sleeping a lot, and I can tell she doesn't feel good about herself."

"Well, your mother has always thought it important to look good, and to present herself well, and she's very hard on herself."

"But when I tell her she looks pretty, she just says, 'Oh, no I'm not.' What am I supposed to say to that?"

My father looks at me and rubs his chin, still holding his coffee.

"Well," he says, slowly and quietly, "thank you for telling me about your concern."

He pauses to take a sip of his coffee and cocks his head to

one side. "Do you know why she might be feeling this way?" he asks, having been trained to diagnose and problem solve; and having been trained, growing up in the forties and fifties, to treat his wife with respectful distance.

I tell him I think she's bored, that she can't find a role for herself, that her surgery has been harder on her than she's willing to admit.

"She keeps buying those miracle creams and videos on facial exercises," I tell him. "She's not happy. I think she needs to see somebody," I say.

"Okay, dear," he says. "Well, again, thank you. I'll try to talk to your mother."

As he excuses himself to go see patients, leaving me with a bag full of sample drugs, I feel as though I have violated some sacred territory. That as his child, I shouldn't bring up these things; I should not invoke my mother's unhappiness in conversation.

I'm afraid, I tell the counselor, that they're not moving at the same pace. That he's restlessly avoiding things, and that she, in sleeping, is attempting some kind of preservation.

"What they're doing is really none of your business," says the counselor. "You need to deal with your own avoidance. How are things going with Michael?" she says.

"Not so good," I tell her. "He's always either playing soccer or working."

"That's Michael," says the therapist. "Those are his priorities."

"He got mad at me the other day because I was acting silly in the grocery store again."

"You want a playmate," says the counselor. "And Michael has other priorities. You need to focus on your work."

I do not bring up again with my father my mother's sadness. It is obvious that it's not worth bringing up, which makes it sound like some kind of rusty sea relic, which is maybe what it is. Lifted out of the ocean depths, salty and deteriorating in the fresh air.

Our Temporary Survival in the Forest

Flo calls on Michael's birthday and wants to know if we'd like to "stop over" for birthday dessert after we go out to eat. Flo has yet to realize that forty minutes out of the city doesn't qualify as "stopping over" unless you're flying from Minneapolis to Chicago, but I "stop over" a lot anyway.

"I'm making that boozy, spongy thing that we had on your birthday," she says.

"Trifle?" I ask.

"Yes, that's it," says Flo. "I've got lots of it. And then you can pick your brother up at the airport on your way out here."

Michael and I play miniature golf before going to the one Italian restaurant he likes in Minneapolis. He calls every other Italian restaurant in town "Meatball Junction." The restaurant is cool and dimly lit, a relief from the late-August heat of our apartment. I don't get to drink, because I am driving, and that kind of irritates me, because I would sure like a beer. And Michael won't sit still so that I can take a nice birthday picture of him; he keeps fidgeting and covers his face with his napkin.

After dinner we go to the airport to pick up my brother, who is flying in from Chicago for his annual end-of-the-summer camping trip to the Boundary Waters with my father. Occasionally I go camping with them, but being allergic to almost everything in nature, and confused by the unfamiliar greenery, I spend most of my time paddling into rocks, tripping on plants and pacing in circles trying to figure out what we're supposed to be doing next to ensure our temporary survival in the forest. Often that means finding the bag where we've packed the chocolate.

My brother, more seasoned in survival, arrives safely with all of his equipment stuffed in a huge duffel bag, and he and I and Michael, who is still burping garlic from dinner, head for my parents' house.

At home, my mother and father are just finishing dinner with Conrad, one of my father's old partners in medicine. It's a funny thing to see them all sitting at the table together, sipping wine, talking and picking at what's left on their plates, since, barring Christmas and Easter celebrations with the relatives, my parents haven't entertained in years.

The last time I saw their friend Conrad his hair was black. Now it's gray, his wife has left him and he tells my mother and father stories about dating and bachelorhood at sixty.

My mother is eager to show off my brother and me; we are her accomplishments, semiproductive adults working on advanced degrees, not in prison or on welfare. My choice of a boyfriend, one who is friendly and smart, is further proof of her good work, and she sits us down eagerly, telling Conrad a little something about each of us, grabbing coffee cups and retrieving the spongy, boozy trifle from the refrigerator.

There is something incongruous about this dessert—the whipped cream and buttery pudding of it refusing to blend with the rum-soaked sponge cake—your tongue must deal with each thing separately, the whipped cream leaving a slippery, buttery coating on the roof of your mouth, the back of your throat feeling the burn of the rum, which moves through you with a kind of hazy sharpness, an intensity of feeling buffered by the Jell-O pudding.

I am thinking about this as Conrad asks us why we didn't like *The Bridges of Madison County*; all the women he is dating now, he says, weep over this book.

Well, basically, I say, it's Robert Waller's own narcissistic fantasy about being a sensitive new-age guy and screwing a beautiful farm-wife who isn't a virgin but is an almost-virgin because she doesn't love her husband.

"Now see," says Conrad, "That's not what the women I know say about the book. They all say it's a story about finding true love, a companion."

"Well, I think—" says my mother, who is interrupted by my father.

"But it's crap," says my father. "I read this thing in the paper, I think it was by Jon Hassler."

"Jon Hassler's a friend of mine," Conrad says to me, and I nod; my mother moves forward in her chair and places her elbows on the table, raising a finger as if to queue up, or to emphasize a point that was never made.

"Well, so, you should know this," my father continues. "He just railed against this book, and I thought, Geez, what a strong reaction, and so I read it. All the critics hated it so much, I thought I better read it. And it's true. I mean, the writing is very simple and plodding and clanky and uninteresting, and I thought, Hell, I could do this."

My mother moves farther forward, now leaning on the table, her finger still in the air, and begins to take a breath. My brother and boyfriend, not having read the book or seen the movie, are silent. "I thought—" says my mother, who is again interrupted.

"You're right, Jon Hassler did *not* like that book," says Conrad.

"I think Robert Waller looks like a lesbian phys-ed teacher," I say.

"Did you see that send-up of the book? *The Ditches of* . . . oh, what was it?" says my father.

"*The Ditches of Edison County,*" I say.

"What a riot," says my father. "Now, I understand that the movie is supposed to be better."

"It's boring," I say.

"I thought the movie was good," my mother finally blurts out, facing Conrad. "It's a lovely story, Connie, and you can see why—"

"Why it's so popular is beyond me," says my father.

"You, who have absolutely no sensitivity, shut up!" my mother turns to my father, pointing a finger at him like a small fleshy gun.

My brother and I exchange glances, shifting restlessly in our seats. Michael sits silently, arms crossed. "Well," mutters my father under his breath, "at least we used to be civil."

"Anyway, Con," my mother says, turning and continuing as if nothing has happened, "you can see why that story appeals to so many women. We all want to believe in romance."

Conrad nods, doing his best, I think, as a guest, not to acknowledge any tensions. "You know, Florence," he says, "I would love to borrow your book on Japanese art. I've developed a real interest in that."

Our Apartment

Late at night, when Michael comes to bed, I go to my computer and try to work for a while, but often he calls out to me from the other room, "Excuse me, excuse me! I'm lonely in here! Hello? I'm *nude.*" It's hard to work under those conditions, too.

One of the things I love about Michael is that in bed, he's careful, and when I say that I'm not in the mood, which is more and more since the strange itching started, he will go sprinting around the apartment with his arms up in the air shouting, "Hooray! Hooray! No means yes! No means yes!" and then we will watch *Jerry Springer* together and analyze Jerry's guests, trying to solve all their problems, deciding in many cases that it's just too late to fix anything.

I get my work done late at night, after Michael's gone to sleep, and usually at the last minute, and Michael always seems surprised when I get an A on something.

"But you threw this together late last night," he will say, seeming stunned. Michael has all of his time scheduled, filled out in blocks on a notepad. He works at scheduled intervals, plays soccer or lifts weights during the times he has scheduled for that, does his own work at scheduled times, plans his classes during the blocks that he's scheduled for planning classes, though he often spends more time on that than he's budgeted, not wanting to disappoint his students with a shoddy lesson, and leaves some time each week to go over his finances and to set next week's schedule.

He showed it to me once and I said, "Where am I?"

"I've got time for us blocked out on Friday evening,"

Michael said. "See? 'Entertainment.' And really, Shanny, I see you all the time."

I didn't know what to say. I had no schedule, no plan for today or the next, or the week after. Everything in my life just seemed to kind of roll together, collect speed and go thundering downhill.

"Shanny, this is the only way I know how to get through graduate school," Michael said.

In the mornings our new apartment gets plenty of light, but I still have trouble getting up, and Michael is usually in the study hours before I'm awake, and then we head off to school together. At school, I go to class, work for Professor Nelson, who says she's pleased with my research and is keeping me on for the year, and try to avoid some of the older male professors who stare at my breasts as if they were pedestrian traffic signals, as if something about my chest said, "Don't Walk. Please stand right here and say something stupid, like, 'The quest for knowledge, as I'm sure you know, can be quite sensual.'"

And then each evening is pretty much the same as the one before it.

It's nice to be at home with Michael. It's warm and the apartment always smells good when Michael cooks, but sometimes, when Michael has been in the bathtub for several hours reading theory or Italo Calvino, and I have to pee and I know he won't leave the bathroom and that I'll have to pee while he's in there, because he's reading and he's *comfortable,* and I know that he'll say that he can just close the shower curtain so he won't see me, and he can turn the water on so he won't hear me, and so what's the problem?—I just start crying.

I just start crying and when I'm done I call Flo, and I don't tell her anything specific but instead I tell her what I heard on Minnesota Public Radio that day, what we had for dinner (roast chicken, steamed artichokes, carrots, potatoes), and where I park at the university (because she asks).

"It sure has changed since I was there," says Flo. "I don't remember those lots."

Inevitably she will say, "What's your friend doing tonight?" meaning Michael, and then she will say, "He sure does work a lot. Does he ever give himself a break? He reminds me," she says, "of your father."

Plant Killer

When my brother was in high school, he made a cooker out of old metal barrels and boiled maple sap during the winter. He would spend hours waxing his cross-country skis, then ski out into the woods behind our house to check on his maple taps. In the middle of the night, he would have to go outside in the freezing cold to check his syrup and stoke the flames that burned underneath it.

My sister and I could never understand all this trouble for maple syrup, since we had Log Cabin in the refrigerator, but we agreed to try our brother's homemade version at our mother's request.

That Sunday morning we kids made our own custom pancakes. I made a pancake shaped like Mickey Mouse, though I couldn't get the nose right and it wound up looking like a third ear. My sister, seeing my Mickey pancake, decided to make one in the shape of the family dog. Our brother made a stringy pancake that read $E=MC^2$. The syrup he'd labored over had a smoky flavor and was more watery than Log Cabin. My sister and I chewed thoughtfully, not sure what to make of this new "real" syrup. To us, Log Cabin, with its corn syrup, starches, and polysyllabic chemical combinations was real, because it was familiar.

I remember now that before my brother turned those barrels into a maple syrup cooker, we had used them to roll down the hill next to our house, curling up inside with a piece of carpeting for padding, and spinning, spinning, spinning to the bottom.

The tricky part was not to hit the tree in the middle of the hill, and actually, I ran into it most of the time, probably because I was trying so hard to avoid it.

Well, that's interesting, the counselor says. *Now, how does this relate to you?*

She keeps telling me to stop telling stories and to talk about my feelings. How did I feel about what happened? I am supposed to provide meta-emotional-commentary, instead of getting mired in detail.

The point, I tell her, is that my brother was always doing his own thing, following his own interests, always on to some new project, running rat brains through the blender, or playing the violin, while I just got used to what was available. I just kind of got used to the nothingness.

And?

It's like trying to write a research paper without doing any research; all you have are your own blind opinions.

You are definitely one of my more challenging clients, she says, *I'm still not following you.*

It means you get to the bottom of the hill and you have no

idea what to do with yourself. So you go up and down, bumping into the same damn tree again and again.

The counselor just looks at me.

I'm stuck, I say.

Your Original Language

I think I'd like to learn Italian, I say to Michael one night while we're in the kitchen heating up chicken broth, cutting up tofu and vegetables for soup, another one of Michael's creations. We have been living in our new apartment for over a year. Four seasons in our new space.

"Why don't you find something of your own to do, Shanny?"

"But you're always speaking Italian on the phone with your mother and it drives me crazy," I say. "I can't understand what you're saying."

"Aha, there's the real reason," Michael says. "Surveillance. Why don't you find something that interests *you*?"

"But it does interest me," I say. "Because you interest me. And you're always talking about Italy and what the people are like, and I'd like to know."

"What about Russian novels, Shanny?" he says. "Maybe you should take a course in that. Or what about Tai Chi?"

"I just thought it would be nice," I say, "if I could speak a little bit of your original language."

Okay, says the therapist, enough about Michael for today. How's your work going for Professor Nelson?

You're not going to believe this, I say, but the press that's publishing her book said that they'd never received such a clean manuscript.

Really? says the therapist. What does that mean?

It means that I got most of that fucking MLA formatting right.

Well, I'll be darned, says the therapist. Now, you get them to put that in writing, so you can put it in your file.

What file?

Your career file.

I'm supposed to have a career file?

You don't have one? says the therapist, that's your assignment for next week. You get that letter and you make a file. Now, let's talk about your thesis project. How's that going?

Hello? says the therapist.

Hello? says Michael. *Earth to Shanny?*

"I'm sorry," I say. I have zoned out while cutting vegetables for stir-fry. Michael wants us both to be in charge of cooking, but he doesn't like the food I make—"It's Minnesota food," he says, when I make Tuna Casserole—and so I bought a book on Chinese cooking so I could learn how to cut the vegetables correctly, how to make the sauces, when to add what, since it all seems to depend on timing.

Where did you just go, little chopper? Michael says, with a hand on my back. *Where do you go when that happens?*

I had been watching *The Joy Luck Club* again, in my head. Michael and I had rented it last week and I was thinking about the part where Andrew McCarthy says to his wife, who had dutifully made herself the most supportive wife she could be, "You've made me bigger than you," or something like that. She had become the perfect mother, the perfect cook and home-maker. He wondered where the intellectual and activist he met in college and married had gone. And then the wife, who had been throwing parties for him and his clients for years, says something like, "But I thought this is what you wanted me to be?"

Michael and I were lying at the end of the futon. He looked over at me and said, "You make me bigger than you, Shanny."

So, I had been chopping vegetables, thinking that in some ways that was true. When Michael and I met, I believed he was right about everything. He had grown up in Rome and New York, gone to Columbia University, while I'd been eating donuts at Saint Olaf, a place surrounded by cornfields. I loved showing Michael off at weddings and family gatherings. He could talk about almost anything and people always liked him. Even my grandma liked him; she'd get this big grin on her face and blush whenever he went over to talk to her. It did bother me that he didn't like me to hug him in public; it seemed oddly Scandinavian of him, but he had once explained it by saying that since he moved around a lot when he was younger, from Rome to New York, to Boston for a little while, and then back to New York, and to different neighborhoods and schools, he always felt like he had to keep a low profile, that he should learn the local customs instead of making a scene. Michael was a good teacher and always got good student evaluations. He could speak a language that I didn't understand—of course, he couldn't speak French, but French never came in handy for me anymore. It was true that I let Michael drive us around most of the time; I just liked it better when he drove, his car had more pick-up. When Michael and I had met, I believed he knew everything. He knew, for example, what transcendentalism was, while I, not knowing, had thrown out a guess, "Does it mean you have really super teeth?"

It was maybe true that I made Michael bigger than me, but I wondered, in our small apartment, if there was room for both of us to be life-sized.

"I don't know," I told him. "I don't know what I was thinking."

In the spring, I have to take the master's qualifying exam, a right of passage where the professoriate checks your academic passport to make sure you can finish your trip. All of the master's students have to take it, and any Ph.D.s who want their M.A. credited along the way. There are just two books to read, and three essay questions. We have four hours to write the test out in the graduate student computer lounge. We can bring only the two books in with us, for citations, and the professor overseeing the test checks our belongings at the door, as if we're at the airport.

They told us to begin studying for the test at the beginning of the quarter, and to read the books several times, but I put off studying for it and start reading the books two weeks before the test, and scramble at the library for corollary materials, research and analysis on the books we've had to read.

Professor Nelson gives me two weeks off and tells me I can make up my hours later so I can study for the test. I'm up late every night and I get a cold. I have a cough, a fever, my body hurts. Michael makes me soup, brings me crackers and Kleenex. He makes roast chicken with lots of vegetables when I start feeling better, and he cleans the kitchen every night. He makes a point of letting me know that he's happy to do this, but when the test is over, it's my turn to cook.

I lie in bed, underlining entire paragraphs, taking notes on theme and structure, symbolism. "God," I say, to Michael, who is putting dishes back in the buffet, "what if I flunk this thing?"

"Do you really think you could flunk it?" Michael says. "Does anyone ever flunk it?"

"Someone flunked it last year," I say. "Actually, two people did."

"Well, how are you doing, sweetie?" he says.

"I don't know," I say. "I have no idea what they're going to ask. I found out that some of the other masters students had formed *study groups*."

"God forbid," says Michael.

"I know!" I say. "And read every other book by the two authors. Will you still be seen with me in public if I flunk this test? Will you still be my boyfriend?"

"I'll still be your boyfriend," Michael says, kissing me on the cheek.

When the test results from the qualifying exam come back, I go bounding out of the English Department and run all the way across campus to the fitness center, where Michael is playing racquetball. I get there just as he's finishing up, covered in sweat and still wearing his goggles, shoving his things in his gym bag.

I bounce over to him, give him a kiss on the cheek, and whisper, "I passed. With distinction."

Michael just stares off at the clock near the gym entrance. He has this kind of blank look on his face.

"Did other people pass with disctinction?" he says.

"Just me," I say.

"Wow," he says, "that's great."

"So we should go celebrate," I say. "My treat."

"Not tonight," he says. "I've got things I need to do at home."

Therapy

It all goes so quickly, I tell the counselor. One minute you're dating a guy who tries to fuck you in your sleep and the next minute you're living with a guy whose attention you can't get. Still, I get them mixed up.

"You're selfish," I find myself saying to Michael, who looks confused. He has just made us salmon steaks. "I feel like you want to control me," I find myself saying.

Are you allowing that control? the counselor will ask. *Are you enabling it?*

My first boyfriend, each time I threatened to leave, each time I made overtures in the direction of maybe "cooling it for a while," would clean my entire apartment, bring me flowers, scrub the floors, dust, make the bed, which he otherwise wouldn't do, have dinner ready for me when I came home. This was, supposedly, to make my life more simple, a kind of treat.

Is it possible that Michael is just trying to do something nice for both of you, by washing the dishes? the counselor will say. *Is it possible that he just needs that kind of order for himself?*

It's confusing, I will say.

"I can't be myself around you," I say to Michael, who looks confused. I am stomping around and angry. "You expect me to be this perfect, productive person," I say, throwing a plastic hairbrush on the bathroom tiles. It breaks in pieces and careens across the ceramic floor, settling into the corners, taking refuge behind the radiator. In the middle of my rage—at what? at the hairbrush?—I have to suffer the embarrassment of cleaning up after myself.

"Who expects you to be perfect?" says Michael, scrubbing and rinsing, shaking off the excess water before placing the dishes in the drying rack.

"You're always trying to get me to organize, to budget, to cook different foods."

"I just don't want you to throw away your future by being in debt," he says. "I just want you to feel good about yourself."

I get out the broom and dustpan. Because I, myself, am so frightened—of what?—it doesn't occur to me that it might be frightening for him to live with somebody like me. I am so certain that he wants to control me and keep me there, that it doesn't occur to me that my behavior is unattractive, and that *he* might want to leave.

And maybe it is me who wants to leave.

On a calmer day I say to him, "Maybe we're just not right for each other. Maybe I don't know how to be with you and still be myself."

"That scares me," he says, "that scares the shit out of me. I'm not a rock, you know. I'm not this strong, infallible person you make me out to be. I need support, too," he says, "I need help sometimes, too."

"But you never act like you do."

At a dinner party, the subject of dangerous occupations comes up and Michael whispers to me, "I think the most dangerous occupation is being a hairbrush in our apartment."

Ever since Michael and I moved in together, I've been having problems, this itching that won't go away. The gynecologist couldn't figure out what it was, so he sent me to a dermatologist, who gave me special soaps and lotions. Told me to stop drinking coffee and not to eat acidic foods.

I spent the first week eating egg salad sandwiches, while Michael made a huge pot of spaghetti with a clam marinara sauce.

We sat at the dinner table, Michael swirling his pasta, "Hey, Popeye," he said, "have you been swimming lately?"

"No," I said. "Why are you calling me Popeye?"

"Your arms are starting to sag," Michael said. "Your biceps are moving toward your elbows."

"Thanks, Michael. That's a really nice thing to say."

I looked down at my sandwich, its hard crust and creamy colors. My sandwich could get lost in a snow storm.

Michael starts to sleep every night with his back to me, and when I ask him not to, he tells me it's the only way he'll get a good night's sleep. That he has to teach in the morning.

"Couldn't we at least talk a little?" I say.

And so we talk for a couple of minutes and then he rolls to the wall again.

"I feel like typhoid Mary," I say. "You know, we could fool around a little, even though I'm having problems. There are other things that we could do."

"I don't think so," Michael says. "I'll just get revved up and then there's nothing we can do about it."

"There are other things we could do about it," I say.

"When you're better," Michael says.

Some nights I just stare out the window at the dark buildings across the street, the one street lamp illuminating the neighborhood liquor store, where a few months ago, a guy tried to beat up the checkout clerk with a tap from a keg. He ran out before anyone could catch him, but then a week later the bicycle shop across the street had been broken into, and the meters up the street bashed open. The police figured it was the same guy, but they still couldn't find him.

"I'm not saying it's all his fault," I say to the counselor.

"Well, yes, you are," she says. "And it's not." Relationships are like bathwater shared by a family, she says. *Who knows whose dirt is whose? The water is just brown.*

"That's gross," I say.

"People used to have to do that," she says.

"I can't do this anymore," I say one night. "Maybe we could still be friends, but I can't stay here anymore. Maybe we could work backward. I think this was all just too much, too soon," I say. "Maybe I just need a break."

"A break? Shanny, is this it? You just drop this bomb?"

"I love you, but—" I say.

"Friends?" Michael says, and starts crying. "Shanny, I'm willing to work this out. To work out anything. But I don't think I could just be your friend."

"This is just too much for me," I say.

"And you're not going to try and work it out?"

"I'm not happy."

"Then," Michael says, "you need to leave."

"I'll start looking for an apartment," I say.

"Tonight," he says.

I move in with my sister and her boyfriend until I get my own apartment, a tiny studio in Saint Paul, in a big old building, decorated like a rest home with floral carpeting, plastic flowers on the stairway landing and old orange curtains.

Michael puts everything in storage and lines up a new apartment for the fall, when he will return for school. We talk a few times to make sure we haven't mixed up each other's things, that no one took the wrong book, the wrong CD.

"You know," the counselor says, "Michael was not like your first boyfriend. They are not the same person."

"I kept getting them mixed up," I tell her. "I felt trapped. It was too much too soon. I couldn't breathe."

My phone rang in the middle of the night last week, I tell her, and I thought it was the ex-boyfriend.

"Not Michael?" she says.

"No," I say, "the other one."

I had gotten up to go to the bathroom, and on my way back to bed the phone rang and I stumbled over to grab it, tripping on a pair of shoes that I'd left in the middle of the room. "Hello?" I said. Someone sat quietly on the other end; I could hear a trace of a breath. "Hello?" I said, and then again, in the most menacing voice I could muster, "Hello!" When the someone disconnected, my heart was pounding fast and hard. I climbed back into bed, gathered up my blankets and pulled them to my chin. When I had fallen asleep earlier the room had been almost suffocatingly hot, but the night air through the open window had now cooled the room. I wondered if someone was watching me; I almost never close the shades up in my new, third-floor apartment. I began to wonder if it was the ex-boyfriend, checking to see that I am still alive, still out there. After all this time, almost three years, I still think it is the ex-boyfriend every time I get a hang-up call, even though my number is unlisted.

"You're lonely," the counselor says at our next session. "You have trouble letting go. Maybe you like to believe that he's still out there thinking about you."

"But I hate him," I say. "I hate that son of a bitch."

"It's like the seduction of depression," says the counselor. "It's familiar. Even if you feel miserable, it's known."

"Depression is that comfortable sag in the middle of your bed," I say.

"Exactly," says the counselor. "Which, in the end, is not good for your posture. Michael and your first boyfriend are not the same person," she says. "You need to learn to separate them."

Separating Them

Before Michael and I met, I had noticed a good-looking guy in the hallways of the English Department. Whenever our eyes met, in the hallway, at department events, he didn't smile, he just looked at me, or looked away. I decided, before even talking to him, that he was mean. The truth was, he looked a little like my ex-boyfriend. Green eyes and light blond hair.

A good jawline. Because of that vague similarity, I decided he was cruel. Though, when I saw him, I couldn't keep my eyes off.

About a month after Michael and I started dating, I was walking down Washington Avenue, on the East Bank of the university, crowded at lunchtime with faculty, students and the staff of the nearby hospital, busy with honking traffic, and littered with empty coffee cups, gum, and cigarette butts. I was looking at the sidewalk trying to decide where I would go for lunch—Bruegger's, McDonald's, The Big Ten for greasy fries and a hoagie?—when I looked up to see Michael, with this guy I had already decided was not, was definitely not, a nice person.

"Hi, sweetheart," Michael said, "I want you to meet Matt."

Matt and I just stood looking at each other while Michael, in my mind and in my peripheral vision, almost disappeared entirely. I couldn't believe my bad luck. They were friends, had shared a big house with two other guys last year. If there was anyone I would want to date besides Michael, it was Matt. I told myself that he seemed harmful, that I should head for the basement, under the stairs, away from windows. Except when Michael introduced us, Matt didn't seem mean or harmful. He looked as stunned as I was. He looked like he'd just got to the cash register and found he didn't have his wallet. Or maybe it was me who looked that way. Surprised and disappointed. A hole in my stomach.

"Matt and I were talking about going to a Twins game this weekend," said Michael. "So Matt is going to see if Elizabeth could come with us."

"Okay," I said. Michael had told me about his friend Matt, about how he and his girlfriend, Elizabeth, were having trouble. About how Matt wasn't sure she was the right one for him. But I had no idea that the Matt who Michael talked about was the guy I saw in the halls.

And I have no idea now what I had for lunch that day, but I remember distinctly what the counselor said to me when I went in the next day for my session, "Not in *this* lifetime you won't date him. He's Michael's friend and you are not going to do that to Michael. That's against the rules."

"But I get the feeling he might feel the same way."

"It doesn't matter," said the counselor.

My sister came with us to the game because Elizabeth couldn't. We met Matt at the gates of the Metrodome; he locked up his bike and we all went through the yellow turnstiles together. I worked hard, mentally, not to be attracted to Matt, to remember that I had chosen Michael. But when I saw Matt, I could feel myself blush, I could feel my insides sort of disintegrate and sprinkle down into my toes like fallen ash. He said something about Milt Jackson and I said something about the Modern Jazz Quartet, even though that was all I knew, that Milt Jackson had been with the Modern Jazz Quartet, and I only knew it because Flo listened to them, and the first time she had mentioned Milt and said the word *vibraharp* it had made me giggle. I told myself that I did not like this person and I was only being polite for my boyfriend.

But about twenty minutes into the game, Michael decided we should all switch seats. "I want to talk to Greta," he said, and he moved us all. He went to sit by my sister, and he put me on the other side of Matt, away from both of them.

And the next thing I knew, the game was over. Matt and I had talked about books, about his undergraduate time at Berkeley, where my brother had gone for graduate school. We talked about the navy, because Matt had been in the navy, I had a friend in the navy, my only Republican friend. And he told me about how, when he was little, his dog ran away and he took it personally.

When he talked it was like a set of double doors swinging open into a bright room. He told me that he wished he were in grad school for philosophy, like my brother, but that he didn't think he'd make it. He told me graduate school in English was kind of an experiment for him, a compromise. Since I always felt like an experiment, like my whole life was one, big, chance combination, it was like walking across a room to greet an old friend and getting a shock from the carpeting. It was both strangely exhilarating and familiar. Michael wouldn't admit to ever questioning himself; it would take me years to figure out that he did, almost constantly, and by that time, it would be too late.

We all went out for tacos and beer after the game, and once we all got seated and began smothering our food with salsa and sour cream, Matt asked Michael what he was going to do for the summer.

"I'm going to Oregon," Michael said. "I'm spending most of the summer with my family in Manzanita."

"Did it ever occur to you, Shannon," Matt said, "that Michael might not come back from Oregon. You know, *he might not come back*. What would you do then?" I just sat there, holding a taco, thinking, "If Michael didn't come back I would have sex with you, Matt," except of course I couldn't say that and I shouldn't even be thinking it, and I wondered how he could be such a bad friend and even ask such a thing, right in front of his friend, *what bad manners!*, which eclipsed me having to think about what kind of girlfriend I was, sitting there wanting to have sex with my boyfriend's friend. I had already told Michael, before meeting Matt, that I was falling in love with him. With

Michael. Michael had gotten rid of his old down comforter, after all, so that my asthma wouldn't act up. He'd bought a hypoallergenic blanket so that I wouldn't have trouble breathing.

On the way home, when Michael and I were in the car alone, he said, "What was that all about, Shannon? What was going on tonight? You were flirting with my friend, right in front of me."

"You're the one who put us together," I said. "And I wasn't flirting. I think he was flirting with me, which is so inappropriate. I can't believe he said that thing about you staying in Manzanita."

"We're a couple now, Shannon." Michael said. "You just don't do things like that."

"You're the one who wanted us all to switch seats."

"I wanted to get to know your sister better."

"Well, you could have asked to switch seats again," I said.

"I looked over at you a couple of times so you'd know that I was ready to go back to our seats, but you weren't even looking at me. You never even looked over at me. We're a couple," Michael said. "We're supposed to take care of each other. In a room of people, we're supposed to take care of each other. To be tuned in to each other."

"Well, I don't read minds," I said, "I had no idea."

"I'm so angry with you," Michael said. "I would never do that to you."

"I didn't do anything," I said. "All I did was something I didn't even know I'd done, which was not to be able to read your mind."

"I sent you signals," Michael said. "Maybe this was all a mistake. Maybe you should stay somewhere else tonight. Maybe you should go stay with your parents."

But I was already attached to Michael. I had told myself, on our first date, that Michael was the one. Some bells had gone off. He had said the magic words, something about supporting his family someday, and he had the same name as my imaginary friend. We were meant to be together. Michael seemed to know what he wanted and maybe it was me who'd been misguided. I was the one having trouble being an adult. What a lovely impulse, to want to get to know my sister better! And I had spent the entire game talking to Matt and had forgotten all about both Michael and my sister.

"I want to be with you," I said as we were driving down Cleveland Avenue on our way to Summit, and I began to cry.

"I don't know, Shanny," he said. "Do you?"

That night, Michael slept facing the wall and wouldn't talk to me. I lay facing the small space that we had shared for the last month. I'd been there almost every night since we'd met, in this old, cramped apartment where the fridge was in a big closet outside the bathroom. Michael felt like a storm shelter to me, thick, heavy walls. There was comfort in that.

I lay on the futon with the covers thrown off my body and looked at the space we shared, moonlight falling across the kitchen table, the table he would give me almost four years later, when he was leaving Minnesota for good.

Part Four \ A Marriage

Miss Right

As I type I am sitting amid and on top of a pile of papers, some of them bills I haven't paid because I have no money. Some of them papers and handouts from classes I took last year. Many of them clips from articles my mother has sent me. Let's look at some of them now:

"Hang on to that property tax or rent bill: Rebates coming your way."

"Secrets to staying together: *ABC News*'s John Stossel tells what he learned about making marriage last while researching a special to air this week." I wonder if he only had to make his marriage work during the week that he researched the special, or if this is just a syntactical accident.

The next article: "Guidelines: Looking for 'Miss Right.'"

"But I'm not looking for Miss Right," I had said to my mother when she gave me the article, along with the faded yellow towel.

"Miss . . . Mister," said my mother. "I'm sure it's the same both ways. I just thought it would be helpful."

I am supposed to look for Miss Right in a supermarket or church. If she tells me she is married or that her husband doesn't understand her, I should *run*. If she expects me to pay for her mother's operation, I should be careful. Is her apartment clean and orderly? If not, I should *not* expect that to change. I should pay attention to how she treats others. If she is hung up on her father and *he* isn't very fond of me, that could be trouble. Is she trustworthy? Don't marry her just because she looks good on my arm. A woman is more than a pretty bracelet or watch. If you feel you need a woman to complete your life, choose her, don't let her choose you. Be selective. Does she expect her daddy to bail her out every time something goes wrong? If so, it means she needs to grow up.

When my car breaks down, I call my mom and dad. I have maxed out all my credit cards, their level of debt now exceeding my annual income, which is not that hard to do, since as a graduate student I make $8,000 a year, but still, there you are. On my credit cards I have put dinners and groceries, books, gas, cheap clothes from Target and Marshalls, and expensive boots from Dayton's, which I justified because they were on sale. Mascara, lipstick, nail polish. An eighty-dollar shirt for which I had no justification, except that it is brown, and *brown* is this year's *black*, and all my other shirts are from Target and Marshalls, so I had been *good* and deserved a more expensive shirt, even though I had charged the cheap shirts, too. Birthday cards and cleaning supplies. Presents for my friends, family and for Michael. I had finally stopped writing checks for anything that didn't require immediate payment and had just begun to charge *everything*.

I call my mom, who says that they will help me, but that it will only be a loan, and that she wants this to *hurt*. She wants me to understand the kind of mess I've gotten myself into.

"It's not my fault my car broke down," I tell Flo.

"No," she says, "but these are the things that happen in life.

And you need to learn to plan for them. I want you to realize that being in a position like this leaves you fewer options."

Then she tells me about the new microwave she just picked up for our neighbor Millie. And how, when she was sitting at Millie's kitchen table the other day, the tiny woman with a glass eye said to my mother, "You know, I have never seen you get mad about anything. You never raise your voice or get angry."

My mother had nodded and smiled, knowing how many years Millie had lived under the critical, angry eyes of her sister and husband.

"On the other hand," Millie had continued. "I don't ever see you get real excited about anything, either."

I have never enjoyed the unpredictable. Or rather, I have never been able to plan for and imagine the future. Here is how, for example, I chose a college: I always assumed I would go to college, and took the necessary tests when the time came to take them. I had long since stopped working to *my potential,* whatever that meant for girls and women, even in the seventies and eighties. Even today, for that matter. I knew that going out of state was out of the question, mainly because my mother was afraid that all of us kids would die if we went too far from home, and I believed her.

My brother was at Carleton College, in Northfield, Minnesota. I really liked Northfield, but my brother was a *genius;* he had begun listening to classical music in junior high school. He read Isaac Asimov during church while my sister and I played hangman on the weekly bulletin. He spent hours playing chess and Risk with his nerdy friends who wore thick glasses. I had all the episodes of *Love Boat* memorized. I enjoyed Barry Manilow and feeding peanut butter to the dog.

I wound up at the Lutheran school in Northfield, even though we were Catholic; it was across the river from Carleton, across the river from my brother. I would go visit him sometimes, to eat lunch in their cafeteria, which was better than ours. They had a good salad bar, while our cafeteria served big blocks of white fish and sandwiches labeled "Roast Beef *Au Jus* with Juice." They wouldn't sell cigarettes on campus, or condoms, and so my greatest excitement in my four years at Saint Olaf was getting hopped up on weak coffee and donuts. Still, it was the principle of the thing, having so few vices available. The campus bookstore would not sell magazines, but they had all kinds of Norwegian sweaters and plenty of cups that said "UFF DAH!" I never realized that being Norwegian was a kind of religion in and of itself. I had grown up mostly with Catholics who felt varying degrees of shame and guilt about their very existence. Now I was in school with people who could use the word *Fellowship* without giggling; who said things like, "My God is a Kind and Understanding God." I waited for irony. I waited for a snicker or some flicker of amusement, but there was nothing underneath those blanket statements. Underneath all those thick, decorative Norwegian sweaters there were just, well, matching turtlenecks.

I went across the river to visit my brother fairly often. Things seemed more vital there. He lived in a co-ed dorm where the girls and boys actually shared the same bathroom. My brother had a roommate named Leo, who was from Texas and whose mother was Mexican. I had never met anyone who was from Texas and whose mother was Mexican. Leo played the guitar and drank Kool-Aid for breakfast. He came home from a party early one morning wrapped in a bedsheet and dragging his guitar and a bottle of wine. My brother told me this. That Leo had walked across campus in nothing but the bedsheet.

I wished I had gone to Carleton. I wished I could wander around in a bedsheet. But I figured I was not *intense* enough, not smart enough. And besides, none of my brother's female friends shaved their legs or armpits, and that frightened me. Also, they ate vegetarian chili and I figured that was a prerequisite for entrance to the college. I did not want to eat vegetarian chili. Where was the protein? At home, we had always had meat at dinner.

At the end of my freshman year at Saint Olaf, my brother graduated from Carleton College, one of eight students in his graduating class with a 4.0 or better grade point average. He hadn't told anyone in the family that he was doing so well. Whenever my mom asked him about his progress in school, he would say, "I'm learning a lot."

Maybe this is a strategy I should adopt. When my mom asks me how my thesis is going, I could answer, "I'm learning a lot," without extrapolating. I'm learning a lot about what it means to be addicted to television. I'm learning a lot about what it means to run your credit cards up to unmanageable levels. There is an interesting dust bunny behind the door in the bathroom. I am learning that these things don't go away by themselves, that dust bunnies need some encouragement. There is a pile of paper around my desk that almost goes up to my knees. It's like wading through a swamp to get to my computer; I lift my legs high, step over things, try not to get stuck in the muck. I am learning about the nature of stasis, how piles do not change until tripped over or physically shoved aside. I am learning the laws of physics through practical experiments. How a body that is not in motion seems to have trouble leaving her apartment. I am learning a lot.

I hated Saint Olaf, but once it became familiar I didn't know how to leave.

When I graduated after four years from "Uff Dah U," as I'd begun to refer to it, my brother giggled. He sat in the bleachers, counting the Andersens, Andersons, Hansens and Hansons. There were four Eric Johnsons graduating in my class. Johnson, Johnson, Johnson, Johnson. Son of John. Larsen, Larsen, Larson, Larson. Son of Lars. Olsen, Olsen, Olson, Olson. Son of Ole. I was one of many people whose name identified them as their father's child.

Of course, I knew that this didn't really begin to explain anything, that, being so many generations removed from the motherland, the name had long since lost its meaning. My father was Myron and Margaret's son, was Swedish and Irish, raised Catholic. My mother was Bill and Helen's daughter, Norwegian and German, raised Lutheran; her great-aunts had broad, soil-tilling shoulders. I was the child of two people—though, from what I could tell, my brother, sister, and I were the result of three miraculous virgin births.

But I had blond hair, like everyone else. And I crossed the stage, like everyone else. Like everyone else, I smiled and shook the president's hand, took my diploma, was thankful that I hadn't tripped. And like everyone else, I wore a black gown that made me look like an eager bat, ready to go flapping around in the dark. Though I would have preferred to remain hanging upside down in my cave.

Labels

The problem with trying to make sense of life is this problem of getting it wrong the first time, of hearing the story differently the second time and wondering how much of the first story you've become. How much of what you heard the first time shaped you in a way that is now wrong? And now, being in that wrong shape, are you in any condition to correct things? to fit things into the right place? Or, will you be making those corrections based on another faulty set of assumptions, a permutation of memory? You could be calling it a bunch of bananas, having forgotten long ago that bananas do *not* grow on vines as a cluster of small purple fruits. "I'm bananas!" you could say, when it's clear that you are not. That you mean grapes. And this could go on and on, until your identity is this sort of horrible, disfigured pretzel, hurtling through time and space—which makes it sound like your identity is this very self-contained thing, twisting in on itself, which it isn't. It has arms, too. It has ways of reaching out, affecting the way someone else is putting things together. When it comes right down to it, we are all just a bunch of self-interested contortionists, twisting around ourselves and sticking our toes in someone else's eye by accident, kneeing someone else in the back.

Meanwhile, I can't find my car keys.

"Well, your father can never find the things he's in charge of," says my mother, when she calls and I explain that I've spent the morning rooting around my new apartment without success. A studio apartment, I should have found them by now.

"What kinds of things is Dad in charge of?" I ask.

"Well," says my mother, "his billfold. His keys. Those things. Which he can never find."

Edward Olson was a straight-A student, an athlete, and also he chewed on the collar of his shirts, which is something his older brother did, too. Later, Flo would develop theories about this—or maybe it was I who developed these theories, based on other stories my mother had told me. Anyway, the theory was that my father and his brother chewed on their collars because they did not get enough affection from their mother. That they sat in class and gnawed nervously on their collars in the same way that a baby monkey with no mother will curl up nervously to an artificial mother, the wire frame of a mother wrapped in a blanket. The monkey will choose the blanket-wrapped mother before the wire mother with a bottle attached to her. Will choose warmth over food.

"Maybe they had fleas," I said to Flo when she told me the collar-chewing story, picturing an agitated dog.

"Maybe," says Flo. "Our grammar teacher used to say, 'Ole, quit bothering the girls.'"

"See?" I say, "he *was* a dog."

"It was really the girls who were bothering him," says Flo.

"It would be hard to chew on your collar and bother girls at the same time."

"Mhmm," says Flo.

My mother saw my father in ninth grade and knew he would be her husband. "That's who I'm going to marry," she said to herself, sitting in the back of Yvonne Andersen's grammar classroom. From time to time my mother will tell me how she struggled with grammar, how it never came easily for her, though she has never connected, in her storytelling, the presence of my father in the classroom and her wrestling match with the requirements of the English language.

My mother and father would date during high school, would go to their junior and senior proms together, though my father did not ask her to the senior prom until very late. "I cried and cried," she says. "Everyone in school knew I wanted to go with your father and he didn't ask me. Finally, he said that he hadn't wanted to keep me all to himself. That he thought, since he'd taken me the previous year, that he should let someone else take me."

"But I want to go with you," Flo wailed.

And so they did.

In college they dated off and on. My mother was a Home Economics major at the university, and my father attended a private Catholic school in Saint Paul. They both paid their own way, being the first generation in both of their families to go to college. My father was busy with his premed courses, and though my mother wished he wanted to spend more time with her, she kept herself busy with other dates.

After college, my mother moved to California to teach Home Economics. She lived on the beach and spent her evenings sitting out on the balcony of her apartment in San Diego with her roommates and the navy guys who lived upstairs. Sometimes they'd wander up the beach to hear some live jazz.

One day, my father showed up at her doorstep. He'd decided to do his medical residency in San Diego and wanted to know if he could sleep on the couch for a night. I don't know why, but I have always imagined that the floor of my mother's apartment there was covered with sand. That as my father entered her apartment that night, dumped his duffel bag down and surveyed the couch where he would only sleep for one night because my mother's roommate was an Orthodox Jew and didn't approve of the arrangement, that their feet had been covered in sand. That in crossing the room, their feet had created a light sandpaper scraping, a kind of friction that comes from bringing nature into artificial surroundings. The soft grinding of flesh and sand and floor.

They dated off and on in San Diego—my father being busy with his residency, my mother dating one of the navy guys who lived upstairs for a while. My mother taught girls how to sew, taught them about texture and quality and cutting on the bias. Once one of her students came up to her with the sewing needle from her machine jammed into the tip of her finger; it had stuck there and snapped off. "Miss Tillman," the student said, "now what do I do?"

My father was attending to the chaos in San Diego General's emergency room. Once, a man with a terrible migraine came in with a knife stuck into his temple. "My head hurt so much," said the man, "I just thought this would relieve things a little." Though it seems impossible, he had been lucky enough to jam the knife into a negligible part of the skull, and he retained all his functions. "I think he was schizophrenic, too," remembers my father. "I don't think he'd been taking his medication. Anyway, the trick was," says my father, "to pull the knife out without causing more damage."

My parents dated off and on in San Diego until my father was drafted into a M.A.S.H. unit in the Korean War.

They wrote overseas letters then, and often my mother was angry with him for supposing that if they got married the children would necessarily be raised Catholic.

"It wasn't that I *minded* if you kids were raised Catholic," says Flo. "Because I was never very fond of being Lutheran. It was that he *supposed* that you would be. He never thought to ask me if that was okay. Of course, I wrote him back and let him know how angry I was. I said, 'It's over.' I was so upset. I cried and cried."

From Korea my father brought my mother some lovely teak salad bowls, which she still has.

And we were raised Catholic.

Food Shortages

This morning I am curled up in bed between two blankets, having torn the sheets off a few weeks ago for washing and not having washed them, awake with a small audience of people who are interested in the Ronco Electric Food Dehydrator.

The man who demonstrates the necessity of the food dehydrator speaks with enthusiasm about his product, but he never really looks at the camera, which follows him around the studio, from the beef jerky area, to the area where they've dehydrated flowers for use in craft projects, to the area where a young girl is preparing fruit roll-ups for dehydration, and never, ever do I feel I've got a good look at him. There is what you see on the outside: a tan, well-built man with better-than-average but somehow indescribable features. Sandy blond hair. Some eyes. A starched shirt. A clean white apron. "I know you can afford this," he says to the camera, to the studio audience. "Please call the toll-free number that you see on the screen below."

"The rule of thumb around our house," says a member of the studio audience, "is, if it's moist and you slice it, you can dehydrate it."

Before I've had a chance to fully consider how dangerous that could be, the demonstrator says, "For folks who have a hard time chewing, you will bless this machine." He runs some corn-on-the-cob across the front of the corollary product, the Dial-O-Matic food slicer, and small bits of corn fall in loose, limp rows onto the countertop. "Squash is so easy," he says, "and onions," he says, "the only tears you'll cry will be tears of joy." He really says this. But I must admit that the idea of making my own dried fruit is sounding better and better.

Now we are making our own raisins. At the bottom of the

screen, in flashing yellow letters, it says, FRESH, JUICY GRAPES; FRESH JUICY GRAPES, and we see fresh juicy grapes, and then their condition one day later when they are SUCCULENT RAISINS AFTER ONE DAY, and then TWO-DAY TASTY RAISINS, TWO-DAY TASTY RAISINS. Things move quickly on television, time is bent. "Why don't you call?" says the spokesman. "Why don't you call right now?"

Next, the tanned man starts talking about natural disasters. Just think, he says, about tornadoes, earthquakes, floods, hurricanes. At the bottom of the screen flashes, TORNADOES, EARTHQUAKES, FLOODS, HURRICANES. "Natural disasters," says the man, "can close grocery stores. You know that happens," and the audience kind of gasps, seeming to remember the jeopardy they've felt at various times when food has not been available to them, the deprivation, the panic of having an empty cupboard, NATURAL DISASTERS, NATURAL DISASTERS, and I think, but it's electric, it wouldn't work in a *natural disaster,* and plus, who would wait two days for raisins? and in a flood, wouldn't much of the food rehydrate?

Another studio audience member says, "I recommend it to anybody who wants to save money and just enjoy themselves."

I think about the fun you could have in a flood with your Ronco Electric Food Dehydrator. Why not just play with it in the bathtub? Why wait for something natural, a natural disaster? Why not just make one?

The Weight of Each Day

It's been five months since we broke up, and I am still missing Michael. We have bumped into each other a few times at school and it's always awkward.

"It's gray outside," I say when Flo answers the phone.

"Yah," she says, in her Minnesota patois, a kind of noncommittal affirmation, strong agreement with no commitment, no harsh consonants.

"It's a good day to stay in bed and read," I say, even though I've been watching television, not reading.

"Yah," she says, "I agree. Elaine and I were going to go walking and just as I was ready to go, the phone rings and it's Elaine and she says 'Let's wait awhile and see if it gets any warmer.'"

Flo is sitting around drinking coffee, too, reading the paper, watching the farmer in the fields behind the house. "Oh, there goes a load of manure!" she exclaims. In the fall, after harvest, the farmer dumps manure all over the fields, keeps dumping it all winter, and then, when it thaws in spring, the whole neighborhood smells.

I tell her how I have a new schedule, how my counselor and I have developed a new schedule for me where I get up and do my schoolwork in the morning, and then go to work at the department in the afternoon.

"And when do you work out?" asks my mother, who once commented that I had a way of involving the world in my own minutiae. I explain that I work out at night now.

"Isn't that interesting?" she says. "How you're just figuring all of this out, like a little kid. What it takes to get through a day."

"Real interesting, thanks, Mom."

"No, I mean really," she says, "how you need help doing this, this kind of remedial organizational help. You're just like your father."

I ask her to tell me again the story of how my father always forgot to cash his paychecks when they were first married, how he neglected to pay the bills, which he couldn't have, anyway, since he had three months of paychecks sitting on his desk, littered among medical journals, charts and prescription pads. How my mother got to Dayton's, up to the counter to pay for our little saddle shoes, and how the card was rejected because my father hadn't paid the bill.

"It was embarrassing," says my mother. "Humiliating. I felt powerless, not to mention inconvenienced. Oh, here it comes back again," she says, "it's all empty."

I believe, briefly that she is referring to her life, to her history with my father, but I can hear the farm machinery, faintly, in the background through her open window. I realize she is talking about manure.

"Oh, Flo, you're just full of shit today."

"The thing that has always bothered me with your father," says Flo, since we are, again, talking about organization, "is that every change, every significant change in our relationship, has always been initiated by me. Everything has always had to hit the bottom of the barrel and then I'm the one that does something about it."

It occurs to me that when a system is working for the person in power, he will see no real need to change it.

"The final straw," says Flo, "was when I went to the grocery store. I had about seventy dollars' worth of groceries and I got to the register, and I realized that your father had the damn checkbook. He always forgot to give me the damn checkbook after he wrote his check in church on Sundays. I had to ask them to spot me for the groceries, and then I'd go back and pay for them. That happened a few times and then I thought, this is humiliating. I had to say things like, 'Well, you know the doctor, too busy saving lives to remember the checkbook. Too busy saving lives to pay the bills.' The phone company kept calling and threatening to shut off the phone, and I'd say, 'Too busy saving lives to pay the bills,' which is such bullshit. That's why we have so many unnecessary jobs in the world; that's why everything is so expensive; because people like your father don't pay their bills and then they have to hire someone to call you and remind you. It's an inconvenience to everyone."

"Well, they couldn't have cut off your phone," I say, "because then they couldn't have called to remind you about the bill."

"I suppose not," says Flo.

The thought that my father's negligence might in some way be responsible for the fiscal disorder of the world is more than I can imagine at the moment—the lines of complication too sticky—but I know that in some ways this is true. Cause and effect is like this; we affect each other in small ways, small ways that spiral out into the world, creating waves of jobs and unnecessary paperwork and a kind of ill will that keeps us all occupied and looking for relief, a kind of mental leisure that never comes, that perfect state of relaxation and total lack of responsibility, a kind of lawn-chair state of being that is, it seems, unachievable. Still, it is a place I'd like to be.

"I felt abused, not respected," says my mother, "not an equal partner."

I want to know these things, and I also don't.

"Your father insisted on writing the checks," she says, "because *his* father always wrote the checks. I always had to wait for the complete failure of a system before I felt like I could change anything. The respectful thing to do," concludes my mother, "if, in a partnership, one partner cannot meet all of his responsibilities, is to ask for help."

"I think Dad has a hard time asking for help." I know this, I say, because I am the same way. It's a weird perfectionist thing, I tell her. The feeling that you should do everything and do it well.

"I've just learned to accept limitations," says my mother, "not to expect perfection."

But this is absolutely what I cannot do. Not now, not yet. Even though I couldn't really say what I *am* expecting.

"Your father," says Flo, "always felt that tomorrow would be better. Tomorrow would be a better day. That everything he couldn't be and do today would magically happen tomorrow. The thing he has never understood," she says, "is that you have to make those changes, you have to take steps to change things, or the next day will be the same," she says, "with all the weight of the day before on top of it."

Thanksgiving

Flo and I have isolated ourselves in my aunt Mary's breakfast nook. We sit on the same side of the bench, sipping wine, alternately facing each other and the floral-papered wall in front of us.

"It's kind of strange," she says. "Not to have Michael here."

I tell Flo that I know it's hard for her, that I know she really liked Michael, that I miss him, too, and that I'm sorry it didn't work out, but that it's the right thing right now.

"Well, do you ever talk to each other?" she wants to know. And when I tell her that we talk occasionally, she seems relieved. "Maybe you'll get to the point where you can at least meet for coffee," she says.

When I ask her if she could please take the picture she has

of Michael and me *off* of the refrigerator, she looks at me suspiciously, as if I've been spying on her. "Well, have you been home?" she says. "How do you know it's still up?" she says, putting a hand to her heart, as if she were experiencing chest pains.

"I was home last week to have dinner with Dad," I say. "When you were in California."

"Oh, well, okay," she concedes. "I'll take it down. If that's what you want. I just hadn't really gotten around to it. I hadn't really thought about it," she paused. "You're not rubbing him out of your life completely, are you?" she says, as if we are members of the Swedish Mafia.

"I'm not rubbing him out," I tell her.

"Well, you know," Flo finally concedes, maybe only because she's had a few glasses of chardonnay, "I could see you and Michael having the same relationship as your father and me."

The wine I've just sipped stings my throat, mixes badly with the chocolate-covered pretzels.

"Not that that's all bad or anything," my mother continues. "Not necessarily. I mean, I married your father for certain reasons. And, you know, whatever they were, having to do with the type of person he is. And Michael is a good person, too. He has integrity, good *values*," she says, which I think makes him sound like Kmart. "But it's a matter of what you're willing to put up with, what you want your life to be like."

The thing is, I have no idea what I want from life, but I know that right now, I don't want my mother's. What frightens me is that it seems I've been moving toward it unintentionally all along.

My mother looks at me with tears welling up in her eyes.

"I don't mean to criticize your father," she says. "In fact, I hope this doesn't sound like criticism. I just want you to have an accurate picture of things, of relationships, of marriage. No one ever told me *anything*. That's why I have always tried to be pretty open with you kids, to answer your questions and to be available. Now, I can't do anything to change your father, but I feel like I should tell you these things so that you don't wind up marrying someone just like him, just because you have unfinished issues. I don't want you not to be able to work through things, just because your father is never around."

She also tells me that after thirty-three years of marriage, and having known each other since ninth grade, she feels she knows almost nothing about my father. About what he really thinks. What he really feels.

"It's not like Grandma Olson would bring out the sensitive side in anyone," I say, "plus, it's the wrong generation. Dad's generation of men didn't grow up watching *Oprah*."

"You're probably right," she says.

"You know what, Mom?"

"Huh?"

"If you were married to some touchy-feely guy who was always trying to share his *feelings* and his *reactions* to things, I bet you'd want to swat him like a big fly. If some guy was always following you around saying things like, 'Chrysanthemums remind me of a song by James Taylor,' I know I would."

"Maybe," says Flo, "but I would have liked more intimacy."

"Your life isn't over," I say. "Your marriage isn't over."

"I've given up," says Flo, taking a big swig of chardonnay.

Where You Left Them

The following Saturday, my father, Flo, my sister, her boyfriend, and I drive to Willmar to see my grandmother, my dad's mom, who's had a minor stroke and has been moved from her assisted-living apartment to a nursing home.

My sister, Greta, and I tickle each other in the backseat, burp and sing the theme song from *Love Boat,* like we did when we were little. Her boyfriend, Cliff, sits hunched in the corner, trying to have a conversation with my father about different options for backing up computer systems. My father knows nothing about computers, but he is trying to learn. My mother picks at her teeth with a toothpick, the way her mother always used to, and my sister makes some kind of joke about her system being backed up and when can we stop for the bathroom? This sends the two of us into a fit of hysterics, though I am twenty-nine and she is twenty-seven.

"You girls have never outgrown that potty stage of humor," says my father.

We try to distract him while he is driving by taking the price tag off of a candy bar and sticking it to his ear, curling it around the curve like an ear cuff. We tell him we are marking him so that we can track his winter migration through the wilderness. We tell him he is lucky we haven't had to tranquilize him with our dart gun. We scratch his bald spot and giggle.

"Hey, cut that out!" says my father. "Can't you leave a poor old critter alone?"

"It's called love," says my mother, giving him a reproachful look. "They're pestering you out of love. Do you know what that is?"

My father does not respond and keeps looking at the road ahead.

"Your head's soft like a baby's bottom," says my sister, imitating Benny Hill.

"You know how to get to a guy where he's most vulnerable," says my father, also using an English accent, for no apparent reason except that it's perhaps easier to say what's most true when you can pretend you're someone else.

I sit behind my father, combing his hair back over his bald spot with my fingers, wondering exactly what the difference is between pestering someone out of love and loving to pester someone. And maybe there is no difference. "Your hairs are all back in place," I tell my father. "Right where you left them."

"You taught Michael to fall out of love with you," the counselor said to me once. "Michael left because you kept telling him to. You kept telling him you weren't sure; maybe he wasn't the right one; maybe it wasn't the right time. Wouldn't you leave, too, if you kept getting those messages?"

But my first boyfriend didn't, I said, he just clung that much harder.

"They aren't the same person," said the counselor. "And you're not the same person now that you were when you were with either of them."

Good, I say, that's my favorite part of the story. Tell me again how I've changed.

"Why don't you tell me?" says the counselor. "Why don't you tell me what's different?"

When my sister finished her B.A. at Madison, Wisconsin, her boyfriend Cliff was one year behind her. She stayed and worked as a waitress the extra year while he finished up, and they rented an apartment together on the outskirts of town, a prefab building that seemed like it would blow over in a storm.

My sister called me one night when they were living there and asked me what I thought about Cliff. *Did I like him?* Some of her other boyfriends had been more wild, she said, but they, in the end, got to be too much. But still, *was he going to be enough?* Living there was hard, she said, and most of their friends had graduated and moved. The walls were thin, she said, and they could hear the neighbors fighting. *Did I like him?* She wanted to know. *What did I think?*

I remembered my ex-boyfriend before Michael, how we had fought in the middle of the night, how I was sure we had woken my neighbors. Who was I to give advice?

When we get to the nursing home, it's clear that my grandmother is trying to starve herself to death. On Tuesday she will be eighty-seven, and she weighs less than her age. She is tiny in the mauve easy chair that the nursing home staff has brought from her apartment.

My mother is already talking about my grandmother's funeral. My grandmother wants us to give her dresses to Goodwill because she doesn't wear them anymore, but later, after we leave my grandmother, as we ride the elevator down to the lobby, my mother will remind all of us that we should save them so that "Margaret has something to wear for her funeral." I can't decide whether this is practical or callous.

My grandmother ate the brownie that the nurse brought

her, but I think it was mostly for dramatic effect. She thinks that if she shows us that she's eating, we'll bring her back to her apartment.

"Can we get you anything else before we go, Mom?" my father said.

"You can take me back to my apartment," my grandma had said, still holding part of the brownie.

"You have to eat more and get stronger before you can go back," said my father.

"I think I ate better there," said my grandmother, though she knows this is not true. She has taken to lying lately—about most anything—and then admitting later that she was lying, which causes us to wonder if she is lying about lying. She had been telling us for months, for instance, that she was still meeting with her bridge group, until her friend Dora told us that she hadn't been. "Oh yeah," said my grandmother when she got caught. "I was lying about that."

In the elevator I ask my sister if she thinks the double lie evens things out, like in math, where two negatives equal a positive. "Maybe the lies make her happier," I say.

"I don't know," says my sister. "I sucked at math."

When my sister was still living with Cliff in Madison, she called me and told me that she was sleeping on the couch. She wasn't talking to him. She was tired of washing all the dishes and doing all the cooking and laundry. She didn't want to be there anymore.

She slept on the couch for a month while Cliff said, "Are you ever going to stop being mad at me?"

She did only her laundry while Cliff said, "Are you ever going to talk to me again?"

She did only her dishes and cooked only for herself until Cliff finally said, "Oh."

He came home one night with a dozen roses and did all the laundry, cleaned the apartment, and made them spaghetti. He kept cleaning and doing the laundry and bringing flowers, and after a couple of weeks, my sister went back into the bedroom and curled up next to him again.

She went to El Paso the following year to teach elementary school, while Cliff did an internship in Madison, and when she came back from Texas, they moved to Minnesota together.

When I talked to her on the phone a few weeks ago, I asked her how things were going, were they going to stay together? Were they glad they were back here? Did she ever think about getting married?

"I told Clifford that I'm ready," she said, "I'm just waiting for him to ask."

Plant Killer

Evelynn no longer lives next door but believes she still owns the house, which she doesn't. Peggy lives there now, a divorced woman in her fifties who is a Lutheran pastor. Peggy has a riding mower, which she drives with one hand, holding a Lite beer in the other. Sometimes Peggy gets going a little too fast on her riding mower, and you'll see her on the peripheries of the lawn, turning a tight corner, the mower up on two wheels, balancing the Lite beer in the air above her head.

When I ask my mom where, exactly, Evelynn is now, she's not sure. "She's in a home," says my mom. "Some kind of state-

or federally funded nursing-home-type thing. You know, for alcoholics, probably. I *think*."

What is clear is that Evelynn would like to be back in her house, and calls my mother occasionally to tell her so. She called on Christmas Eve one year, just as my mother was pulling the broiled oysters out of the oven. "I have a house in Chaska, you know," Evelynn told my mother. "I want you to come and get me. I want to come home."

"She also thinks," my mother says to me, now, on the phone, "that she has an original Norman Rockwell paintings in storage in Eden Prairie somewhere."

"Well, that's kind of ironic," I say. "Do people in Norman Rockwell paintings smash Mason jars in the garage?"

"She's very confused," says Flo. "She doesn't remember signing off on the papers to sell her house. She doesn't remember selling and signing."

"Soiling, selling, and signing," I say.

"That's the truth," says Flo. "That's a nice use of alliteration," she adds.

I'm not sure that my mom ever told Pastor Peggy what the house had been like before she moved in, the kind of bacteria that had been growing there, the smell of urine that wafted to the door each time my mother came over to clean or make sure that Evelynn wasn't dead. Evelynn would pass out for days, and then wake up and begin again the same furious activity that had previously knocked her out, drinking and clanging around the house, and then pass out again for a while. And so on.

Peggy, on her small pastor's budget, has done a lot of redecorating. Painting her own walls, refinishing furniture that she finds at Goodwill and painting her own designs on the floor, designs that *look* like rugs, and don't slip when you walk on them, but also offer none of the padding and comfort of a real rug, though I suppose she also saves on vacuuming time. "Peggy is very creative with limited resources," my mother has said on a number of occasions. "I remember those days, in college and when I was first working," she tells me. "It can be exhilarating to rely on your own resources."

But it's really hard to do that in America, I say to the counselor. I mean, everything is so *convenient.* McDonald's, for instance. Automatic car washes. You can have almost anything done *for* you.

It doesn't help you grow as a person, says the counselor.

I look down at my thighs, which have begun to spread a little from too many Big Macs.

That's true, I say. But you have a whole country founded on this principle. This principle of convenience. *I'm a victim!* Just for today, I say, could we blame some of my troubles on America? *America, with your high-calorie promises of convenience,* I say. With each new product and service comes new paperwork. *We are drowning in a greasy vat of efficiency.*

Just for today, says the counselor. If it would make you happy, you can blame some of it on America.

I'm an American, I say. I deserve to be happy.

When you're really in your own life, doing your work, says the counselor, you'll be happy.

Is that what everyone else is doing?

Pretty much, says the counselor.

But a lot of people eat at fast-food places, I say. Billions have been served. If no one's eating home-cooked meals, how come I have to? I mean, metaphorically.

Because you'd eat *every* meal that way, metaphorically, says the counselor. You don't know where to set limits.

Birdsitting

I run into Michael at a Christmas party thrown by one of our mutual friends. Because I had been invited, I assumed he wasn't.

"No one else cares about that except you," the counselor will say later. "Of course she invited both of you. You're the one keeping all the drama alive."

It's a small party, only a few blocks from my apartment, and Michael is there with a tall, thin brunette who is laughing at his jokes and gently rubbing her hand over her neck and across her collarbone. She has the kind of skinny legs I've always wanted. Legs like a baby deer. And when I go up to the drink table to make myself a gin and tonic, I think about tripping her, which seems like it might be easy.

At that moment, she heads off for the bathroom, and Michael walks over to me.

"Hi, Shanny," he says. We haven't spoken in six months. "How are you?"

"I'm fine," I say. "Actually. How are you?"

"Good," he says. He has new glasses, a lighter frame.

"Actually," I say, "I was just taking an olive for the road. I have to go." I grab a green olive and head out the door, running all the way back to my apartment. Arriving with my olive, sobbing, I call my brother in California and cry and bitch for about an hour on the phone. "He's always dating someone," I say. "He's always got some new somebody."

My brother is like my dad. He just listens and says things like, "Yep, love's the pits."

In college, when my brother was going through a breakup,

he would eat frozen burritos and listen to Bob Dylan. Now that he is married, he has complete meals most every night.

"You'll be okay," my brother says. "You'll find somebody."

The minute my brother and I hang up, the phone rings. I figure that it's my brother again and that maybe he forgot to tell me something, maybe he forgot to recommend his favorite brand of frozen burrito, but it's Michael.

"Shanny," he says, "that was a blind date. I didn't know that you'd be there. They set me up with her, and so I figured you weren't going to be there. I'm sorry."

"I miss you," I say.

"I miss you, too," he says.

"It was weird to see you with her," I say.

"It was weird to be with her. I would rather have been talking to you," he says.

"Do you want to come over?" I say, blowing my nose into the phone.

"I don't know if that's such a good idea," he says.

"Oh," I say. "Okay."

"Okay," he says. "I'll be right there."

When Michael and I had broken up, Flo had come over to my new apartment with some helium balloons.

"This is a chance to celebrate a new start for you," she said. "Take all of your worries, and all of your sadness, and put them in these balloons."

"Have you been watching *Oprah*?" I had said. "Have you been drinking?"

"And then," she said, "let them go."

We stood in the alley behind my apartment building. I had

taken us around to the back of the building, because releasing my anxieties into the air wasn't the kind of thing I wanted to do on one of Saint Paul's busiest streets. I looked at the balloons, their bright, transparent colors. I could see Flo's face through the bunch. I wondered what would happen to me next, *Would I ever meet someone?*, *Maybe I was meant to be alone,* and then I let them go, watched them float high in the air, up and over my apartment building, heading northeast.

Going exactly in the direction of Michael's new apartment.

So, Michael and I are going out again, tentatively, the way old people move, trying to control their shaking on even short trips to the dining hall. We spend more time apart than we used to, more time alone at night in our respective apartments, just a few miles from one another. On those nights, we talk on the phone before we go to bed.

And my sister gets engaged. She comes home from work one night, and her boyfriend is making salad, baked haddock, and baked potatoes. He lights a candle and sets the table. When they are almost finished eating, he says, "I have something to ask you, but I want you to clean the salad out of your teeth first."

My sister says she knew something was up when he wasn't making frozen pizza for dinner.

And so, when my sister and her boyfriend, now fiancé, go out of town for the week as a kind of engagement celebration, Michael and I stay at their apartment in the suburbs, taking care of their cockatiels. My mom and dad call the birds their "bastard grandchildren," hoping that something better without feathers will come along soon. The birds squawk and shit all over the place, like Evelynn, our next-door neighbor, used to, but Michael agrees to come out for at least part of the time because my sister has cable. We move back and forth between our apartments in the city and my sister's place, taking turns feeding the birds pizza crust and letting them sit on our shoulders while we watch all the channels that we don't normally have.

Today, maybe because it's gray again—it's been a gray year—or maybe because I've watched *Father of the Bride* the night before—my sister has already rented it to get ideas—all I can think about is that marriage and television and homeownership are inextricably linked and created to dull us into complacency. I had left Michael with the birds this morning so that I could go to campus for a while, and all I can think about on my way back to my sister's is how difficult it is to function when so much free entertainment exists, and that the government is perhaps trying to keep us docile, trying to keep us busy with mowing the lawn and barbecuing, to keep us from noticing how boring and violent our lives are, how violently boring: the way you can sit and watch TV for hours and hours, and watch people be arrested, thrown down on the ground; watch car crash victims come bleeding and writhing into the emergency room; watch Steve Martin plan his daughter's wedding; watch Cindy Crawford put on lipstick; and all the while there are plenty of real things going on in the world, people who don't have enough to eat and rampant racism and plastic sitting in a hole in the ground where it will stay forever, never breaking down completely. I know about these things because I listen to Minnesota Public Radio. A line, twenty-five miles long, of Rawandan refugees. The world is violent, I think today as I drive on the gray expanse of freeway back to my sister's place. Cars are violent and NutraSweet is violent, occupying your body like foreign troops, your body having no way to manage the unfamiliar compound. Fluorescent lighting is violent. There are so many ways to irritate the body, to agitate the mind. And the world is like a body; it can't possibly manage all this, digest all of it. It curls up, goes to sleep, instead.

Later the counselor will say, "You're displacing again. What are you really angry about, in *your* life? Be specific."

And Michael will say, "It's not like you couldn't get out and do something about any of those things."

"I wouldn't even know how to start," I say.

I stop at Target before I go back to my sister's and I try on lipsticks. I try hydrating formula, wondering if it will smudge. I try smudge-proof formula, wondering if it will dry and crack my lips. I try the kind that is not supposed to leave any marks on *him*; Michael hates it when I wear lipstick. Next fall I will teach my first writing class, Beginning Expository Writing, and so I imagine myself in front of my classroom of young, eager composition students, my lipstick looking just right, validating my feigned expertise with paragraph structure, thematics and grammar.

"Go ahead and split those infinitives, kids," I will tell them, wearing Matted Huckleberry. "To not have fun with infinitives is such a crime."

I leave Target with a picket fence of lipstick marks on the back of my hand, where I've tried Paradise Plum, Riveting Red, Sun Coral and Surprisingly Mauve. I ask the saleslady if she has any Kleenex, and since she doesn't, I use the register receipt to wipe it all off.

Back at my sister's, Michael is sitting on the couch with the birds, watching *Babe, the Gallant Pig*. We have rented mostly movies for kids, and although I don't mind them, it disturbs me in some way because it seems to indicate a growing problem in our relationship. I have wanted to watch a French film and Michael has vetoed this, saying that he's not in the mood for translation and heavy French gazes. He never is. Michael has wanted to rent action/adventure movies, which he then deconstructs as "texts," analyzing the accidental racism, the conservative family values portrayed, the right-wing take on crime, the way that men can enjoy themselves together only when they are fighting something else. I agree with him about all of it, but on the other hand, I say, "These are very stupid movies and everyone knows it."

"Not everyone knows it," says Michael.

And I suppose that is true.

So we wind up with *Babe, the Gallant Pig, What's Eating Gilbert Grape* and *James and the Giant Peach*. In just a short time of going out again, we have become more like brother and sister, sitting on the couch together in our sweat pants, farting in front of each other and vying for more of the blankets and pillows. We hardly ever have sex—or anything remotely like it. Still, we stay together, the way the elderly hang out together in nursing homes, fighting over the remote control.

I walk around in my sister's life for the week that she is gone, taking care of her plants and her small birds. Soon she will be married, and she may buy a house and have some children. She and her fiancé already own a sport utility vehicle, and they keep

M&M's in a dish near the couch. I don't even have a couch. Their computer is much nicer than mine, and I panic when it freezes up while Michael is trying to play games on it. I don't want us to break anything here. It seems like adult property.

Later the counselor and I will talk about Target and credit cards, and I will reiterate my fears about having to work for things, to patiently build something.

"I've never had much patience," I tell the counselor. "That's why I finally quit piano lessons. I couldn't stand practicing. The teacher kept shoving Schubert at me, and I just wanted to play Barry Manilow songs."

"You really haven't worked for much in your life," the counselor says.

"But let's say that I work to earn everything I have before I buy it, and then later I get sick of that thing," I offer, "then I'll feel like I've been gypped."

"That's life," says the counselor. "You work at something, when it wears out, or no longer fits, you make it into something else, you give it to someone who can use it, you move on. You work at something else. Life is about choices, and constant maintenance."

"Not if you do it on credit."

"Then you're stealing a life."

But I want to sample everything, I tell her. In Target I'm like a dog looking for a comfortable place to sit, I circle and pace, sniffing everything. I go there for laundry detergent and I come home with a new CD, two shirts, a bath mat, a plant, some magazines and contact solution.

"Those aren't experiences," says the counselor. "They're things."

"I keep getting them mixed up," I say.

At the end of *Gilbert Grape,* I tell the counselor, when the mother dies, Gilbert decides that he can go anywhere. He can do anything.

"You're the only one," says the counselor, "holding yourself back."

"Yesterday that new lipstick made me very happy," I tell the counselor. "But today, it just doesn't seem like enough."

Voice Mail

I keep having to explain to my mother the virtual reality that is voice mail.

"Where are the messages, then, actually?" she wants to know. "Do you have to go someplace to get them? I don't understand why there's no machine. There's no machine, really?"

At first, not trusting in the technology, she leaves brief, tentative messages:

"Hi. Um. I never know if this thing is actually working or what it's doing. Call me."

But then as she becomes more comfortable, and because I have made the mistake of telling her that there's really no time limit on voice mail, that she can talk pretty much as long as she wants, she does:

Okay, Shannon, I'm off of your back. Now, you may not like to hear this, but your father had looked and looked for his green waterproof jacket, and he looked in the front closet and the back closet and every closet we have, thoroughly. I just found it in the front closet. So we can all live in peace now, and I'll stop bothering you about it. Bye.

Shannon, I was kidding you. You know that I give you a lot of rope, and I am not a picky, fussy mother. So, I was just giving you a hassle on the phone, so, no I am not angry with you, and I completely understand, if I were in your shoes I would be off having fun, too, rather than going to my mom and dad's house, so, no sweat, dear. Um, I guess I'll have to quit kidding. Talk to you later. Bye.

Shannon, I have a major policy, a major *personal* policy, that I would like to share with you. I don't believe in being indirect, and therefore, if I get angry over something, I will announce it, and I will say, "I'm ticked off, or I'm upset, or I'm angry or whatever," so that you will know, you will have a clear message. And I apologize for giving indirect messages—if I have—so, and that was meant to be funny, so, you can call me later if you want. Bye.

Oh to be a twenty-nine-year-old and out gallivanting around. Well, I hope that you're out having a good time. It's ten o'clock and this is your mother, and I just thought maybe you could use a phone call, and also, I wanted to find out what this thing is that I got in the mail. It says on the outside, "Try America Online, the nation's number one online service," and it says "fifteen free hours." And it looks like there's some kind of, I don't know if it's one of those disks or whatever, that goes in the *thing*, you know what I mean, but anyhow I thought that maybe you could enlighten me. Well, I'm going to clean up the kitchen now. Dad and I just ate, and we—I'm—going to go to bed. So, I hope you're out having fun. Bye.

And because my mother has begun to have a personal relationship with my voice mail, and because she's never really been able to get along with her mother-in-law—has always said that my grandma doesn't like her, believes that she has never accepted her because she wasn't raised Catholic—this is how I learn that my grandma is dying:

Shannon, it's seven thirty on Monday, and I'm just calling to tell you that after Dad had gone to the office this morning, he was called to Willmar, and the nursing home said that Grandma was, um, it appeared to be that she was dying, that she had taken a turn for the worse, and so he and your aunts are out there and have been out all day, and he just called now and she's been, you know, continuously going downhill, and her breathing is becoming *labored*, and so um you know she will, you know, I would imagine will die tonight or tomorrow morning or something. But, anyhow, I just wanted you to know so that you, as you plan your week, you'll have, you can keep ahead enough, to know that there's going to be a funeral and that type of thing. I can't answer when or where, but I'll let you know as things progress.

Last

My grandmother's last word was, *No,* and this would begin to change everything, would be the first brick to fall out of a crumbling wall.

My sister and I stand over our grandmother's casket, our father's mother, who looks better now than she has in months—quiet, her skin creamy. Like all the dead who needed spectacles in life, she is still wearing her glasses, but this is for our vision and not hers. To see her without her glasses would be to see her differently.

We hold in our hands a small piece of green polished glass with a shamrock etched into it and the word LUCK. Our Irish grandmother, with her sharp tongue, who I will understand later never meant a word she said. Our Irish Catholic grandmother, who would not acknowledge her great-grandchild, my cousin's daughter, born out of wedlock. Who herself had six children, twenty-four grandchildren, eight great-grandchildren (to her mind, only seven). Who kept asking me when I was going to get married and recommended that I have twelve children of my own.

We place the little glass stone near her hands, over the button of her jacket.

"It looks funny there," says my sister. "It looks like it's going to slip. Put it near her shoulder."

But the small green stone is too close to hands that I know are heavy and cold, despite layers of makeup. "I can't do it," I say.

"Cliff, you do it," she says, turning to her fiancé. "You were an altar boy."

"Where do you want it?" he says.

"By her shoulder," I say.

"On the pillow," Greta says.

"Here, I'll do it," I say. "Never mind, I can't do it," I say.

"I'll do it," says Greta, reaching quickly and precisely, trying not to disturb my grandmother's hands. "Here," she says, placing the small stone on the pillow, next to my grandmother's head. Now, resting in the coffin, is my grandmother, with this little green rock by her ear. "How does that look?" says my sister.

"Kind of goofy," I say.

"What are you kids doing?" says my mother, coming up behind us.

"We wanted to leave this with Grandma," I say. "It's the luck of the Irish."

"We don't know where to put it," says Greta.

"Why don't you put it in her hands?" says my mother, but this is immediately rejected because it would look like she was holding a casino chip. "Well then why don't you put it *by* her hands, over that button?" suggests my mother.

"They already had it there," says my sister's fiancé.

"Well, I don't want to stand here all night moving this thing around," says my sister.

I am holding the glass stone, turning it around and around in my palm until it is shiny and clear with sweat and oil. What was meant as a gesture of goodwill, a parting gift, has now become a matter of accessorizing.

"Put it here," says my sister, taking it and placing it again by our grandmother's shoulder.

"That looks good," says my mother. "Now move, kids. Give someone else a chance to see your grandmother. Oh, my eye is dry today," she says, digging around in her purse, wandering off toward the bathroom holding her special eye drops.

"That looks good," says my sister's fiancé, looking into the casket.

I nod, wondering if we should have even brought it in the first place. My grandmother never liked *things*, not the way I do. When my sister and I brought her new slippers in the nursing home, warm, fleece-lined ones, she wouldn't keep them. "Take them back," she said, "I like the ones I have." The ones she had were terry cloth with hard, rubber bottoms. The elastic on them was too tight and her feet were cold to the touch. "Your feet are freezing, Grandma," we said.

"I'm fine," she said, "I don't need new slippers."

My grandmother who never gave a straight answer about anything. Now I think that perhaps I've been selfish. What I have really wanted is to give her something that she can't give back, so we stand over her now, treating her body like a gameboard, moving this small piece around and around, hoping that somewhere, it will fit.

"I left my football jersey with my dad when he died," my cousin says later, and I think about the small green stone we have left with her, which will undoubtedly slip off her chest and bounce around in the coffin.

My grandmother had already lost two of her children, four siblings, and her husband, Myron. At eighty-seven, she had decided she wanted to die. She stopped eating and got smaller and smaller until she looked like a baby bird, fragile and curled up in her bed, long and bony, accepting only small amounts of food and water, lifting her head off the pillow to receive them.

The last time I saw her, she was whacked out on painkillers and more congenial than she had ever been. She was a grandmother I didn't know, small and frail and smiling up at me, rubbing her head against the pillow. "My head itches," she whispered. "Scratch my head." She had never been so vulnerable.

At eighty-seven, she had decided that life was no longer interesting. Her husband was gone. She was tired of bridge. She was tired of *Wheel of Fortune.* She no longer had the energy to read trashy novels about naughty priests. She had spent a life cooking for six children, cooking in the restaurant she and my grandfather owned, cooking for the prisoners in the county jail when my grandfather was sheriff.

As she lay dying the priest spoke soothingly to her, "Margaret," he said, "it's okay. Let yourself go. You've wanted to die for some time now. Aren't you ready to let go? Aren't you ready to go be with Myron?"

Her eyes flew open like window shades. "No!" she said.

And that was all she said before she closed her eyes again for the last time.

Now that she is gone, we will never know if she said, "No," at the last minute because she suddenly changed her mind about dying, or if she just didn't want to spend eternity with my grandfather.

But my sister and I did learn, after the funeral, that our grandma had been pregnant when she got married. That it had been a great scandal because not only was she pregnant, she was Catholic and our grandfather was Baptist; their families didn't want them to be together.

"Why didn't you ever tell me?" I asked my dad.

"I don't know," he says. "I never really thought about it."

"I think it would have made a huge difference," I say. "I always saw Grandma as this Irish Catholic martyr."

"I think guilt moved your grandmother more than anything. I think she wanted to make sure you kids didn't make the same mistake she made."

"It would have helped to have known there had been a mistake in the first place," I say. "Grandma was always so reserved and crispy. This makes her more human."

"That's interesting," says my father.

"How long have you known?"

"Since high school," says my father. "One of your aunt's friends told her and she told me. I mean, it was a surprise at the time, and then I just forgot about it. And," he says, "I guess I just didn't think it was my story to tell."

Holding

"I kind of wish you'd come to my grandmother's funeral," I say to Michael.

We are sitting around my apartment eating bagel sandwiches and watching TV.

"I told you, Shanny," he says. "I needed to finish that project."

"I know," I say. "It's just that she liked you." My grandmother had always asked me when Michael and I were getting married. "And I would have liked having you there," I say.

Michael has started a new internship at an architectural firm in town. The pay is good and he really likes the people he works with. They go out for drinks a lot after work, and sometimes they go dancing. Still, he's been talking about applying for fellowships to Italy, to live in Rome.

"I'd really like to go back there," he says, "I haven't been back to visit since I was in high school. And my Italian vocabulary would improve."

Michael starts buying new clothes for work. He gets new glasses and a new leather jacket.

"Do you ever think," he says to me once, "do you ever worry that we're keeping each other in a holding pattern?"

I know he might be leaving, keeps talking about leaving Minnesota for New York, or Rome, and in some ways, it makes it easier to be with him.

"It's easier to be in the moment," I tell the counselor, "When it has some definition. When it's not just stretching into infinity."

"That's the depression," says the counselor. "For depressed people, each moment has the weight of a lifetime on it, and no hope for change."

The Bananas You Picked Out

My sister's wedding is in one month. Her fiancé has a new job in Portland, so he's moved out there already. She's moved back in with our parents until the wedding. Her fiancé will come back for the wedding and then she will move out to Portland, and I will drive out there with her, even though I can't drive a stick shift.

"You'll learn," says my sister.

My sister is also house-sitting for Pastor Peggy, who is on safari in Africa, so she spends most of her time next door at Peggy's, and takes most meals over at our parents' house.

"This is an interesting system you've got worked out," Flo keeps saying to my sister. "All these free meals."

I think because of Flo's constant comments, my sister finally went out and bought some groceries for them to share.

Tonight Greta and I are in the bathroom getting ready for

the bridal shower that one of her friends is throwing. This is the big bachelorette party, the one where everyone buys her plastic penis paraphernalia. She is in the tub shaving her legs and I'm putting on makeup. We can hear Flo puttering around in the kitchen, putting away pans and closing cabinet doors. I can hear her make a phone call, and then she putters around some more, and then out of the blue she begins to call my sister's name, "Greta!" she calls. "Greta!"

"We're in the bathroom!" I shout.

"Greta!" she calls again, still not hearing me, as she now often doesn't.

"God," says my sister, one leg smothered with shaving cream and propped up on the edge of the tub. "She always wants something when I'm on the phone or in the bathroom. Some things don't change."

Flo knocks on the bathroom door, "Greta, are you in there?"

I unlock the door and open it.

"Hello," says Flo from the doorway, a banana in her hand, her mouth stuffed with the fruit. "Greta, I just wanted to tell you that these bananas you picked out are just perfect," she stops to swallow. "They're not too ripe and they're not too green. They were just absolutely ready to be eaten." She pauses. "What are you two talking about? Can I come in?" she says. "It's lonely out there."

The Survival Table

Here's what happens at the bridal shower: we go from bar to bar to bar, drinking. My sister is wielding a giant penis-shaped squirt gun filled with Schnapps (a gift), and a T-shirt covered in Life Savers that reads "Suck for a Buck" (also a gift). My sister's friends and I round up men who are willing to pay to suck a Life Saver off her T-shirt, and by the end of the night, my sister has accumulated about one hundred dollars.

When most of my friends got married in their mid-twenties, I went to plenty of these parties. Part of me sees them as a necessary American rite of passage, like watching the Super Bowl and eating nachos. The part of me that's now had a few more feminist literature courses is mortified and wants to save my sister from all of it, wants to take her by the hand and go bowling or to see a nice movie. Mostly I don't know what to do, and I'm feeling sorry for myself and so I just get really drunk and start smoking, and find myself at the last stop of the night, a strip club, putting dollar bills into a dancer's underwear and saying to him, in very slurred English, "You must hate this job. What do you really want to do?"

As I'm shoving money in his red bikini briefs he tells me that he wants to be an actor. Even though I'm drunk I can see the dark stubble growing back on his arm from where he's shaved the hair off. He smells of baby oil. "You should," I say. "You should be an actor. You're beautiful." I give him my phone number and tell him that I will try to help him with his career.

I have no idea what happens after that, except for what my sister will tell me the next day, when I am on the couch at Pastor Peggy's, where she had deposited me in the middle of the night.

I wake up with my head pounding, feeling like a shell of myself. Like someone looking down on myself. There is someone else living behind my eyes. I look around Pastor Peggy's basement and see my sister folding the clothes that I now remember throwing up on, the ones she'd taken off me in the middle of the night and has already washed this morning.

"I'm so sorry," I say to her when she comes over to set my clothes on a corner of the couch. "I'm so, so sorry," I say again.

"Shannon," she says, holding up a hand, "don't even start. That just makes it worse."

For the rest of the day I lie on the couch, drifting in and out of sleep. My sister comes and goes, running errands and then returning. In bits and pieces, and because I ask, she tells me the things I can't remember:

I had the hiccups, she says, and then suddenly I threw up out the window, and kept throwing up the whole way home. They used her friend's extra jeans shorts to wipe it all up. I should send her some money for new shorts, says my sister. They took the car through the car wash around three A.M., she says, and I begin to vaguely recall standing outside the car wash. And I begin to remember resting my head on the window of the car, laying it in my own vomit, beer and gin and nachos, the car being stalled in traffic in the middle of the city, young men yelling "gross!" and honking their horns.

For the rest of the day, I watch men's golf on TV while my sister works in the other room on her masters thesis in bilingual education. My dad comes over with a shot of Compazine around three P.M., after I've not been able to keep water down all day, after I've thrown up nothing but my own insides three times.

"Oh, dear," says my father, pulling a syringe from his bag, "I remember those days."

"But not when you were almost thirty," I say to him. "Don't you think this is a little pathetic?"

"Almost thirty is about when you finally stop it," says my father, who instructs me to pick a cheek and to roll over. "That's about when you finally say to yourself, 'I don't think I want to spend a whole day of my life feeling this way.'"

The shot burns, but once it takes hold, I can sleep. It's just like the good old days, me in my little asthma tent, my dad with his old-fashioned leather doctor's bag that smells like mothballs and cotton and tongue depressors. He opens the bag to retrieve a shot of something or another and I know that in a few minutes I will be able to breathe again.

I fall asleep remembering all the times I got drunk in high school because I didn't know what else to do with myself, because I felt uncomfortable, because once I got going I didn't know how to stop, because I always felt different than everyone else. My friends all had boyfriends who were older than us, so I would just get really drunk and wind up talking to some girl in the laundry room who was also sad, and then on Monday we'd just see each other in the hallway and nod, like nothing had happened, like we hadn't pledged our undying friendship over Budweisers.

I fall asleep in the house that is now Peggy's and used to be Evelynn's. The difference between me, I think as I fall asleep, and Evelynn, is that Evelynn passed out *upstairs,* not in the basement. The basement, with its workshop, was Ray's space. At least I picked a different floor.

My mom used to come over here to clean up after Evelynn; now my sister cleans up after me.

When I wake up, Andy Rooney is bitching about his eyebrows and combing them for the camera. I shut the TV off and go next door, where my parents are sitting in the living room eating pasta and drinking chardonnay, which I can barely stand to look at.

The addition is finally really in progress, and so there are building materials everywhere—lumber, tools, and sheets covering the furniture—and my mother has begun to clean out and pack up all of the kitchen cupboards, which will soon be ripped down and rebuilt, new wood in a new configuration.

My mother, always a planner, always an organizer, has set what she considers to be emergency food stuffs on a card table in a corner. She calls it "The Survival Table." On it, she's placed the coffeemaker, the toaster, a can of Hills Bros, saltines and peanut butter, bread, cereal, a few bowls, silverware, plastic cups and paper plates. "Almost everything you need for the week that they'll be working in the kitchen," she tells my father, "is on the Survival Table." The rest of the food is in the fridge, ready to be microwaved. The coffee can be made on the Survival Table; the toast toasted. When my father can't find a fork for his pasta, and so goes rummaging around in a box over by the front door, my mother says, "Ed, I already told you not to look in there. That's all packed. Go check the Survival Table."

I want to throw myself across the Survival Table. I want to stay here where the rent is free and the nice older couple who own the place are quite affable. Where there's good pasta and my mother seems to have put *fresh* vegetables in it for once, not the ones that are about to go bad. I want to throw myself on the Survival Table like it's some kind of life raft, but I know it would go crashing to the ground beneath me, sending the Hills Bros and the saltines clammering across the kitchen floor. And that is how I feel, like it is safe here, but that if I stay, I will bring it all down with me.

Totie Fields

It's a Saturday heavy with clouds, the day after Independence Day, and in just two days I will be thirty. For my birthday, Michael and I are going mini-golfing and out to eat with my parents, to an expensive restaurant in Saint Paul, a place where you have to make your reservation two weeks in advance, which is not a common thing in Minnesota. On our birthdays, Flo usually asks us what we'd like to eat and makes a special dinner; we get to design our menu, including dessert. But since it's my thirtieth birthday, my parents thought we should do something extra. Actually, it was my idea and they agreed to it. Michael was always talking about this restaurant, an Italian place that the two of us would never be able to afford, and so I chose it for my birthday.

In three weeks my sister will be married. It's almost noon and I am still in my pajamas, in my tiny apartment, watching planes in the distance. On most days, when I look out of my kitchen window, I notice only the clouds, the trees in my neighbors' yards, the chimneys that poke up into my view here on the top floor. But today, for some reason, I am noticing a whole army of planes taking off, jets from the Minneapolis airport that are tiny in the distance, one after the other, heading northeast. They look hopeful, optimistic, their noses turned up like girls from the wealthy suburbs. But they are also tiny from here, fragile, buglike with crisp skeletons.

I call Flo, who has spotted, at Mervyn's, what she believes will be the ideal shoe to go with my maid of honor dress, "But you better hurry up and get over there. They move merchandise through quickly, you know. They're always moving things through. That wedding's coming up fast. You need shoes."

I tell Flo about a guy who was interviewed on Minnesota Public Radio this week. A psychologist who has a book about how our thinking creates our life; we are what we think.

"That's not new," says Flo, "that's Norman Vincent Peale."

"I always thought I would be married by the time I was thirty," I say.

"I think you'd have better luck finding someone if you *didn't* think about it so much," says Flo. "These things happen when you're not looking for them."

Flo always labeled things around the house so that we wouldn't have to go looking for them, but relationships aren't the same way. I tried labeling Michael as "The One for Me" and it didn't work. He wouldn't stay put, kept surprising me with his own personality, different from the one I'd created for him on our first date.

"Maybe I should move to the woods," I tell my mother, "to clear my head. Maybe I need to walk around with dirt under my feet more often." But looking around my apartment, I know that I already do this; there is plenty of dirt.

"You would just find something wrong with the woods," says my mother. "You would probably start saying that you needed to get out of the woods because you couldn't see the forest from the trees. Or something."

"The woods would probably not meet my expectations," I agree. "They would fall short."

"Probably," says my mother.

"If your expectations fall short in the woods," I add, "does anyone hear about it?"

"Oh, I'm sure you'd let me hear about it," says Flo, laughing at her own joke, as usual.

"I'm always missing something," I say to Flo, "but I have no idea what it is. And I have no idea how to figure out what it is. I always want more, or something different. Maybe if I just started pretending that I was really happy, I would start to feel really happy. I'd be like a big happy idiot."

"I think of it like the food groups," says Flo. "Say you never eat fruit. You have meat and potatoes and vegetables, but you've never had fruit. Your body is craving fruit, it's sending you messages, 'I need fruit,' but you don't know what fruit is. You just know something's missing," Flo concludes. "You're missing those vitamins."

I think about my diet briefly and know that plenty of vitamins are missing. Meanwhile, planes are still taking off in the distance. "So I don't get it," I say.

"Well, maybe you need to take stock of what you have, and what's missing. Maybe you need to start figuring out what *you* can do to fill in what's missing, instead of expecting someone else to do it."

"But if I've never had fruit, how will I know it when I come across it?"

"Well, fruit will not just arrive at your door, you have to go out in the world."

"But if you're a member of the Fruit of the Month Club, then fruit does arrive at your door," I say. "See? There are all kinds of loopholes."

"You really don't want to be happy, do you?" says my mother. "You really kind of languish in your own misery."

"It fills those empty spaces," I say.

"You know," says Flo, "it's the Totie Fields philosophy of life. Do you know who Totie Fields was?"

"I have no idea."

"She was this comedienne who was short and as round as she was tall. And she had this whole routine about why she was fat. She would tell the audience that it was because she ran out of potatoes, and the audience would sort of look around, knowing that couldn't be it. And she would say, Yes, it was because she ran out of potatoes. You see, she had too much gravy on her plate, and so she had to add some potatoes. But then, when she ran out of gravy, she had too many potatoes, and she had to add more gravy, but then she would run out of potatoes again. And she always said that the thing she wanted most in life was to balance out her potatoes and gravy."

"Hey, that's pretty good."

"She died recently," adds Flo.

"Of a potato overdose?" I say.

"I don't know," says Flo. "But that's my whole philosophy of life. I've always said that I want enough money to live until I die, and if we run out at the same time, well that's just fine."

"Okay," I say. I don't know what to say. I do not want to talk about my mother dying, so out of the blue I ask her, "Do you still like *stuff*?"

"What do you mean?"

"I mean, do *things* still make you happy?"

"Well, some things. Things that will facilitate my growth and living. My journey."

"Like those exfoliating gloves I got you to use in the shower?"

"Yes, I love those," says Flo. "I always use those after water aerobics. You know, I look around this house and I see so many things that I don't know what to do with, because they're things that at one time were important. Like when your brother was little, for instance. He went through this phase of wanting to grow plants, and so we had to go out and buy about fifty pots, and then he was into fish, so we had a bunch of aquariums. And these were things that facilitated his growth and learning as a person, so that he could get to his next stage. And there are all kinds of things like that around this house, things I needed at one point but don't need anymore where I am now."

"And you have an attachment to them," I say, thinking I am one step ahead of her.

"No," she says, "I have a respect for them. A respect for

what they gave at that time. And I'd like them to move on and be useful to someone else in the same way."

"I have a feeling they're all in a bag marked 'Shannon,'" I say.

"Well, no," says Flo. "I think I need to have a garage sale."

I go that afternoon to Mervyn's. Flo is right. The shoes are perfect.

And on my thirtieth birthday, after a quiet dinner at the expensive Italian restaurant with my parents, Michael is sick with food poisoning.

A Bad Puppy

When we break up for the second time, Michael says things like, "You're number one. You're my favorite person in the whole world, and I can't imagine a life without you, but I don't want to be in a relationship with you. I mean, I don't think we're the right partners for each other. This just isn't working. And, anyway, I'm leaving," he says.

Michael has decided that he will definitely leave Minnesota by Christmas. He doesn't want to spend another winter here.

Michael goes to bed for two days. He buys a TV and watches it and has diarrhea. That is how he mourns the loss of "us."

Then "we" are out of his system.

"The thing is," I said to him as we were breaking up, "is that I like you so much better now than I ever did when we were going out."

This summer we had actually been going out and having fun. Playing miniature golf, going to movies. We had no sex life, but we didn't fight over stupid things, either. It's almost like we're dating again, except when we were dating it was never this easy, we never got along this well. We were never honest enough with each other; we kept trying to make it romantic, to make it perfect, to make it something it wasn't. It was strained, stressful. And now that there were no expectations, I was enjoying him. And I'm horny again.

I want to touch him all the time, to pet him and pat him, to wrestle around with him.

"I'm like a little dog to you now," he says, "an adorable pet."

"That I can't have," I say.

"That you can't have," he says. "It's the Catholic girl in you," he says. "Now that I'm forbidden I'm attractive."

"You were always attractive," I say.

"Not like this," he says, "I used to have to beg you for back rubs."

"Same here," I say.

"Now you can't keep your hands off me."

"Sorry," I say. "I'll stop."

"It doesn't bother me," he says, "I just think it's funny."

I want to stick my hand down his pants. We could be anywhere, the car, a restaurant.

"Shanny," he says, "sex with me made you nervous."

"It wasn't sex with you," I say, "it was just sex. Period. I wasn't ready yet, we jumped in too soon. It wasn't anything you did. You didn't do anything."

"Oh, thanks," he says.

"That's not what I meant," I say, "Maybe it was just an issue of timing before," I say.

"Or maybe we're just better off as friends," Michael says.

"What happens if you choke a puppy? If you wrap your fingers around its little neck and tighten your grip so tight that the puppy can't breathe?"

"It will look to you for help, even as you're choking it," I say.

"The puppy will die," he says, releasing his fingers from his tight grip on the air of the car, from his tight grip on nothing. "Life is the puppy," he says. "Let go," he says, "let go."

"Life is a bad puppy," I say. "Naughty puppy. No biscuit." I pat Michael on the head and continue driving.

"You're squeezing the life out of life," says Michael. "You can't control everything."

Anyway, Being with God, or What Have You

I stand in the church during my sister's wedding, kind of discreetly smelling my upper lip, remembering how my mouth was on fire the other day from Kung Pao noodles. Today is a day to be serious. We are getting married. Or some of us are getting married and the rest of us are here for support, says the priest. A community is needed to support this young couple, which couldn't, incidentally, get married outside, on the green grass, even though they wanted to on this god-forsaken hot day, but had to get married in here, and they agreed to that, says the priest; they understand that God is in *here,* in *his* house, where his woman will bring him a pot pie and a cold beer at the end of the day.

I make up the last part. I've never been able to pay attention in church.

My sister and her husband are gazing at the priest, while he tells them about marriage, even though he's never been married. It takes commitment, he says, and communication, he says, and my sister and her husband-to-be nod. My sister's legs swing because they are shorter than the stone chair she sits in, a stone chair with an orange ecclesiastic cushion on it. Her legs swing the way a child's do when the furniture is too big, or just because she is happy, or both.

I wonder what my sister is thinking while the priest is going on about raising a family in the church, since the two of us could never pay attention in church and always got sent to the corner of separate parts of the house afterward. I've developed a twitch in my eye today, and sweat is dripping down from the crack where my thighs and butt join. Women's magazines will tell you that if you fit a pencil in that place and hold it there, that you've got work to do, that your butt is too big. I could hold a permanent marker there, or a big piece of that sidewalk chalk, and today it's Lake Michigan, which has begun to drip down the back of my thighs and to pool around my knees, which I notice now are locked, which Flo has warned me repeatedly not to do since childhood, which she has warned me about again today, "especially when it's hot, you know, it cuts off your circulation."

"We are here, today, with this young couple, and with God," says the priest, holding his palms open toward the ceiling.

And without central air, I think, and suddenly the organ player bursts into song; she is rocking at her bench, feeling the music in her fingertips, and I start to giggle. I try to get myself under control by looking down at my flowers, but my flowers just remind me of bees and our camping trip in the Boundary Waters last year, when I got stung on the boob, which felt like I'd just got out of the shower and stuck my boob in a toaster. I had this big red spot that my sister said looked like a third nipple, because of course I had to show someone my injury. "That looks like it hurts," said my sister, "I bet you're thinking, 'Why do I have to be the victim?'," which was exactly what I had been thinking, and I was grateful she knew me that well. At the same time, she had been the one who told me to step on the bee that came into our campsite, and just as I was doing that, one of its friends came along and stung me on the boob, right through my T-shirt. "It gives new meaning to the term B cup," I told my sister, even though I was crying and feeling like the one camper who got singled out this year by the bee community for special pain.

I realize my knees are locked, and I bend them a little and look over at my sister, who is nodding at the priest as he says, "Greta and Clifford understand the gravity of what they've decided to do, and they ask for your support, O Lord." I think of them falling from a tree, a couple of apples on Newton's head. My sister keeps nodding and my new brother-in-law looks much the same way he does when he is watching football, an interested observer who is wondering if there are more potato chips in the kitchen. The priest starts talking about their shared activities, including hiking and golf, and I think, "farting," which is easily just as true if we're going to talk about shared activities, and I'm thinking that ceremonies hardly ever have anything to do with what they're supposed to commemorate or symbolize, and that mostly they make everyone crave alcohol and music, and when the priest says something about bringing children into the world and into the church, I assume my parents are grinning so widely that they might be pushing people out of the pews with their hopefulness.

When I was walking up the aisle as slowly as I could, which is what you are supposed to do as Maid of Honor, and which I couldn't do and so kept walking kind of fast despite myself, I looked for Michael's face and when I found it, behind his black-rimmed glasses, I was relieved. He had said he still wanted to come to my sister's wedding. That he loved my sister and that it was important to him to be there. When we broke up again, we decided that we'd stay friends, since he's leaving, and who knows when we'll see each other again?

But then last weekend, Michael was supposed to meet me with my sister and some friends to go sailing, and he never showed up.

I had called him on my friend's cellular phone, left messages wondering where he was? It wasn't like Michael to just not show up.

As we were driving to the lake and the cell phone got out of range, I made us stop at a gas station so I could call one last time, before we hit the water. "I'm sure he's fine," my sister had said.

"It's just not like him," I had said.

Then earlier this week he had called me and said, "I'm sorry I missed you guys on Sunday. I was up north with some friends. From work." He has a whole host of new friends from work that I've never met. "We had horrible weather up there and the power went out, and so I couldn't call you. In fact, we were trying to leave but the weather was so bad that we could barely see, and the roads were horrible, so we turned around and went back to the cabin."

"I was really worried about you," I said.

"I'm sorry," he said. "I just figured that if I didn't get back in time, you'd go without me."

"Well, we waited for a while," I said. "And then we left. It's just not like you not to call, Michael."

"The power was out."

"It sounds like you weren't planning on coming back, anyway."

"Listen," Michael said. "I should tell you. I'm seeing someone else. You should know that."

"But you're leaving," I said. "You said you were cutting ties here."

"I want you to know that our friendship is important to me," he says. "You're my favorite person. I'd actually kind of like you to meet her. I think you'd get along. I've told her all about you."

"Meet her?"

And so today he is wearing his linen pants and a white linen shirt and one of the ties I gave him, and I know he's hot, too, in this warm barn called God's House, which could use central air. I was relieved to see him, and yet he looked at me like he barely knew me, which is perhaps when my eye started twitching. It's a way he looks at me a lot lately. In the way that a movie camera will suddenly back off a character, making them appear far away, Michael always looks like he's moving backward, away from me, even when he's standing still.

My sister and her husband-to-be are exchanging vows and I can see that the priest's nose is dripping while they are promising to love each other and take care of each other and heat up frozen pizza together and feed their birds together and pay car insurance, and the priest's nose is about to drip into the Bible, I think, when my eye starts twitching so hard that I kind of grab my face by reflex, hoping to stop it, and Greta looks over at me and Cliff looks over at me, sweat beading on my upper lip, pooling around my knees, dripping down to my ankles.

Is there a pool on the floor? do people think I have wet myself? and out of the corner of my good eye, which has not seized up in a kind of retinal coronary, I can see my mother wearing a peach dress with some alstrameria on her chest, smiling and then kind of frowning, and my father in his tuxedo, and suddenly my chest heaves and then goes tight, as if a rope has been tied around it, the way you'd lasso a horse, and the horse slapped, *Hey! my chest is attached to that rope,* that horse, being dragged though the dirt, across the desert, get along little doggie. I can't even get one that's small. I can't breathe, I can't breathe, and the harder I try to breathe, the harder it becomes and soon my sister is moving toward me, where's Michael, where's Michael?, my new brother-in-law is moving toward me, dear Jesus I'm having an asthma attack just like when I was little and the girl scouts brought me a little peanut cup and a card in the hospital, an asthma attack with steam and vapor, going down, underwater with a priest who is standing over me now and I try to grab his collar and he grabs my wrists to let go of his collar and so I grab those pretty things that are like table runners or a stripper's boa, that hang down from his dress, what's it called? if I had paid attention I'd know, robe. Where's my mom? Dad should have his doctor's bag, old and black cracked leather smelling of mothballs. I can feel my shame rising like a hot air balloon. *What the fuck is wrong with me? I can't breathe, Father, forgive me, for I have stopped breathing.* When I was little and this happened, my brother and sister took the go-cart out and went up and down the neighborhood, *Jesus Christ,* up and down our dead-end street in the dark.

Amen.

I am coming to in the ready room, the same room where I'd fretted before the wedding about my makeup and noticed how stupid my hair looked, like a little kid performing at her first piano recital, and how my breasts were spilling up over my dress, making me look like a big pink cupcake, and how beautiful my sister looked, so much like Mariel Hemmingway, an angel hovering over me now, kind of blurry, holding flowers, am I dead?

Vision focusing, I remember that it is her wedding, her veil is pushed back over the flowers in her hair. The ring is on her finger. For a brief second I think she is a nun. My dad is next to me, taking my pulse.

"Where is Greta going?" I say.

"Here's your bag, Ed," says my mom, still in her peach dress, handing him a briefcase stuffed with papers, a stethoscope and some drug samples.

My dad listens to my chest. It's coming back to me now. I can hear people milling around outside. I can hear one of my uncles, a manic-depressive veterinarian shout, in the church's entryway, "Greta, you were magnificent! I laughed, I cried! Two thumbs up!"

"Take a deep breath," says my dad, holding the stethoscope to my chest.

My brother wanders over. "How's she doing? What's going on?" he says. He still has the flower in his ponytail that I stuck there.

"Maybe it's the heat," says Flo. "And the humidity."

When we were small, my brother and I both got overwhelmed in Dayton's, the local department store—got overwhelmed by the marble floors and the chrome and the endless racks of clothing. But my sister just wandered off happily, knew how to find my mom anywhere in the department store by the snapping of her gum. Mom's noise.

I stayed close. Was there anything on those racks that was worth risking your safety for?

"Do I need to go to the hospital?" I ask my dad.

"I don't think so," he says, "just sit here for a while, and your mom's getting a cold cloth."

"Okay," I say. I am looking for Michael, but he is not here.

"For a second there," says my dad, "I thought you and your sister were up to your old church tricks."

Puffins

Our parents drive to Portland, Oregon, with my sister and me the week after the wedding. It was supposed to be just the two of us, me and my sister, but Flo and my dad decide they should come, too. It's a long, hot drive. Hard on the car, especially when you're towing all of your belongings. Plus, I can't drive a stick.

Michael is still in Minnesota. For once, I am in Oregon in the summer and he's not.

Once we get my sister settled in to the apartment her husband had already rented for them, we drive out to the coast for the weekend, and we go to the Newport Aquarium, where Keiko the Killer Whale, the real Free Willy, has been kept, recuperating in a giant saltwater tank. Soon he will be freed to a huge pen off the coast of Iceland. He will adapt there before being let out to sea, to the great, chilling expanse that is no longer familiar. His trainers are not overly optimistic about his resilience. He has become used to people, to giving them rides. His fin is bent from swimming around and around in the same direction, in the same small tank.

My sister and I watch Keiko from the underwater window until he takes a huge crap, and then we go to the zoo's Coastal

Aviary and watch the puffins swim around. They dive over and over for the same thing; hard to tell what it is, something vaguely shiny that keeps getting away, slips just a little, every time the puffin has it in its beak.

I ask the aviary volunteer, an old man who looks something like the puffins, with long bushy eyebrows like Andy Rooney's and a beaked nose, if it is food that they are trying so hard to get.

"Oh, no," says the volunteer, who wears a button proclaiming him volunteer of the year—he has clocked thousands of unpaid hours during his tenure at the zoo, "they're just playing."

The volunteer goes on to tell me that they were having something of a drama in the aviary today.

"Oh, really?" says my sister, "what time does that start?"

"No, a real drama," says the man, who has come to love each of these birds. "It's hard to watch."

He says something about how the black-legged watchamacallits have kicked their adolescent black-legged something-or-another out of the nest and have sent it to live across the way with an older brother.

"You can't imagine how this little guy feels," says the volunteer. "The parents just love them up like you can't imagine for the first two years and then, suddenly, one day, every time he tries to come near home, they peck at him and screech at him. He has no idea what's going on. Everything he does is wrong. They won't talk to him the way they used to. They won't let him near the nest. They turn their backs on him until he finally goes away for good, crying and confused. Oh," the volunteer says, stopping at the sound of fluttering feathers. "Listen. Here we go again."

My sister and I watch the aviary drama and the happy puffins diving until it's time to meet our parents in the Deep Sea room, and knowing that they will be late, we stop and watch the otters swim on their backs for a while, until one of the otters takes a crap, kicks it around with its feet and plays with it a little, which makes me gag so hard that I throw up in the wastebasket next to the display, and my sister has tears streaming down her cheeks from laughing at me.

"Oh, Lord," she says, dabbing her eyes with the paper napkin left over from her ice-cream cone. "Aren't you glad you don't live underwater?"

By the time we get to Creatures of the Deep, my sister and I have calmed down a little. I have stopped gagging and she's finished her ice-cream cone. Our mother is there, watching a huge case of angel jellyfish. "They look like lingerie," she says. "Like they're all wearing nightgowns."

Flo has always worn nightgowns and I imagine she feels some kinship with these creatures. In the winters, she wears a Lanz nightgown to bed, along with Ben-Gay on her legs and old socks with the feet cut out around her elbows. "My joints ache," she always says. She's been doing this as long as I can remember; sometime in her forties, my mother started practicing to be old.

"Where's Dad?" says Greta.

"I think he got hung up in turtles," says Flo.

"I'm going to find Clifford," she says, "I think he's still watching that dumb whale movie."

In Creatures of the Deep, Flo and I discover how nature maintains itself. There are fish, of the same exact variety, who are two completely different colors, having adapted to their varying environments for survival. These flat fish used to have eyes on each side of their heads, but since living on the bottom of the ocean affords you only one good view, soon their eyes began to migrate, with both of them winding up on one side, on the top. Some of these fish are sand-colored, some completely black, depending on the color of the small pebbles in their habitat. The trick to survival is to have two good eyes, and not to stand out.

"The trick with these guys," I say to Flo, thinking that she's still standing behind me, watching the fish, "is that they weren't too proud to change." But when nothing but silence follows, I realize that Flo is no longer behind me, that she has moved on.

Honeymoon

Greta and Cliff and I take the train up to Seattle to meet my brother and his wife. We're going on a weekend sea kayaking trip in the San Juan Islands. Cliff can get only a few days off of work so we'd arranged this sort of Appalachian honeymoon where the family would get to go along, three days of kayaking and two nights of camping on the islands. Our parents fly from Portland to San Diego to visit friends. "You kids enjoy yourselves," my father had said, giving us the thumbs up, "*To the extreme!*" We had been watching television together at my sister's, and I'd been teaching him youthful catch phrases.

"Do I have to paddle with the guide the whole time?" I whine to my sister on the ferry ride to the main island. "I hate being single."

My brother and his wife stand on deck with their binoculars, trying to identify some hovering bird.

"We can all switch around," says Greta, rolling her eyes, as her husband snores with his head in her lap.

When we see the guide, my sister kicks me in the ankle and says, "I'd like to roll his kayak."

"Hi, I'm Dave," he says, extending his hand to my brother, who arranged the trip. "You must be Peter." Dave has a broad smile and is tan from being outdoors year-round; his brown hair has been streaked blond. He leads kayaking tours around the San Juan Islands in the summer and in Baja during the winter.

"I've always wanted to see Baja," I say

"Ba ha ha!" says my sister, and starts shaking with laughter.

"Is she okay?" asks Dave.

"Oh," I say, "she has issues. The water there must be beautiful."

"Crystal clear," says Dave.

"You don't even know where Baja is," my sister whispers to me later as we're dragging the equipment down to the beach.

"Yes I do."

"'*The water there must be beautiful,*'" she snorts, putting on her life jacket.

"My zipper's stuck," I say, pulling my life jacket tight across my chest.

"I think maybe your jacket's too small," Dave says. He is standing in front of me, watching me try to squish my boobs into this tiny light blue life vest. "I think you got the junior jacket. I had a bunch of kids on the last trip."

I can feel my face go bright red, and for some reason I remember a *Saturday Night Live* sketch from the eighties, where they did a list of fake children's books. The one that made me laugh really hard was "Pooh Gets an Aching in His Loin." At the time I thought it was funny without really understanding what it meant.

"Here," says Dave, smiling and holding out a brand-new bright red jacket. The hair on his forearms has been bleached by the sun. "This one's made for women."

"For the full-figured gal," says my sister, who didn't inherit what my mother calls, "The Tillman Breasts," our own genetic collection of Fabergé eggs. Even my abridged versions are bigger than my sister's.

Dave has us lay our backpacks, tents, food bags and day packs next to the kayaks. He explains how to load the boats and how to paddle, how the person in the back should steer, and how to feather our paddles in a strong wind. He explains how to skirt up in strong waves, gives us each one of the aprons that attach to the boat, the "skirts" that will keep everything dry. He lays a map out on the sand and anchors it with rocks, shows us with a stick where we'll be headed for the first night, explaining where we'll be taking detours to accommodate the tides. He has fine crow's feet spreading out from the corners of his eyes, long eyelashes and a dimple in one cheek. It's hard to tell how old he is, but he looks younger than I am.

"So, we have about a four-hour paddle this afternoon before we get to our campsite. Did everyone follow that?" he says. Of course, I wasn't paying attention and I have no idea where we're going. "Who's riding with me?"

"Me," I say.

"*'Do I have to paddle with the guide the whole time?'*" my sister murmurs as she and Clifford are packing their kayak. Clifford looks at me and shakes his head. "She's torturing you," he says.

"It's not too late to get an annulment, Clifford," I say.

My brother and his wife are applying 45 protection sunscreen and making sure their bird book is in the day pack, and I have finished stuffing the boat with equipment and am looking at our unsteady craft.

"Do these ever tip over?" I ask Dave.

"It's almost impossible to tip these things," he says. "These are sea kayaks. No one's ever tipped over with me."

I look out at the broad expanse of water before us.

"Go ahead and hop in," says Dave, and once we're in the boat he says: "Okay, Captain. You set the pace."

It takes me a while to get used to the rhythm of paddling but once I do, I love it. I like being at the level of the water, just on the surface.

"You're good," says Dave. "You've got a strong back."

It's ninety degrees outside and not a cloud in the sky, which Dave says is very unusual. We're floating so that my brother and sister and their spouses can catch up with us, and I've taken off my life vest to put on some more sun lotion.

"I used to swim," I say.

"What strokes?"

"Mostly backstroke."

"Me too," he says, "How are those guys doing?" The kayak jiggles as he looks back to make sure everyone's okay. I look back to see that Dave's got his feet propped up on the boat and so I pull mine out of the hull and prop my legs up, too. "So, Greta's your sister and they just got married, and then that's your brother and his wife?"

"Mhmm," I say.

"We should have tied some tin cans on the back of Greta's

kayak," says Dave. "I have some shaving cream. We could decorate."

"Wouldn't that ruin the kayak?"

"These things have been through a lot," says Dave. "So, where's your boyfriend?" he says.

I think about Michael, back in Minnesota, probably out dancing with his new girlfriend and their friends from work. He'd gone on our family camping trip one summer and I know he'd like this. Earlier that afternoon Dave and I had paddled past a huge rock with seals stuck to it like mussels to a boat's hull. I could practically hear Michael's voice saying, "Shanny, this is *amazing*." Then we'd gone around the corner of the island to a quiet inlet and Dave had whispered, "Stop paddling and look to your left." There had been a baby seal, taking a nap on a bed of seaweed. It woke up, looked at us, yawned, and went back to sleep. I could have reached out and touched it. Michael would have said I'd found my soul mate, another unflappable napper.

"I don't have a boyfriend," I say.

"Now, I find that hard to believe," Dave says.

I turn around to look at him and he hands me the water bottle, just as everyone else catches up with us.

"Do you think he's one of those guys who's got, like, a million women tucked away?" I ask Greta when we're cutting vegetables for dinner. Dave is making chowder and has given us all jobs. Greta and I are balancing a cutting board on a rock. My brother and his wife are making sure the boats are secured. Clifford is putting up their tent. "Clifford, put up Shannon's tent, too," she shouts in the direction of the tent sites. "You remember Shannon," she shouts. "She's single and she gets her own tent."

"Stop it," I say.

"I don't know," says Greta. "He is cute. What did you guys talk about all day?"

"Well," I say, "I told him about school, and he told me that he had started graduate school in marine biology, studying whales, and then decided to take a break. He's twenty-eight. His dad's a doctor and he keeps wondering if he should have gone into medicine. He has relatives in Minnesota. In Detroit Lakes."

"I like that he's not one of those super-asshole-nature guys," says Greta. "He's pretty mellow."

"He has three sisters."

"That explains it," says Greta.

After dinner we sit around the campfire and drink wine, remembering things that Evelynn did when we were growing up. How she knocked over the lamppost at the end of our block with her Chevrolet. How we could sometimes hear the wild dogs in the fields behind our house and occasionally mistook them for Evelynn. How Flo wouldn't let us cross the highway, except my brother and sister did, anyway—my sister to go to Dairy Queen, and my brother to buy beef jerky at the Ben Franklin and to sit in the park downtown reading *Mad* magazine.

"How about you, Shannon?" Dave says.

"Shannon wore blue eye shadow in junior high school," Greta says.

"Thank you," I say. "Everyone needed to know that."

My brother and his wife get their star chart out and try to find the constellations. Greta and Clifford go off to sit on a big rock.

Dave pulls out a sleeping bag and parks himself under a tree near the fire.

"Don't you sleep in a tent?" I say.

"Not when it's like this," he says. "No rain. No bugs. Do you guys want coffee in the morning?" he says.

"Coffee is my favorite thing in the whole world," I tell him. It's still kind of hot out, and he's sprawled out on top of the sleeping bag, wearing shorts and a torn blue T-shirt. "We all drink coffee."

"Your family is nice," he says. "Your sister's a hoot."

"Yeah," I say. We just sort of look at each other for a while. I can't tell if I should leave him alone. "Do you like doing this?" I finally say. "Leading groups?"

"It's good for now. Sometimes it's really hard to figure out what to do with people." He is propped up on one elbow and I wish I could lie next to him. "Last week I had all of these little kids, and the adults were really out of shape—I thought one guy was going to have a heart attack—so it was hard to keep everyone together. And the kids were up half the night singing Neil Diamond songs."

"Jesus," I say. "But no one tipped?"

"No one tipped," he says. "You guys should come back and do one of the longer trips," he says. "That way you get away from all the boat traffic. The next two days you'll see a lot of boats. Probably some whales, too, but you'd see more further north."

"Whales, really?" I tell him about a special I'd seen on whales. It talked about how some whales hang upside down in the water and sing, with their tails sticking up above the surface, and how all the whales in the same herd know the same songs.

"Were they Neil Diamond songs?" says Dave.

"I don't think so," I say.

Then we are just kind of looking at each other again.

"Those are humpbacks," Dave finally says. I blush at "hump."

Greta and Clifford come walking by and head off toward their tent. "Goodnight," says Greta. "Don't stay up too late."

"Well," I say, "I should go to bed, too."

The next morning I hear footsteps outside my tent. Dave is humming, "Forever in Blue Jeans." "Shannon," he whispers. "Your coffee's ready." And he leaves the cup outside.

Michael was always trying to get me to stop drinking coffee. "It's bad for you," he'd say, listing various facts he'd read over the years about what coffee does to the system. "And Shanny," he'd say, "you get kind of bitchy after too much coffee."

I unzip my tent and lie on my stomach in my T-shirt, drinking my coffee, looking out at a sky that is again blue, the sun already beginning to burn the dried grass on the island. Dave is over by the fire making eggs and oatmeal, and suddenly turns to look at me, smiles and motions me to come over.

I paddle with my brother that morning and with Clifford in the afternoon. Dave takes us to an island for an afternoon hike and a swim in the salty water.

"It's freezing!" says Greta, sticking her foot in.

"You have to breathe out and sink into the water at the same time," says Dave.

"Fuck that," says Greta.

"It will feel good afterward," I say. It's ninety degrees again today and we've been sweating in our kayaks all day.

Greta and I move out on a rock until we're knee-deep in the water.

"My feet are going numb," she says, and takes my hand. We

each take a huge breath, then let it out as we jump off the rock we'd been standing on.

"Christ!" Greta says when she comes to the surface, and she paddles back to the shore, scrambles up on a rock and grabs her towel.

My brother and his wife jump in, too, while Dave and I have a little swimming race, which of course he wins, and then while everyone is up changing clothes behind bushes, Dave and I dry off on a rock. I pull my towel around me and Dave says, "You should think about trying one of the Baja trips in the winter."

"That would be great," I say. "I mean, it's hard for all of us to coordinate our schedules to go at the same time, but it would be really fun."

"You could come by yourself," he says.

That night, after everyone else has gone off to bed, Dave and I go down to the shore where we've secured the boats, we take out a kayak and paddle around in the moonlight, in the quiet absence of boat traffic. When we get back to shore and get the kayak tied back up, Dave leans over and kisses me, a long deep kiss.

"God," I say, "it's been a really long time since I've had a kiss like that." I think quickly that I probably shouldn't say things like that, that the counselor would tell me not to.

"What's wrong with Minnesota?" he says, "I don't understand."

We are pressed up against a rock on the shore, his body pressed up against mine and soon we're kicking up sand like crabs, moving sideways on the beach, making out like teenagers. I take it as a good sign that he doesn't carry condoms on these trips and that this is all it will be, just hours spent in the sand on a hot night, half skin half clothed, with something maybe to look forward to.

The next morning, Greta says, "You came back to your tent awfully late last night."

"We were up late talking," I say.

"Mhmm," she says, batting her eyelashes. "Did you find the Baja peninsula?"

On our last day, on our way back to the landing, I paddle with my brother's wife for a while, and then with Dave after lunch. We are paddling at a regular pace when out of the blue Dave says, "Quick, pick it up," and switches direction so that we're speeding, relatively, toward one of the huge ferries.

"Where are we going? Are you trying to kill us?"

About fifty yards in front of our kayak a killer whale surfaces.

"Holy shit!" I say. Breath just leaves me.

"Yep," says Dave.

"How did you know that? How did you know he'd surface?"

"Experience," says Dave. The ferry is honking and the passengers are hooting and waving, happy to have seen a whale from their perches on the upper deck, toting binoculars and cameras instead of harpoons.

"So," says Dave as we're unpacking our equipment on the beach and piling our backpacks into his van, "you know where to find me."

"Mhmm," I say. My sister-in-law is standing behind Dave, giving me a funny look.

"Think about a trip to Baja?" he says.

"I will," I say.

On the plane ride home, I'm seated next to a tall man named Branford who does custom research at the business library in downtown Saint Paul.

"I've been there," I say. "That's a pretty library. I spent an afternoon there once, sitting around reading the paper with a bunch of homeless guys. They have free coffee."

"Yeah," says Branford, "The guys come for the coffee and the paper. Some of those guys are really smart." Branford has these big gentle eyes and beautifully tapered fingers. His skin is a light brown and he's shaved his head. And when we're getting off the plane he holds out his hand, smiles and says, "It was nice to meet you, Shannon. Maybe someday we can have coffee at the library."

I had no idea, going back and forth to campus everyday, parking in the same lot, walking down the same corridors, sitting in the same office, heading back home to the same apartment, what I'd been missing. Like Flo's theory about the body craving fruit. Who knew these fruits existed? We'd been living on potatoes.

"Well, how was your trip?" says Flo when I call her later in the week.

"It was really great," I say. "We had perfect weather and we saw baby seals and a whale."

"You're kidding," says Flo. "And the guide was good?"

"Yeah," I say. "He really knew what he was doing. He knew the tide schedules and the currents. We all felt safe."

"That's good," says Flo. "And you all got along?"

"We all got along," I say.

"I always encouraged you children to get along," she says.

In Motion

Michael's sister visits in the fall. In the time Michael and I have known each other, she's never been here, to Minnesota, and I've never met her. He wants us to get to know each other, and even though he's leaving for Italy soon, going back to live in the place where he grew up, he thinks his sister and I will get along. "You'll probably be lifelong pals," he tells me. "You're so much alike."

Michael still calls me, asks me to come over for dinner, to go to movies, to play miniature golf. I am teaching now, and he helps me figure out lesson plans; strategies for controlling slackers. Sometimes I think I am a complete idiot for spending time with him, and yet, I can't seem to help myself. I call him, too.

Tonight Michael invites me over for dinner; later he and sister are going dancing with Michael's girlfriend and her friends. I am invited to come along. "They would all love to meet you," Michael says.

Michael's sister laughs wildly at his every utterance, his every move. He is dancing around the apartment like a stripper who has no rhythm and I just can't laugh. Michael's been with his new girlfriend since the middle of summer and I don't want to think of him this way; anything smacking of sexuality at this point makes me uncomfortable. For instance, the other day they were playing with the Play-Doh I got Michael for Christmas. Michael's sister made a big penis, which she felt was "very accurately rendered," and then she made a big Georgia O'Keeffe flower; then she squished the giant penis and made from its remnants a big monster with a small penis. Then she took the big monster, trotted it over to the Georgia O'Keeffe flower, thrust the monster into the flower's middle and closed the flower's petals around the monster, until it had been devoured entirely. "There," she said, "that's every man's fantasy." She laughed wildly and Michael laughed wildly.

The whole thing made me a little nervous, so instead I concentrated all my energies into sculpting a chicken out of green and red Play-Doh. She had interesting feathers, a nest, and she managed to lay three eggs. She had one leg slightly lifted, as if she were walking. I called her "Chicken in Motion." At first she was walking away from the nest, but then I moved the nest in front of her, so that she'd be moving toward it.

Later, when I wasn't around, Michael's sister disassembled my chicken, telling me on the phone that she had wanted "all the colors to go back in their separate containers," which made me sad, because in the brief time I had spent assembling "Chicken in Motion" I had become quite attached to her. I had even grown fond of the eggs.

So, anyway, on this evening when Michael is dancing around the apartment, and his sister is shrieking with laughter, "Shannon, look at Michael's strip dance!" I feel the muscles in my neck tighten and seize upon my skull. It's a goofy dance, a pretty harmless thing, but it's the kind of thing that only a sister thinks is funny. A sister filled with adoration, or a lover, maybe. Michael used to dance around the apartment for me, but those dances had more humor and irony; this one I find uninteresting, there is a neglect of choreography. I try to relax and enjoy it, but I can't, so what I do instead is to take the plastic Target bag that Michael's been whirling over his head and I tie it over his hair like an old lady's scarf, a kind of babushka, so that his glasses and his lovely, large nose are peeking out from the plastic hat. I take a magic marker and write, on top of his head, on the bag, "I like bananas!" On the back of his head I write, "Follow me to paradise."

When he looks sufficiently ridiculous, but in this more interesting way, which I've created, I can relax, a little.

So you had to make him ridiculous? says the counselor. Which is the same thing you try to do to your mother. What purpose does that serve?

Things seem more manageable that way, I tell her. Less threatening.

But most things aren't threatening, says the counselor. They're just what they are. You make them threatening.

Okay, I say. All right. And then I make them ridiculous. It evens things out.

Why couldn't you have just let Michael and his sister fool around and laugh?

Because I thought they were expecting me to laugh, too, they kept looking at me and I couldn't laugh.

Why is so hard just to relax? asks the counselor.

Maybe it's a good defense mechanism. I can relax when things are more on my terms.

You're missing out on a lot when you do that.

So what's to miss out on? It wasn't that funny. It wasn't such a funny dance.

You really do isolate yourself, says the counselor.

Well what was I *supposed* to do? I say, and I can feel the tears welling up.

Why? says the counselor. *What do you mean?*

I just get uncomfortable when they talk about sex so much in front of me, I say. You know, my brother and I never talk about that stuff, except for when I had breast reduction surgery and he made a "Good Luck" sign and decorated the kitchen with pink balloons. *But that seemed more like support,* I say, honking into a Kleenex, *no pun intended.*

You had breast reduction surgery? says the counselor.

I've told you that, I say. Maybe I only mentioned it.

Maybe, she says. I can't remember everything. Anyway, what does this have to do with you? Why are you crying?

Because Michael and I had no sex life, I say. I mean, most of the time. He kept turning his back to me. And you know, Michael has a new girlfriend. *Already.* Why is everyone else having sex, except me?

Well, you had fun with the kayaking guy, says the counselor.

But he's not *here.* And I don't wave it in Michael's face. I don't say, "I wish you could meet the sexy kayaking guy. *I think you'd like him.*" Michael kept saying that he needed to leave Minnesota. That he needed to cut ties here, and then *poof!* New girlfriend. Except he still calls me. He says I'm his *pal. Do I look that bad nude?* What's wrong with *me?* It's painful, embarrassing. It feels lonely, shameful.

Okay, now we're getting somewhere, says the counselor. *My God!* she says. *We're finally getting somewhere!* See? You don't have to analyze and judge everyone else in order to get to your own material. You can *start* there. You can start with, "I feel lonely and ashamed. Shame, by the way," says the counselor, "is not very useful."

Okay, I say, but those are abstract terms. Sometimes, I say, it's easier to start with the details.

Say it, says the counselor, you need to say it.

Say what?

How you feel.

I can feel my own tears begin to well up. The counselor offers me a Kleenex and I accept it with a hand that is shaking, that seems removed from my own body. I blow my nose and look over at the pastel paintings on her pink walls, at the fake-wood shelving, piled with dusty self-help books from the seventies, remnants of free love and naïveté. I look at the footstool where the counselor is resting her feet, where every week we both rest our feet. I examine the worn beige carpeting. The counselor is waiting patiently.

"I feel lonely," I say, and I really begin to sob. *I'm lonely.*

The counselor pats me on the hand and then squeezes my fingers. "Good for you," she says. "You've finally realized you're lonely."

And in that brief moment, that small moment of contact, I am not.

Part Five \ Entering the Solar System

Our Level

At our level my mother put the potato drawer, the pots and pans, the measuring cups, "Anything that I thought you might be interested in," she says, "that you could play with and not hurt yourself. I didn't want to run around saying *no, no, no* all the time." She put things with interesting textures at our level, and things that would make interesting noises. She put everything dangerous out of reach.

I tell her now, that in some ways I wish she hadn't done this. *I was in no way prepared for what came next,* I tell her. *For the world.*

She put pictures down by the baseboards and at the bottom of the refrigerator. "I wanted things to be interesting at your level," she says, "I figured your little lives should be rich down there near the floor. That you should have plenty to look at."

She taped a Picasso print underneath the cupboard so that she could set my sister's baby seat on the counter, and so my sister would have something interesting to look at. And she hung things from the underside of the cupboard, empty spools of thread, and big old buttons on a string, so that my sister would have things to play with while my mother cooked. "You kids were always close by," Flo says, "because I always made sure there was plenty for you to do. When you got sick of everything else," she says, "I just opened up the cupboard with the spice jars and let you kids look at those. For some reason you were all always fascinated with those spice jars."

My brother spent one entire afternoon, she says, taking potato after potato out of the potato drawer and placing them in a pile on the rocking chair in the living room. "I kept praising him each time he brought in a new potato," says Flo, "because it's very good for kids to have methodical activities like that. They can create order in their lives that way. They feel in control."

I think of the stories Flo is always telling me. In some ways they are like those potatoes, discrete efforts at order, at making sense of things.

"Well then what did he do with them?" I ask. "Once they were all in the rocking chair?"

"Well then he put them back in the drawer," she says, "one by one."

Plant Killer

Flo was a child during World War II and enjoys telling me how she and her friend Eva made their own shoes at that time, out of plywood and rubber, some sandals.

It has never been clear to me that this was absolutely necessary, that they would have gone barefoot without them, or whether it was just a kind of fashionable deprivation, a kind of *Good Housekeeping* wartime craft project, so that even on the Minnesota prairie you could feel you were contributing something. Suffering in a pedestrian way.

"That's a joke about feet," I tell the counselor.

"I get it," she says.

When Flo was growing up, you just assumed you would get married. You could be a teacher, a nurse, and/or get married, and you could wear plywood shoes. You could be a kind of composite character: Imelda Marcos as Rosie the Riveter. Flo was a teacher, and then she got married. And then she stayed home with us kids.

"One time Flo got so bored," I tell the counselor, "that she waxed the couch." My brother was a baby and I hadn't been born yet, so maybe there was less to do. My parents were living in a basement apartment in downtown Chaska, less than a mile from the Minnesota River that would be flooded when my sister was born, when we were no longer downtown but had moved up the hill near the Dairy Queen. Anyway, Flo ran out of things to do—my brother was napping and she'd already cleaned the house and it was too early to make dinner, so she waxed the couch. Took some polish to the vinyl. My dad came home from work and sat down and slipped right on the floor.

"What do you envision for yourself?" the counselor asks.

"In life?" I say, still thinking about furniture.

"Mhmmm."

I am embarrassed to share the ridiculous variety of my dreams, a buffet of the experimental and the ordinary—a kind of odd combination plate of escargot, cottage cheese and Jell-O.

"Well," I say, "in a weird way, I have always pictured myself staying in Minnesota, having a house and a family. You know, a husband and some kids. Maybe a dog."

"Really?" says the counselor. "Don't you want to get out and live in a bunch of different places?"

"I'm a Cancer," I say. "We're homebodies."

"I've already told you," says the counselor, rolling her eyes, "that if you want to keep working with me you have to carve out your own life, not hand it over to some astrologer, or psychic."

"Or a man," I say. "We're still working on that, right?"

"Right. You're in charge."

"And for me, looking for a husband has meant looking for someone else to take responsibility for my life, since I don't want to. Have I got that right?"

"Historically, yes, that seems to be what it has meant for you," says the counselor.

It is true that I would prefer to hand off my destiny like a baton in a relay race: "Here, I'm tired. *You* carry it for a while."

"Then *you* won't get to the finish line," the counselor keeps having to remind me. "And you'll miss so much along the way."

"Like an arm shot off in the war," I tell the counselor. I'd have this stump of a life—a kind of itching absence.

"If you want to think of it that way," she says.

Marriage, I tell the counselor, for Flo's generation, was like that, I think. And maybe it still is. The men were sent out to run this long, lonely marathon, but at least they got to see the world. The women got stuck on a treadmill, left to jog around in the same small spaces like hamsters in a Habitrail.

"Mhmm," says the counselor. "And do you really want to limit yourself in that way?"

"Sort of," I say. "I like limits. My mother always said that children need limits in order to function. Also, I'm a middle child. I like being boxed in. When I was little I had this fantasy about being in prison. I thought it would be neat to be a prisoner because you would have this small clean room with a tiny window and it would be quiet and you could read all day and no one would bother you."

"You know now that it wouldn't be like that, don't you? Prison?" says the counselor, shaking her head.

"Oh, sure," I say. "I know that now. I think I believed prison would have all the fringe benefits of being sick, without having to be sick. Prepared meals, maybe some Popsicles. Time to read and stare into space."

"What else do you envision for yourself?"

I am embarrassed by the disparity. "I'd like to be on *Oprah*," I say. "I think it would be neat to be on TV in general, but I'd especially like to sit and chat with Oprah."

"How do you suppose you could do that?" the counselor asks, in the same way that my mother used to encourage us to develop our own strategies for dealing with "issues that came up," as if "issues that came up" were like geysers, and you could throw yourself on top of them to stop the spouting water, to plug the hole. Or as if "issues that came up" were like regurgitated food. A sudden mess that needs to be dealt with.

"Well, it used to be," I say, "that to be on *Oprah* you could just go sleep with your best friend's boyfriend, but it's more of a feel-good show now." In a weird way, I tell the counselor, without all the drama of obvious catastrophe, the stakes are higher. "Now," I tell the counselor, "I have no idea how you'd get the media's attention. Except I know a woman who was running a 10k race and it turned out that Oprah was running the same race, so they chatted for a while as they jogged. That would be good, too."

"What would you and Oprah talk about?"

"Our struggles," I say. "Our personal struggles."

"You don't *have* any personal struggles," says the counselor. "Not the way Oprah did. And you know it."

"That's true," I say.

"Okay, what else?"

"Well," I say, "when I was younger I always dreamed about waking up in the morning and swimming laps, naked in my own indoor pool. Then I would shower and put on a clean, white robe, the really soft kind, and have some kind of nutritious fruit shake. That's how I would always start my day. Then I would go off to my job as a highly paid therapist in a really posh office space with tasteful furniture, expensive rugs and abstract paintings."

The counselor is smiling at me and rubbing her chin.

"I was much more interested back then in nutrition," I say, thinking of the fruit shakes. "Now I eat a lot of junk food."

It is difficult to explain the limitations I impose on myself, and it's only later that I will find a way to describe how the possibility of infinite possibility frightens the daylights out of me: *I picture myself in a hot air balloon just floating off somewhere, higher and higher into the cold, dark air. Eventually that balloon is going to pop. My family, and this place—Minnesota, this silly place with its terribly cold winters and emotionally repressed Scandinavians—are like the sandbags that weigh the balloon down, the stakes and the ropes that tether it to the ground. Without them I'd be frightened to death of where I might wind up.*

Advent

I am home on the first Sunday of Advent. Michael is at home packing. He and his girlfriend have broken up, though he won't say why. He spends all of his time organizing his things, closing his accounts, asking me if I want his sweaters, his dishes, his plants.

Tonight Flo and I sit at the kitchen table alone, with one candle from the Advent wreath burning. Flo has lit it with a little gadget that she has, kind of a lighter with an extremely long snout, specifically for candles, specifically for candles in those hard to reach places, the ones hiding at the bottom of a glass, for instance. Though all our candles stick out in plain day from the greens of the wreath, Flo uses the little gadget anyway, and with a quick click the first candle is lit. I tell her she's the Annie Oakley of ambience, the fastest clicker in the Midwest. *"Flo, the Fire Bearer,"* I say in a dramatic voice, and she ignores me, as she often does.

"I've had this thing for a long time," says Flo, "I don't know why I never used it. Except I couldn't find it." She is walking away from me, going to the drawer to put the lighter back in it. "Where did it come from? Where has it been all this time?" she says.

Meanwhile, I am happily eating the pasta and roast beef that she has already set on the table. She has recently been to France on a group tour with the Minneapolis Art Institute, and this afternoon had been reading their new tour brochure advertising a trip to Tuscany. "Have you ever been to Tuscany?" she had shouted to me from the kitchen. I was in the other room, putting up Christmas decorations, and shouted back that I hadn't. "The Minneapolis Art Institute is going there," she shouted, as if I could afford to go along. Now I believe that must have been the point in the afternoon when she decided to make the roast beef into an Italian dish. She cooked it for several hours in a combination of various tomato sauces—one of which, I think, was ketchup—and she added a lot of garlic. Ever since she went to southern France, she's been adding garlic to things.

I eat my pasta and roast beef with mushrooms and tomato sauce, and there is salad, which has been served with this introduction: "Now, here's some salad. It's last night's salad, kind of dressed up."

"If you hadn't told me, I probably wouldn't have noticed that it was last night's," I say.

"Well, you might have noticed some things," Flo says.

"What do you mean, 'things'?"

"Well," says Flo, "in places underneath, it's . . ."

"Brown?"

"Brown," she says.

I eat my salad, brown or not, because I haven't had any vegetables all week. The salad is a combination of iceberg lettuce, precut "Oriental Salad Greens," fresh avocado, and prepackaged shredded cheese with Mexican spices. It is not clear how the diaspora of the salad fits in with Flo's travel plans.

My stomach has been hurting all day, but I eat anyway, because it's the first decent thing, the first thing not pizza, that I've had in several days. Flo is digging around in her CD collection, because the last disc stopped playing. "Put in that Chet Baker CD we were listening to last week," I say.

Flo puts in Chet Baker and as she's coming back to the table, I ask if we can use the fireplace. "Is the fireplace expensive to run?" I say.

"I don't think so," says Flo.

"Can we turn it on?"

"Sure," says Flo, and like so many things, with the flip of a switch, it's running. We never had a fireplace before the new addition, and Flo decided that, though she wanted a fireplace for cold winter nights, she didn't want to mess with a real one. We've now got this gas fireplace with logs that Flo thinks are "pretty realistic." The switch for the fireplace is hidden behind the plants. Flo had the contractors change the shape of the fire after they first installed it. "It was too masculine a fire," she told me. "It was all spiky and unconnected. This is a more feminine fire," she said. "It's relaxing and sensuous."

I could spend days curled up in front of the new fireplace,

fake or not, looking out past the new deck at the cornfields that have always been there, at the gentle, rolling fields and the strip of pasture where the cows lie in the summer. I am, in some ways, I finally realize, like those cows. Those cows are my inspiration, preferring to be docile and clustered in a small familiar group.

Chet Baker is singing "I Fall In Love Too Easily," and my mother and I are eating Tuscany roast beef, sitting around the new kitchen table, a small round table, with an empty plate for my father between us.

"I like this song," I say. "It matches my mood today."

"Can't you just feel his pain?" says Flo, "He was a sensitive and troubled man. Hear the sorrow," she says. "You have to be careful with this kind of music. I can really fall into this mood and have a hard time getting out."

"Me, too," I say. I ask if I can borrow the CD until next week.

"That's fine," says Flo, "but don't get in too much of a funk."

"I'll listen to it until I get it out of my system," I say. "That's what I do."

"I used to love this song," says Flo. She is gazing at the ceiling and chewing. "When I was home on college breaks," she says after a while, "I used to play this song over and over, and moon around about your father."

"Did Grandma think you were nuts?"

"No, she liked this music, too. She didn't listen to jazz, but she liked it when I played it." Flo is staring at the kitchen ceiling of the house she's lived in for thirty years; it's been redone recently, but it's the same foundation, the same frame. I like the idea that she used to moon around like I do, and I wonder if that's why she's always urging me not to. I like the idea that she longed for something, because she often acts now like she doesn't, like she never has. It makes me happy to know that we have this in common.

"You were in love," I say, hoping she will tell me what it was like, what went through her mind, what it was like to be her in her twenties, to be in love with someone, to not know what would happen, to feel *that* deeply about someone you actually *knew,* instead of an imaginary boyfriend, which are the boyfriends I usually pine for, men I've met once or twice, men I can't have, and so decide that they must be my destiny, pining for them in a kind of romantic vacuum.

"I think, with your father," she says, "that it was always one-sided."

The thought of that, that my father might never have loved my mother, or never loved her to the degree to which she loved him, is a little more than I can deal with right now. It's not that I had never thought about it; it's not that she's never hinted around about it before; it's just that she's never said it directly. And then I think that perhaps she has, but that I didn't hear it in the same way, feel it in the way I feel it now. I don't want to be my mother. I don't want to be someone who always feels empty, bitter, cheated, deprived. I don't want to live with someone who is always disappointing me. I would rather live alone. I would rather move to the country and raise goats. The goats would have each other, and they'd nibble happily on the lawn. I'd have fresh goat cheese, and these indifferent companions from whom I'd expect only a little sustenance and some lawn care. Which is maybe all most people expect from marriage. I just always thought there would be more.

Therapy

You really need to stop calling your mother by her first name, says the counselor.

Why?

It establishes a distance that later on seems to alienate you. Let her be your mother. Practice calling her, "Mom," says the counselor. Why did you start calling her by her first name, anyway?

Oh, I say. *That's easy.* I saw *Bye Bye Birdie* in high school, and the lead character started calling *her* mother by *her* first name. I thought it looked fun, and liberating.

Well stop it, says the counselor. Practice calling her *Mom.* In a few years it'll seem right again. Every child, no matter how old, deserves to have a mother, someone who will cradle them when they need to be cradled.

It seems true. I work on that.

Something Fun

I call my dad to find out what we should do for my mom's birthday. He's on call at the hospital that day, which means if he gets beeped, he'll have to go back.

"Well, maybe the two of us can just go and do something fun," she says to me, and keeps saying to me as we're trying to iron out her birthday plans.

"Dad and I talked about the three of us having dinner. And actually, my present to you is an afternoon together, for a different day, you can redeem the coupon whenever you want, but since Dad's on call, I thought we could do something near home. And I was going to bring laundry," I confess. "I thought I would stay overnight."

"Good," says my mom, "We'll have a slumber party."

My mom and I spend the early evening browsing around Target. When she's not looking, I put a big bag of York peppermint patties in her cart.

"Hey!" she says when she notices them at the checkout lane. "Am I supposed to buy these?"

"They're fat free," I tell her.

"Are they really?" she says. "I'll be darned."

We eat some peppermint patties in the parking lot and on the way to Byerly's, where we pick up deli food to take home. My mother has decided that she doesn't feel like going out to eat. She'd rather be at home eating deli food. Since the addition's been finished, she doesn't seem to mind being at home as much.

At home, my mom and dad sit at the kitchen table and sort through mail, while I get all the Byerly's stuff ready. "Okay," I say, pulling some cannelloni out of the grocery bag, "let's pop these fuckers in the microwave."

My parents think it's funny. I think it's *extremely* funny. Nothing much has changed since high school: I still enjoy trying to shock my parents with feigned insolence, without much success.

"I'm going to be a great mom someday," I say, shoving the preprepared food in the microwave.

"You probably will," says my dad.

"I bet your kids will be really conservative," says my mom.

"To make up for me being weird," I say.

"Exactly," she says.

"This is just a little something I whipped up," I say, setting some roasted vegetables from Byerly's on the table. "It's nothing fancy."

While I'm getting more things out of the microwave I tell my dad about the date I was on last week. My mom already knows the story, the one about the guy who stuck his nose in my hair when I was unlocking the car door, stuck his nose in my hair and took a big dramatic whiff, which made me feel like I was on some bad soap opera.

"Well, I bet if you liked him, you wouldn't have cared," says my dad. "Dating's hard," he says. "It's hard for everyone."

"How would *you* know?" says my mom, as she's walking into the living room to get something.

"We're not talking about Edward," says my dad, talking about himself in the third person the way Bob Dole does. "We're talking about Shannon."

At dinner my dad reminds my mom about the office party on Saturday, and my mother becomes indignant. "I told you I'm going up north with Pauline," she says, lifting her chin in defiance, "and I am *not* canceling those plans."

"Okay, Flo," says my dad. "Well, I'm sorry about that. I didn't realize it was the same weekend."

"You could have checked with me earlier," she says.

"I got it mixed up," he says. "I forgot."

"Edward, you lose everything," says my mom.

I am shoveling cannelloni into my mouth and looking down at my plate. I feel like I am about eight years old, and begin to understand why sometimes kids from troubled homes get really fat.

"Well, now we have an extra ticket," says my dad. "Shannon, would you like to go?"

I nod my head yes. My sister and I have both gone to the holiday party before, along with both our parents.

"It's at Lord Fletcher's," says my dad. "It's good food."

"Sure," I say, swallowing my cannelloni. "I've never eaten there."

"Oh, I see how important I am around here," says my mother. "I see how easily I am replaced."

"Well, Flo," says my dad, "you just said that you didn't want to change your plans."

"No, you go and have a good time with your favorite date."

Now I'm shoving salad in my mouth like a starved rabbit, wondering if my parents show this marginal restraint around each other when I'm not here, or if they really go all out and let each other have it. I wish I wasn't here; I wish I could go back to my apartment, or downstairs or somewhere else, but it's my mom's goddamn birthday dinner. Actually, over the past few years, it's rare that my mom's not crabby on her birthday. When we were small she was happy if we wrote her a poem for her birthday, or picked some wildflowers. But now, nothing we do ever seems good enough.

A couple weeks ago, I brought my mom some bath stuff back from Toronto, where I had gone for a conference, and I tried to explain to her how it was all the rage, how it was supposed to be like the new Body Shop, the next big trend. "I hate to say it," she said, "but this is the same kind of stuff I used to tell my Home Ec students to use. This 'all natural' stuff is just a gimmick."

"Mom," I said, "I brought you a present. This is a present from me, okay? For you to *enjoy*."

"Well," she said, "I'm just commenting on something. You know deep down I like it, don't you?"

"No, Mom," I said, "I don't."

"Can't I ever have an opinion?" she said.

We had already had this conversation weeks ago, Thanksgiving weekend when my sister was home. We'd gone to Dayton's and were waiting for my sister to finish trying on shoes. I explained to my mother that she could have an opinion now that I'd been through four, going on five, years of therapy, but that before it had been very difficult for me to separate her opinions and random commentary from my own definition of myself.

"God, I just hate this job sometimes," she'd said. "This job of being a mother."

"Think about it, Mom," I told her, and explained: *You're the one who taught me not to stick my hand on the stove. Not to stick my finger in the light socket. You're the one who taught me to stay away from the boy down the street who was always catching squirrels and torturing them. Everything you taught us when we were little was to help us survive, to help us get along in the world. Everything you told us was true. And so when you have an opinion about something, I've always believed it has some direct link to an eternal and life-preserving truth. Like, I should wear royal blue more often. I would get more dates that way. And, I'm not as pretty without makeup.*

"I never said that," said my mother.

"The other day," I said, "when I was wearing my new blue shirt, and I had just showered and put on makeup, you told me that I should always look that pretty."

"But you were simply *glowing*," said my mother, "I just noticed it. It's nice to see you feeling that good. Shit, I hate this job."

"I can handle it now," I said, "because of all my therapy."

"My mother was always so critical of me," said my mom. "I vowed never to be that way. I made a conscious decision not to be that way."

We were sitting on the floor in the Tommy Hilfiger section, and the security guard sauntered over near us, I think to make sure that we weren't stealing anything or ruining the T-shirt display.

"I'm glad we had this talk," said my mom just as my sister walked up, holding up her shopping bags like a string of fish. "I appreciate that we can talk about these things. I appreciate that you're willing to communicate with me."

Therapy

How is it going not calling your mom by her first name? says the counselor.

It's going okay, I say.

Do you see how calling her "Mom" can be freeing? You don't have to try to be bigger than she is, or take care of her. You can just let her be herself, with her own life.

Okay, I say.

Isn't it nice to have a mother again?

We work on that.

Swiss Cheese

Michael has left now for Italy and says he won't be coming back. He leaves me some winter clothes, his heaviest sweaters, which he says he will never need again. He leaves me his kitchen table and chairs, his mountain bike, his plates and glassware, his bike rack, his plants.

"He left you his mittens," Flo says.

"I didn't need any more mittens," I say. "He took the mittens to Goodwill."

"No, I mean *symbolically,*" says Flo. "Don't you remember that? When you kids were little and you were going to school for the first time, I always left you something small, something you could carry with you during the day, so you'd know I'd be back to get you. I'd leave you a sock, or a glove, or a mitten, something that came in halves, so you'd know I'd be back."

"He took the pair to Goodwill," I say. "Left and right."

"He sure left you a lot of stuff," says Flo. "How does he do that? Just leaving like that? Leaving everything behind?"

I had let him stay at my place the last week that he was here. He had to leave his apartment at the beginning of the month and had been staying with various friends. The last week he stayed with me. He was hardly there, and he slept on the floor, on a little blow-up mattress.

His last day here he had scheduled a breakfast with his new ex-girlfriend, and as he got dressed that morning, I was still in bed, gradually making gestures toward getting up and being in the world. I had slept in pajama bottoms and a long underwear shirt, and had pulled the covers down to my waist. I was entering the land of the living.

"Have a good breakfast with your ex-girlfriend," I said as Michael put his watch on and looked at his hair in the mirror.

"God that sounds weird," I said, propping a couple of pillows up behind me.

"Do you know what she'd say to you if she could see you now?" he said.

"What?" I said, even though I had told him months ago that I didn't want to know anything about her.

"She'd say, 'Nice tits,'" he says, nodding at my chest.

"What is that supposed to mean?"

"She's a lesbian," he said, "but she made an exception for me. And her ex-husband."

"What is *that* supposed to mean?"

"I don't know," he said, grabbing his wallet and car keys.

I am looking down at my boobs as he says from the doorway, "So, we're having dinner tonight, right, and then I'm leaving."

"Right," I said, wondering when he started noticing my boobs again.

I wonder sometimes now if I am stupid.

"I let him walk all over me," I tell the counselor. "I tried to be his friend because he said it was important to him, but then the kind of friend he was to me is not the kind of friend I'd want."

"You weren't ready to let go," says the counselor.

"I let him walk all over me," I say again, "and still, sometimes I would look at him and see this lost puppy. Someone who just wanted a warm lap to rest his head on."

"He could have been that," says the counselor. "And maybe that was you, too. Maybe you were lost. And you didn't draw a clear boundary. You didn't set limits."

"If I had set limits he would have left. He wouldn't have been in my life anymore."

"So then you know that about him. And you've made a choice."

"Sometimes," I say, "for no reason, he'd have this look on his face like he just swallowed knives. I think Michael's need to keep everything in order was his survival mechanism."

"It probably was."

"But there was no room for me. I was part of a schedule, a grid. And when I pointed that out to him, he'd say, 'Shanny, a lot of couples don't make it through grad school. This is what I need to do to get through this.'"

"So he let you know what he needed."

"But I didn't think it would end with graduate school. I thought my whole life would be like that. I'd be worked into the schedule and I'd always want more. I wouldn't be consulted; I'd just be a budget item."

"And that's why you had to leave," the counselor reminds me. "You wanted a playmate. You wanted different things."

"Couldn't we just say that he walked all over me and leave it at that? Couldn't we just say that he was mean and that it was all his fault?"

"That wouldn't be true," she says. "People are more complicated than that."

"I hate that part," I say.

Michael called me around four P.M. at work the day he was supposed to leave Minnesota.

"Hurry home, I'm leaving," he said.

"But it's only four o'clock," I said. "We're supposed to have dinner."

"I want to go now," he said. "Maybe I'll just go and we can skip dinner."

"Then I won't see you," I said.

"I'm feeling like I should just get on the road," he said.

"The other part, I tell the counselor, is that I don't think Michael ever forgave me for leaving him the first time. I'm not sure if it was because he loved me, or because he'd told everyone that I was the one, that we'd always be together. I mean, I told people that, too, that I thought Michael was the one, but everyone expects me to change my mind."

"You interrupted his plan," says the counselor. "And I think he loved you," she says. The counselor always conjoins conflicting things with *and,* which drives me crazy. "And I think he also wanted to do things his way. There wasn't enough room there for you. It's that old Greek machismo thing."

"He was Italian," I say.

"Oh," says the counselor. Sometimes she gets things wrong and I wonder if we've been having different conversations for the last five years. "Where did I get that?" she says.

"You thought my last boyfriend was Middle Eastern," I say.

"He wasn't?" she says.

"Please just stay and we can have a quick dinner," I said. I wanted to go to the place where we had always gone when it was my turn to cook.

"I really think I should be on the road," Michael said. "It's getting late."

"Then why don't you just go tomorrow morning? Why are you leaving in the dark?"

"Okay," said Michael. "But we'll eat fast. And hurry home."

"I can't just leave," I said. "I'm in the middle of something. Why are you changing our plans?"

We went to the restaurant around six P.M. I didn't hurry home and I didn't hurry through dinner. Michael didn't seem to, either, and he even agreed to dessert. We ordered his favorite, apple pie with caramel sauce and ice cream, and I ate most of it.

I put dinner on my credit card and then I drove us back to my apartment building, where his car was parked on the side street. Packed and ready to go.

"Thank you for my dinner," Michael said.

"How far are you going to go tonight?"

"I don't know," he said.

"Is Steve buckled in?" I asked. I had given him one of my plants, Steve, to take along.

"He's in the back," Michael said. Steve was on the back window ledge and had already fallen over. Some dirt had sprinkled out, and his leaves languished in the ledge.

"I'll miss you," I said, and as I leaned over to Michael, seated behind the wheel, his window rolled down halfway, I started crying and gave him a quick kiss on the lips.

"Hey," he said. "That's against the rules. No lip kissing."

I had done it without thinking, in the same way that you'd dive off a flaming boat, no matter how cold the water. "I'm sorry. I forgot. Drive safe," I said, and gave a little wave.

"I love you, Shanny," Michael said as he began to pull out of his parking spot. I don't think either of us had said it since we first started going out almost four years ago.

"I love you, too," I said.

And then he drove away.

Michael always said that the Minnesota winters were too hard, that the people here don't talk about *issues*. They just make small talk, he always said. No one ever talks about the really important things. Poverty. Government policy. Racism. Also, he always said, people in Italy know how to have fun. They know how to *live*.

In many ways I am glad he is gone. It was hard to try and be his friend after we'd gone out, and I am used to the winters. I barely notice them.

Michael always told me that I had to hear the same thing over and over and over again before it sunk in.

"What do you mean?"

"I mean, we always have to have the same conversations, again and again, before you seem to get it."

"Like what?" I would say.

"Like how we've already talked about the fact that I just think of you as a friend now, but you keep forgetting, and you keep making those googly eyes at me like you're going to kiss me. But I'm over you. It took a long time but I'm finally over you. You forget that you wanted to break up with me, too. You broke up with me the first time. And now we're just friends."

"Okay," I would say. "I get it." It would always come up again a few weeks later.

I need to hear things over and over before they sink in, that is true. Maybe it's because I never believe anything the first time I hear it. I believe that the first time I hear it, it has been offered as a kind of experiment, potentially riddled with problems and holes in its logic, a piece of Swiss cheese: Here. Here is some food. Except it has some holes in it. But around the holes, you'll find food, something that might sustain you.

You need to begin to tell your own story, says the counselor.

I have been telling my story, I say.

No, says the counselor, you haven't. It's Michael this and Michael that. My mother this and my mother that. Stories about the neighbors. You talk more about other people than you do about yourself. Those people have their own lives, their own issues. This is supposed to be *your* therapy. Do you realize how much of your therapy time you give them?

"But they affect my life," I say.

And there you go again with the "but," says the counselor. Denial, denial, she says. Tell your own story, she says. *What's important to you? Who do you want to be?*

Okay, I say. Okay.

In the beginning there was me, I say. And my mom and dad, and the people in our neighborhood, and of course, my older brother was already there, too. Did I tell you that he locked me in the family suitcase once? It was a very big suitcase, one of those fabric ones, plaid, with a zipper, and I was small for my age.

This doesn't represent progress, says the counselor.

But before all that there were my grandparents. Of course, they had their own *issues.* My mom thinks that her mother was really smart, *thwarted by her time.* She, my grandmother, had four sisters. One was a fashion model and one smoked cigars. One remarried the same man three times; the *last* time, he really did quit drinking.

Maybe we should just wrap up, says the counselor. I don't see this going anywhere.

My mom once told me that I shouldn't worry about turning into her, in the way that all women are afraid they'll turn into their mothers. I think I had just done something that she does, like hum and rub my chin while I'm driving, and when I said, "Oh crap, I'm turning into you!" she said, "Remember, you're fifty percent me, and you're fifty percent your father." And then she said, *Actually, you're a little bit of everyone who came before you, kind of a composite. Isn't that nice? And in being that, you're completely different, someone totally new.* It kind of takes the pressure off, I say to the counselor. Don't you think? I have all their mistakes to fall back on, too. I can say, "Grandma screwed something up. It's okay if I screw up."

Or you could say, says the counselor, "I'm done picking other people's lives to death. I've learned something from it, and now I'm going to move forward with *my* life, and make the best choices *I* can make."

Well, I do like a loophole, I say. I've learned that in therapy. You taught me that.

Oh, good, says the counselor. You've learned *something*. (She is in a playful mood today. Today she is tolerating me.) You know, she says, your mother is fine. She's a strong person. Your father is fine. You have *good* parents. And you'll be able to stop obsessing about their lives when you are *in* your own life. They had lives before you ever knew them—there are things you'll never know. Start over, says the counselor, with *you*. Don't talk about *anyone* else.

Okay, I say. Okay. Here I go.

In the End

I call my mom to tell her that I have finished my project, but for some reason, telling her that it's done is less satisfying than just feeling done with it. Catholic superstition begins to creep in. I tell her I'm going to read her the last few lines, but then I begin to chicken out. "Maybe this is one of those things that you ruin by saying out loud," I say.

"Like seeing all your Christmas presents ahead of time," says Flo, who has already shown me several of mine, though Christmas is still a few days away. When we were younger, we opened our presents one at a time, one a night, for the twelve days of Christmas. The presents by the twelfth day were small, some socks or markers, but still, we had to be patient. And she wouldn't let us open our gifts until we did the dinner dishes. There was a system of rewards for our labor. As we grew older, she gave up on surprises, giving things to us early just because she couldn't stand having a secret anymore.

"Yes," I say now, with the final pages humming on my computer screen, "it's like an early Christmas." She hasn't read the rest of it, why would the end be meaningful? "Never mind."

"Read me the ending," says Flo. "Now I want to know."

Okay, I say, and I read her the ending.

"I don't remember you fainting at your sister's wedding," she says. "Did you faint? Did I forget about that?"

"I fainted *symbolically,*" I say. "I made that part up."

"Oh," says Flo. "Well, good. Just like when you were little, using your imagination. Good for you. So, that's the end?"

"That's it," I say. "It's just an experimental ending. Kind of a way to cap things off and say, 'Okay, that's it.'"

"Well, good for you," says Flo, and then she says: "Am I

being supportive enough?" I had told her the day before that I was really sick of her badgering me about graduating, that I really could use some unconditional love and support for my efforts, to which she had replied, "Well, do you like *yourself* when you're still in school? When you're kind of dragging things out?" So now she adds, "And I love, love, *love* you. How's that? How am I doing?"

"That's fine, thank you," I say. "I guess the whole project is just kind of like Swiss cheese. It's wrapped and packaged, but you can still see the holes in it." I seem to fall back on cheese more and more. Cheese has become important to me, a big smelly metaphor.

"So, you have to go back and fix some things," says Flo.

"Yes," I say, "I probably do. But it's nice to have something that *looks* like an ending. It's a good feeling to at least *try* it. Closure is hard. Maybe I won't fix any of it."

"It's just today's ending," says Flo. "You can write a new one tomorrow."

Therapy

Most of my dinner plates are chipped, I tell the counselor. And it's bugging me. My chipped life. My hand-me-down chipped life. You know, I tell her, all of my most reliable appliances are from Michael. The things that Michael left with me. What does that say about my own ability to plan and survive?

It shows that you picked a responsible boyfriend, says the counselor. That's a start.

I wonder if he will come back, I say. He left me his mittens.

Oh, the denial! she shouts into the room, a thing she does sometimes for dramatic effect. *Don't do this. He's moved on. It's your time to be in your own life.*

The closest thing I have now to a boyfriend is a microwave, I tell the counselor, spinning around my sustenance, heating it until it pops and sprays the oven walls.

I don't understand what it is that you expect, says the counselor. I mean, chipped plates, everyone has those. And ex-boyfriends. Lots of people have those.

I was hoping I wouldn't have to do so many things wrong, I say. I was hoping for not-chipped plates, metaphorically.

You're learning, says the counselor.

I was expecting an apple to drop on my head, I tell her. Something more decisive. You know? Maybe there are no more big discoveries to make, I tell her. Yet, life expands like the universe, keeps expanding, *and I can't stand it.*

My mother always gave us limits, I tell the counselor. *Which three pieces of candy would you like? Would you like to brush your teeth first, or put on your pajamas first?* I believed I had choices, though the limits were already in place. I was going to bed, no matter what. It was just a question of what would come first. And now, I say, now, I'm standing in life's great open field and you know what? If you build it, they will not necessarily come.

This is the part where I get lost, says the counselor. What are you building? she says, *besides an argument for more therapy.*

She is feeling campy today.

It's like stamps, I say. The price keeps changing, but only, like, one cent at a time, so it's hard to remember. Did it really change? What is the price again, anyway? Do I need a makeup stamp? Life is like that, I say. It changes incrementally, and so you know that things have changed, but sometimes you can't remember what they were before, and if you're attaching appropriate values. The mail is really spiritual that way, I tell the counselor, who is looking up at the ceiling, blinking up at the tiles. I can see up her nose.

You put something in, I say, and you just have to have blind faith that it will arrive somewhere, that it will be delivered. *I want to be delivered,* I tell her. *Do you see?* I want my grandmothers to speak to me from beyond and tell me if I'm doing all right. I want them to tell me if I'm expecting too much. *Should I move to the West Coast, Grandmas? Should I take up dog sledding? Will I ever fall in love? Should I stay single and learn how to knit? Did you get married because you wanted to or because you thought you had to? Grandmas, did I go down the wrong path too long ago? Is it too late?*

The counselor is looking directly at me now and rubbing her chin, which means she has an answer. "Maybe," she says, "it's time for you to start going to church. You know, we are all children of God. Church would teach you that it's okay to be you, just as you are."

"Not the church I grew up going to," I say. "The priest spent a half hour one Sunday going on about how men with beards were all going to hell."

"So we'll find a different church," she says, crossing her ankles on the footstool. "Did you ever call that guy? The one who works at the business library?"

"No."

"Why not?" says the counselor.

"You're the one who keeps telling me not to spend my time chasing men."

"You're not chasing him. He invited you to call him."

"But I've been finishing my thesis," I tell her. "You told me to focus on my thesis."

"Well, you're done now," she says.

"It's probably too late," I say. "He probably has a girlfriend by now."

"Well, you won't know unless you call, will you?" she says. "And what about Baja this winter? Have you thought about that?"

"Since when are you my dating service? Since when are you sending me on trips to have sex?"

"You don't have to have sex. You can do whatever you want. You can bring your sister along. I just think it would be fun," she says. "See a new place. Get to know the kayaking guide better. I have a good feeling about him."

"I thought I was supposed to establish a life on my *own* terms," I say.

"The only way to do that is to get out in the world," she says.

"I keep thinking about Michael," I say.

"What purpose does that serve?" she says. "Michael has moved on."

"How am I supposed to afford a trip like that?" I say.

"Get a second job," she says. "Now that you're done with your thesis. You have time."

Dots

On the phone one night my mom tells me about this nature show she'd been watching. Scientists had done tests on ravens, "because they're really smart, you know," she says, "they have real cognitive abilities. They're real good problem solvers."

I can see why this would appeal to my mother. I would be more attracted to the nature show about the animals that just gave up and decided to lie around. A one-hour *National Geographic* special called "Gorillas in the Midst of Doing Nothing."

"So anyway," says Flo. "This raven was just amazing. They put a piece of meat on the end of a string—you know they tied the string around it—and then they hung it from a branch, but far enough up and out so the raven couldn't get at it from the ground, or from the trunk. So the raven's up on the branch, and he tries picking up the string with his beak and kind of pops the meat up, swings the meat up, you know, trying to catch it in midair . . . hold on a second," my mother says, clearing her throat, and then, holding the phone away from her, she says, "Ed, there's salad in the fridge and rolls on the counter, and lasagna in the microwave."

"Say hello to Dad for me," I tell my mother, when she gets back on the phone.

"And your daughter says hello," says my mom.

"The Saint Paul one or the Portland one?" I can hear my dad say in the background while he's clanging around in the kitchen, looking for silverware, salad, rolls and lasagna.

"Saint Paul," says Flo. "Anyway, and so this raven finally figures out that he can pick the string up with his beak, and then he takes the piece of string he's brought up, and slides over a little on the branch to hold the string with his feet, and then he picks up some more of the string, and then slides over a little more, holds it down with his feet, and he keeps doing it again and again until he's brought the whole string up and the piece of meat is sitting on the branch. Isn't that amazing?"

"That is pretty amazing," I say.

"He dropped it a couple times along the way and had to start over. Ed," says my mother, holding the phone away again, "the lasagna's in the microwave, not the oven. Check the microwave. So anyway," she says now to me, "it was fascinating."

"Here's what I think is fascinating," I tell my mom. "That a raven could figure out how to pull a piece of meat up on a string, but dad needs help finding lasagna in the microwave."

"That's true!" says my mom, who repeats it to my father, who mumbles something in the background about how we should have pity on the less evolved.

At some point when I was in high school, little green dots began appearing around our house. The first place I noticed them was in the upper right hand corner of the bathroom mirror. Little round green stickers on the mirror, inside cupboard doors, and on the refrigerator. I don't think I ever asked who put them up, or what they were for; I knew them to be my mother's work. Something to remind her of something, to do something, whatever it was.

I had grown up with my taped parking spot in the garage, with inspirational sayings on the inside of every cupboard door. Things like, "Bloom Where You Are Planted," and "Children Learn What They Live," and, what seemed to be her favorite and a kind of warning to us kids, a piece of masking tape on the kitchen windowsill on which she'd drawn a ladybug and written in heavy black permanent marker, "Thou shalt not bug." It faded to a light gray over the years.

My mother made lists. Job lists and grocery lists. Every Saturday she made a list of the jobs that needed to be done around the house, and we kids were to sign up for three each. We would hobble out of bed, examine the list on the kitchen table, put our initials by the jobs we could tolerate, and wander downstairs with cookies and leftover cake to watch *Bugs Bunny*. We could watch as much TV as we wanted, but we couldn't leave the house until we finished our three jobs, which had little impact on my schedule, since I never left the house anyway. I did my cleaning slowly and methodically, thinking about how the pioneers had suffered with their chores, pretending I was part of some kind of monastic community. I enjoyed the idea of suffering, the *idea* of labor, and so, for that reason, I always chose to clean the bathroom.

The grocery list was pinned to the same place on the same bulletin board the entire time I was growing up. If there was anything we wanted, we were to write it on the list. The left side was for groceries; the right side was for grocery-related items—staples that weren't food, like lightbulbs and toilet paper, salt for the water softener. Sometimes, on the left side, where we were to write requested food items, I wrote things like "Pringle's," or "Cap'n Crunch," or "gigantic man-eating potatoes," just to see if my mom was paying attention.

So when the green dots showed up around the house, I never asked about them. I knew them to be part of some system. My mom was remembering to do something discreet. Something she didn't want to announce formally, in writing. And at some point, the dots became a part of the landscape to me, a billboard whose worn advertisement is never changed. I always knew the dots were there, and at the same time I stopped noticing them.

I am visiting my parents one day when I notice them again, in the same ways that the film industry enjoins us to see Hollywood movies twice, "again for the first time." And when I ask Flo about them, what they were meant to do, she says, "Oh, those are to remind me to breathe."

Because I've taken some yoga, I understand this. That reflexes sometimes fail us. That the body can occasionally seize up on itself, forget to act in its own best interests.

"I was in some kind of a biofeedback group for my blood pressure," says Flo. "And we were trying to learn to remember to breathe, because sometimes, you know, you forget. You'd think it would be natural, but it isn't. You know, when you get stressed, and all of the sudden you stop and think, 'Hey, I've been holding my breath.'"

The next time I was home, my mother produced some red stickers for me, from a box of stationery supplies that she'd had since the seventies. A sheet of big red dots, bigger than her small bright green ones. "I found these and I thought you might like to use them," she said. "You know, if you're interested in changing things. It helps to just do one thing at a time. You pick one thing, and you focus on that for a couple of weeks, or however long it takes you before it becomes habit. You do one thing at a time or you get overwhelmed."

I took the sheet of red stickers back to my apartment that night and placed one big red dot in the bottom left-hand corner of my bathroom mirror, and stood there, next to the toilet, trying to figure out what one thing the dot could represent.

Where even to begin?

The dot could remind me to stop treating my cups, bowls and plates like petri dishes. To wash them every day.

It could remind me to go through the mail when it arrives, instead of months later.

It could remind me to call old friends, to be conscious of my *narcissism,* to set better *personal boundaries* or to water the plants regularly.

The dot could remind me to read my car owner's manual, to balance my checkbook, to stop eating at McDonald's.

The dot could remind me that I shouldn't buy women's magazines when I go to Target, that I have enough nail polish and shouldn't make any more impulse purchases when I go to Target, that I shouldn't go to Target in general.

The dot could remind me to get out of bed in the morning, to use biodegradable household cleaning supplies. To shut the light off when I leave a room. To limit my caffeine intake. To put clean clothes away instead of tossing them around like decorative household accessories.

The dot could remind me to eat more fiber and to learn interesting vegetable recipes. To do volunteer work, not to honk in traffic unless it's an emergency. To read one article in the international news section of the paper each day, instead of heading straight for the horoscopes and "Mark Trail." To take each thing as it comes. To breathe.

To call the library guy. To go kayaking.

I think of the dot as a great solar system, one bright light from far away, a whole series of interconnected bodies close up, held together by gravity and forces that we can't see or understand. If one thing goes out of orbit, what else might follow by default? How do we know the universe will not collapse in on itself?

The dot on my mirror could stand for anything.

I could begin anywhere.

My mother has always told me that somewhere along the line she had to learn to think differently. She called her old way of being, "The Ernie Larsen School of Stinkin' Thinkin'." I have no idea who Ernie Larsen was, and having heard the story of my mother's reinvention, her personal journey to positive thinking, so many times, I have always thought that she must have been someone entirely different, someone I wouldn't even recognize.

But I'm not sure now that this is true. I think now that

maybe the changes we experience in one lifetime aren't as dramatic as we'd like to think, aren't anything like the immediate refuge of the chameleon, but something more like the flatfish, eyes migrating over generations for a better view. That we are tugged back into shape by genetics and the osmotic misfortune of behavioral inheritance. In the way that my grandmother always walked around with a toothpick, and my mother always walks around with a toothpick, and my sister now reaches for a toothpick every time we go out to eat.

My mother had to become a latter-day Norman Vincent Peale in order to survive. Could no longer stand, she says, living in her own critical mind, hearing her mother's voice in her own head, the voice that found something wrong with everything. She had to take some small step toward change, even if she didn't know where it would lead. It was a leap of faith, which is not what I thought it was when I grew up reading the inspirational sayings my mother had placed all over the house. Things like "Bloom Where You Are Planted" I took to mean "Sit down and die and fertilize the soil." I considered my mother's weakness for aphorisms to be a weakness for the easy answer, but I think now that my mother held on to these phrases like an oxygen mask in a plane that's going down. And I have been the girl with whom she's so nicely shared her little bag of peanuts. It was her way of trying to fortify me, of hoping that I wouldn't struggle with the same things she did.

She had forged a path, why did I still insist on cutting down my own trees, hacking away at the branches?

"Everyone gets overwhelmed. You need to pick just one thing," says my mom, "I'll help you."

"Okay," I say. "You help pick one. These are some of my

ideas: Lose twenty pounds. Work out regularly. Buy groceries at the discount store. Focus on paying off loans and credit cards. Floss teeth. Try to relax. Wash dishes. Live in the moment. Say what I'm feeling instead of letting it bottle up and become carbonated. Don't eat out so much. Pay rent on time. Take antidepressant, asthma and PMS medication regularly, do not skip a day. Stop buying frozen dinners and women's magazines. Don't smoke when drinking. Practice self-acceptance."

"Well, I pick the last one," says Flo. "But why don't you start with something more manageable, like dishwashing? And please don't smoke," she says. "After all those nights that I stayed awake with you, wondering if you'd stop breathing and if we'd have to rush you to the hospital."

"Remember not to tell Mother certain things," I say. "The dot will stand for that."

Acknowledgments

I am grateful to Maureen Howard, for making it all happen; to my agent, Gloria Loomis, for leaping tall buildings in a single bound; to Shirley Nelson Garner, for wisdom and good example; and to my family, especially Flo, who understands that "spinning is more than a Colonial skill." Many people helped and supported me in writing this book, but I'd like to thank, especially, Julie Schumacher and Charles Sugnet, for their encouragement and patience in reading unwieldy drafts. Thanks also to Gretchen Scherer, Elizabeth Larsen, Lynn Bronson, Jan Baker, Steve Swanson, Steven Polansky, Patricia Hampl, Madelon Sprengnether, David Mura, Jim Moore, Katherine Fausset, Alexandra Babanskyj, Carolyn Coleburn, Gretchen Koss, and the staff of the English Department at the University of Minnesota. And finally, big thanks to my wonderful editor, Carole DeSanti, who understands the power of cheese.